NIGHTMARE

PEOPLE OF COLO(U)R DESTROY HORROR!
SPECIAL ISSUE

D0596650

ISSUE 49 | OCTOBER 2016
GUEST EDITED BY SILVIA MORENO-GARCIA

NIGHTARE MAGAZINE: People of Colo(u)r Destroy Science Horror! Special Issue (Issue 49, October 2016)

Publisher: John Joseph Adams

Trade Edition ISBN: 978-1537571881

Published by *Nightmare Magazine*   First Edition: October 2016

To receive news and updates about *Nightmare*, please sign up for the *Nightmare Magazine* newsletter on our website: **www.nightmaremagazine.com**

NIGHTMARE

PEOPLE OF COLO(U)R DESTROY HORROR! SPECIAL ISSUE

FROM THE EDITORS

On the Destruction of Horror: Notes from your POC Editors 1

ORIGINAL SHORT FICTION
edited by Silvia Moreno-Garcia

Wish You Were Here | Nadia Bulkin
Illustration by Maggie Chiang 5
None of This Ever Happened | Gabriela Santiago 18
A Diet of Worms | Valerie Valdes
Illustration by Kimberly Wengerd 26
The Taming of the Tongue | Russell Nichols 34

REPRINT FICTION
edited by Tananarive Due

Cruel Sistah | Nisi Shawl
Illustration by SainaSix 43
The Show | Priya Sharma
Illustration by Reiko Murakami 51
Wet Pain | Terence Taylor 60
Monstro | Junot Díaz 78

NONFICTION
selected by Maurice Broaddus

Interview: VictorLaValle | Maurice Broaddus 94
The H Word: The Darkest, Truest Mirrors | Alyssa Wong 98
Terror, Hope, Fascination and Fear in Filipino Horror | Rochita Loenen-Ruiz 101
Horror, Inside Out | Jayaprakash Satyamurthy 104
The Thing We Have To Fear | Chinelo Onwualu 108
Horror Is....Not what You Think or Probably Wish It Is | Chesya Burke 112
Artists' Gallery | Maggie Chiang, Reiko Murakami,
SainaSix, and Kimberly Wengerd 116

AUTHOR SPOTLIGHTS
edited by Arley Sorg

Nadia Bulkin 125
Gabriela Santiago 127
Valerie Valdes 129
Russell Nichols 131
Nisi Shawl 133
Priya Sharma 135
Terence Taylor 137
Junot Díaz 141

MISCELLANY

Coming Attractions / Subscriptions and Ebooks 144
Stay Connected 145
About the Special Issue Staff 146
Additional Staff 149

ON THE DESTRUCTION OF HORROR: NOTES FROM YOUR PEOPLE OF COLO(U)R EDITORS

SPECIAL ISSUE EDITORIAL STAFF

Silvia Moreno-Garcia, Guest Editor-in-Chief and Original Fiction Editor

What scares you?

When I was growing up in Mexico, I watched horror movies set in the United States. The people there lived in huge houses crammed with luxury gadgets. And as the minutes ticked on, I hoped the killer got all the privileged, snotty kids with their fancy houses and their white picket fences.

What scares you when you are in a horror movie in the US? Your nice house built on Native American land being ransacked by ghosts, unencumbered young people who go camping and have sex in the woods only to face a masked killer, zombies who devour everyone at the shopping mall.

In these horror movies, there was never anyone like me. Never anyone who took the crowded subway and had to fend off men who wanted to pinch some teenage ass, never anyone who lived in an area dotted with factories and a sprinkling of petty crime.

The kids in American horror movies might as well have been living on Mars. It was the same with horror books. Upper middle class, white men faced evil. Four men in Peter Straub's *Ghost Story*, multiple New Englanders in Lovecraft's tales. Sometimes evil touched women, like in William Peter Blatty's *The Exorcist* or the lone girl in Stephen King's *It*, but these were also alien women, as distant as the moon.

This issue of *Nightmare* looks at the people who traditionally have not made it into the pages of horror books. People without white picket fences. People who face no masked killers or zombies who devour brains, but instead wade into more insidious waters.

What scares me? The stories and essays contained in these pages, which chronicle a deeper, darker haunting than anything experienced in Amityville.

Tananarive Due, Reprints Editor

As the reprints editor, I had a tough job selecting these four stories from so many worthy suggestions and submissions of previously published horror by writers of color. They were well-written and disparate and always engaging, so two central questions guided my choices: Do I believe in these characters? Does this story fill me with dread?

Dread is not a fun state in real life, but it's a delicious feeling when we're reading horror. For me, the guts of horror fiction is not the creature, or the infection, or the possession, but the way it forces us to feel about characters facing overwhelming odds. And what it teaches us about ourselves.

Nisi Shawl's vivid storytelling and poetic language in "Cruel Sistah" makes her haunted world come to life. Priya Sharma's "The Show," about a psychic with a television broadcast gone awry, spooked me with its warning not to meddle where we shouldn't. Terence Taylor's "Wet Pain" is an all-too-plausible rumination on the ways the past can creep into the present. And Junot Díaz's plague story "Monstro" is simply one of my favorite short stories (I teach it often), both for the horror it reveals in his fictitious world and in our real one.

They are the kind of stories that make daily headlines easier to read, life's mysteries easier to accept, and our own travails meek by comparison. They are also groundbreaking stories: authentic in voice and experience, and political by their very existence in a genre where writers of color are still vastly absent.

These stories help us better understand the wider world and further illustrate that all of us—regardless of background, age or circumstances—are still very much afraid of monsters, whether they lurk without or within.

MAURICE BROADDUS, NONFICTION EDITOR

The greatest gift my mother gave to me was the ability to dare to dream . . . and destroy. She was the first black nurse at the hospital where she worked, told repeatedly that she shouldn't bother applying. She made us the first black family to move into our neighborhood. She was always going where people thought she couldn't (or shouldn't) go, and often where some people didn't want her. She didn't care about facing down the hard stares of neighbors or dealing with the grumblings of co-workers. She ignored the tidal wave of micro-aggressions that became a part of her daily life for simply daring to exist and pursue the promised American Dream. Hers was a legacy of firsts and being a first destroys—it destroys preconceptions, destroys barriers, and that destruction makes room for something new.

Being in a space where not everyone wants you is not a new experience for any person of color. SQWs (Status Quo Warriors) want to reduce our experience to an obsession with identity politics, somehow turning the reduction of exclusion into a case of white victimhood. The same people who resent our presence try to relegate us to second-class citizen writer status. Demanding that we "earn [our] place at the table" while their place had been assumed. Because, ironically, at the root of their argument is fear. Fear that our inclusion means that we're taking slots from them. So, in the face of losing their ability to dominate and define, they get active and louder. These are the times we live in.

But we've been here before.

Being a first requires that people challenge the assumptions of how things are done. The genre continues to struggle with what it looks like to be inclusive, to not erase people of color from conventions (often relegating them to diversity panels) or anthologies. The genre has more than its share of editors who still proudly proclaim/defend a lack of diversity in their anthologies. Those editors march on, oblivious to the optics that they may be any combination of:

Lazy (because, seriously, how hard is it to reach out to people?).

Not widely read.

Unwelcoming (anyone can submit, as long as they ignore the latent hostility).

Without a very diverse circle of friends/influence.

Over a decade ago, editor/writer Brandon Massey released *Dark Dreams: A Collection of Horror and Suspense*. When the anthology was discussed within the tight-knit horror community, which wasn't very often, the discussion revolved around the series being the equivalent of "reverse discrimination" (ignoring the history of all-white, even more specifically, all-white male horror anthology series). Some writers and editors derided it as an affirmative action anthology, with the not-necessarily-unspoken insinuation that editors of diverse anthologies were actually bean counters produced by a PC culture; the writers themselves dismissed as recipients of some sort of editorial handout.

The defense for those wholly white and wholly male horror anthologies was that those editors were "just about the story." The reality was that they were about a certain kind of story. The problem was that those editors read from the same pool, catered to the same readers, and kept producing all-too-similar product to diminishing returns. Those same critics missed the whole point of an anthology aimed at the black market in an effort to grow the pie of readers. Instead, they focused on their fear of someone else cutting into what they saw as an already shrinking pie.

Being a first also challenges the definition of the status quo. When talking about the legacy of (western) horror, noted horror historian Darrell Schweitzer said: "Lovecraft is a defining writer. He is a figure like Wells or Heinlein in science fiction. The whole field either reflects him or rejects him. Your whole idea about what horror is or should be probably pivots on your ideas about Lovecraft, pro or con. He also defined much of the canon of the field in 'Supernatural Horror in Literature' . . . and he gave us much of the vocabulary of our discourse: weird fiction, cosmic horror."

The entire genre venerates H.P. Lovecraft and this points to the strangeness of the relationship of horror with people of color. Through the long lens of Lovecraft, people of color occupy a space of being viewed as The Other.

Sadly, being a first makes you question why you bother in the first place, and wonder whether putting up with the nonsense is all worth it. If horror is an emotive element, a matter of authorial intent—another common definition of the genre—then the emotions and the history of people of color are included. Which is partly why I'm drawn to the genre. I write from a personal place. Horror is the perfect genre to make sense of the daily horrors around me, make sense of my wounds, make sense of my scars. It gives voice to my despair, hurt, pain, and rage. By that measure, horror ought to be a point of connection between people. Horror should be a bridge to allow us to relate to one another if we're willing to listen to one another's stories. Different voices, different stories, different terrors, coming together since fear and pain are universal and reveal the same human condition.

You'll see these themes play out in the essays I chose. How the definition of horror—both through the lens of Lovecraft and as an emotive element—is seen from the outside and what our fears say to those outside of the U.S./Europe. What it means to be feared or erased. How horror can be a tool to exorcise our demons, deal with our pain, and process our rage. What works should be considered canon and why some works in that canon are problematic. All conversations we need to have as we build toward a better future.

The greatest gift my mother gave to me was the ability to dare to dream. To realize that to be born into a story doesn't mean you have to be constrained by that story. The horror genre is still in its phase of firsts, but people of color have nothing to prove. We are at the table, and SQWs have to deal with it. While the angry cries of SQWs may be evidence of a last, desperate gasp of an outdated mentality and way of doing things, that's also when those voices are the most dangerous. However, I live in hope. The fact that a rising chorus shouts down those SQWs' voices may portend a new day. In the meantime, I dream of a better future.

ORIGINAL
SHORT
FICTION

EDITED BY

SILVIA
MORENO-GARCIA

WISH YOU WERE HERE

NADIA BULKIN

"Tell us a ghost story," said one of the women, the pouty one, the one named Melissa. She was the nice, friendly one for now, the one asking questions, the one who wanted to stop at every little roadside fruit stall and pose next to every possibly rabid monkey, but Dimas knew this kind of tourist. Eventually, she was going to exhaust herself, and then—fueled by a high metabolism and the vengeance of unmet expectations—she was going to become his worst enemy. That was why he was counting on the other woman, Rose, to keep the group stable when they reached their breaking point, which was probably going to be on Day 3. He could already tell that both Melissa's and Rose's men would be useless.

For now, however, the tour was still in its "honeymoon" phase. Melissa was still excited, leaning out of the seatbelt that Dimas had forced her to buckle; Rose's man Ben's cellphone was still fully-charged, and Melissa's man Josh was still full

5

from breakfast, too. Rose was—well, it was hard to tell how she was, sitting in the back row and not having spoken the whole morning except to say that she and her husband had slept "fine." So, Rose was fine.

"A ghost story, eh?" Dimas glanced over at his driver, Nyoman, who shrugged. "Well . . . here's a story. An army unit is sent to a remote village in the middle of the jungle in order to move the villagers to a new settlement that's, uh, less remote. They need the land for an army base. But the villagers have lived there for a hundred years, and even though the government offered to buy the land, many times, they always refused to go. So the army drives up to the village in the middle of the night. They go to the first house on the main road—nobody home. They go to the second house—nobody home there, either. Third house—"

"Nobody home," said Ben.

"Right, nobody home. So the soldiers look at each other and say, where is everyone? Did they evacuate? Why did they leave all their belongings? Then suddenly, they realize one of their men is missing. All that's left . . . is his head. The soldiers panic. They're shooting at shadows, but it doesn't help. One by one, they're all killed by something they can't quite see, until finally, there's only one soldier left, and he's out of bullets. He squats down by a chicken coop, closes his eyes, and prays to Allah as he hears something come out of the darkness. He breaks open the chicken coop and throws a chicken, screaming, 'Take it!' There's a big crunch and so he looks and . . . it's a woman. Except she's got claws on her hands and feet, and her eyes are yellow. She's a tiger-woman. Of course, the soldier starts running back toward the trucks. Except this time, all the houses are full. The villagers are home. And they're eating his comrades."

Dimas laughed uncomfortably. Nyoman shot him an odd look. It was indeed an odd story to tell, one he would never have told two months ago—it involved soldiers dying. But in this new, rapidly-reforming world—this spinning, twisting lump of mud—nothing was off-limits. Or so he'd gathered from the drivers who blasted through Jakarta's red lights, yelling "Reformasi!"

For at least thirty seconds, the tourists said nothing. And then Josh, who had wasted no time telling everyone that he had already been to the island twice and he knew all its "ins" and "outs," said, "That's not really a ghost story, is it?"

Dimas stared over his shoulder at Josh, his plastic work-smile stretched across his mouth like the surgical masks the Japanese tourists liked to wear. "You're right," he said. "It's not."

Josh, clearly uncomfortable, smiled back almost in spite of himself.

Then Rose spoke. "So what happened?" Her voice was flat as the banana leaves slapping the windows of the van. "Did the government leave them alone?"

"Oh, no. The army came back with helicopters and sprayed the village with napalm until everyone left. It's an army base now—"

Without warning, Nyoman swerved violently to the right, unleashing a barrage of screams from the Americans. Dimas jammed his fingers against the window to protect his head. Josh spilled his iced coffee and Ben became very upset about what this traumatic maneuver might have done to the apparently breakable Rose. "Sorry!" Nyoman said, in exaggerated English, and then added, staring meaningfully at Dimas, "Animal ran into the road."

THEY PAID THE SECURITY GUARD eighty thousand rupiah each to enter the historic broken temple complex. Last month, it would have been seventy thousand, and four months before, it would have been forty thousand. The security guard kept it close to triple the cost of a bowl of noodles—one for each of his children. The Americans had no idea, and didn't complain. The dollar was monstrously in their favor, after all.

As the five of them trudged toward the ruins—Nyoman stayed in the van, partly to keep it from being stolen and partly because he would rather read the sports page and fantasize about the World Cup—Rose hung back with Dimas and asked, "Do you know a way to contact the dead?"

Dimas tried not to cringe as he squinted at her. She was hard to read behind those giant sunglasses. "Why, ma'am?"

"My son died in a . . . car accident," she whispered. "I just want to know he's all right."

Gatot, who ran the travel agency from a tiny office in Kuta, said that he had never before seen so many fever-dreaming grief tourists as were sleep-walking through Bali today. Most had lost parents or siblings, through plane crashes or cancer. They were good for business, because even the ones that didn't buy extensive reality-delaying package tours, like Rose's group, bought souvenirs and memorabilia and other *things* that they could wrap up and keep safe and take home with them, unlike the people they had lost. *It's because they think we're dying too,* Gatot said, and then defiantly snuffed out his cigarette on his own desk. *We'll just see who dies first.*

"He's all right, ma'am. For sure, he's all right."

"But how do you know?" A mosquito landed on her arm and deliberately sucked her blood. "I read about something that you have here. Jelangkung. Am I saying that right?"

He shook his head, watching her blood travel from flesh to insect belly. He had played with jelangkung. Ani's grandmother had showed them how, tying half a coconut shell to a pair of criss-crossed, rag-draped wooden sticks. *Give the ghost some respect,* her grandmother explained. *At least give it a head.* He also knew that a tourist would not have found that game unless actively searching for "ways to contact the dead." "Bad idea, ma'am."

"I thought we were supposed to get the full experience," Rose said. She had stopped walking, forcing him to pause as well, and by the way she was throwing out her arms, jangling her wooden bracelets, she was frustrated. "I thought anything was on the menu. That's what we paid for, isn't it? No-holds-barred, all-inclusive, complete-access bullshit. Right?"

He suddenly became conscious of a pain in his palms where his nails were digging. "Ma'am, jelangkung isn't like a person-to-person telephone call. It's like taking a megaphone and yelling, *hey, spirits, come find me.* Maybe your son answers. Maybe someone else. Maybe it's not like this in America, but over here, it's very, very crowded on the other side."

Rose took a deep breath in preparation for another rant, then apparently changed her mind and went hurrying up the hill with a new and soldierly determination. Dimas followed, trying to stop himself from shaking his head. At the crest, they looked out upon the broken temple complex, scattered across the bright green like a giant child's failed attempt to build a block tower. Dimas searched his pockets for his notes, because he didn't know anything about any of this. As a Javanese, all he knew about this island and its people was how good they were at cultivating an exoticism—just wild enough without being savage, *the rest of us can handle savage*—for Australians to fawn over. At the bottom, Melissa was waving enthusiastically.

Ben shouted something at Rose. He was pointing at one of the little half-fallen candi stupas. He was no bigger than a hand. On the hill, his wife was looking elsewhere, at the line of enormous trees that had been continuously beaten back by skidders and diggers, and before that, fires and saws. With his pulse pounding after the hike up the hill and Rose's demand and the thought of Ani's grandmother and the jelangkung, the trees seemed to be trembling. Ben didn't know that his wife wasn't watching, and he moved toward the stupa in large, grandiose steps, like an astronaut walking on the moon. Dimas was about to yell at him not to walk carelessly on the stupa when Ben suddenly slipped from view with a yelp that roused birds from the trees.

———◇———

"Tell me a ghost story." Ben hadn't spoken since he was told that he'd be bedridden with a broken leg for the next two months, and Melissa and Josh had to leave because they started arguing over the merits of alternative medicine, and Rose announced that she was taking a walk to get some sweet polluted air. "Ghosts this time, no monsters."

The quiet, pretty nurse adjusting Ben's IV widened her eyes and smiled. In the next bed over, behind a thick green curtain, a wheezing patient stirred in their bed.

"All right," said Dimas, who tried to focus on summoning his pity for Ben. "A boy moves to a new city to go to university. He thinks he's very lucky because he rents a room in a house that's quite close-by, just two street blocks away. The most direct route to his house is down a wide stretch of street that—for some reason—never seems to be very crowded. The buildings on either side are either abandoned or under construction. Taxis and becak don't use the road. It's very strange, he thinks. He walks down the path a couple times, in daytime, and doesn't see anything peculiar. But most of the time, he tries to avoid it just like everyone else.

"So one night he's at the university very late, because he has exams and he's trying to study and the electricity goes on and off at his house. Finally, he packs his things when he can't stay awake anymore and as he leaves campus, decides that he can't be bothered to take the long way around to his house. He takes the direct route. The first thing he notices is that a strange fog is just sitting in the street, like a landed cloud. The second thing he notices is that there's a figure in the fog ahead of him: a crying bloody man, in rags. The boy has enough sense to know this isn't good, so he tries to swerve around the man, except the man then appears again, right in front of him, weeping *Help Me*. The boy doesn't say anything and picks up his pace and feels someone grab him from behind—it's a woman this time, with her eye gouged out, saying, *It Hurts.* The boy pushes her off and runs straight into a body that doesn't even have a head, just arms reaching out to take hold of him. Eventually he just begins to pray as he runs and eventually the ghosts stop coming so close and he's able to run the rest of the way home. When he gets home he asks his old landlord, who's smoking a cigarette on the porch, what that street is. The landlord says, 'Oh, that's where they killed communists in this city, in 1965. They dumped the bodies in the gutter. Tell me, boy, what did they say to you?' And the boy says, 'Well, I think they were asking me for help.' And so the landlord leans forward and says, 'They'll need it in hell.'"

It wasn't a very good story, but Dimas didn't know how else to finish it. He had heard iterations of the story from several friends of friends over the years, always about a neighborhood that no one seemed to know of, and that cold razor-wire line had always been the ending.

Ben didn't care because he was asleep from all the pain medication he'd requested, but the nurse was staring at Dimas incredulously. "There's a road like that where I'm from too," she whispered. "But why would you go and tell *him? He* doesn't understand what it was like.'"

Neither she nor Dimas would have been old enough to have any real memory of 1965, but she wasn't talking about that. She was talking about institutional, *genetic* knowledge—the amorphous plasma that stitched acquired data together into one cohesive, rational narrative. "He wanted a ghost story," Dimas said with a shrug. "That one has a lot of them."

Half an hour later, the Americans reconvened for a team meeting in Ben's room. Ben was still unconscious, and they didn't want to disturb him, they said, but apparently they needed his body to be their non-voting witness. Rose sat down near the bed and silently held Ben's hand, and Dimas started to excuse himself. But she stopped him, with a set of cool fingers pressed persistently to the spot where his pulse hit his wrist. "We've decided to go on with the tour," she said. Her voice was utterly without affect. Behind her, Melissa and Josh were uncomfortably squirming, sucking mango soda from straws. "Where do you think we should go next?"

<hr />

DIMAS PURPOSEFULLY SAT AT THE end of a row of folding chairs—provided a quick exit, if needed, and allowed the three Americans to hopefully talk amongst themselves—and thanked God that Melissa, not Rose, demanded to sit next to him so she could ask him as many questions as possible about a dance he knew nothing about. But he had his notes, so he tried to explain to her the story of the stolen princess, her avenging husband, and the demon-king. Oh, and the warrior monkeys, which made Melissa's eyes gleam. Every so often Josh would interject, mostly to show that he could. Meanwhile, he could feel Rose staring coldly at him through both of her friends.

"Take a picture of us," Melissa said, slipping her little black camera into Dimas' hands and then leaning back into Josh. "Rose! Are you in the picture?"

Rose had to lean forward to get into view. Her look, naked in its resentment, was so awful that Dimas didn't even wait for Melissa to say *Bali Hai* before snapping the picture. He gave Melissa a thumb's up. His plastic smile was starting to ache.

After the kecak performance started, the audience of foreigners and wealthy natives—all from Jakarta, of course, no locals—prepared their cameras. As one chanticleer led a call-and-response around a fiery torch, the hundred male performers sitting in concentric rings on the ground shook as if inhabited by the splintered spirit of a cackling gecko god, arms outstretched and fingers frantically twitching. Dimas wondered how it felt, pretending to be possessed every sundown. He imagined them on their smoking break, sneering at tourists while they argued over where to buy shabu.

The fire leapt as Australian winds brought the night in, and the heavily made-up princess, legs wrapped so tightly that she seemed to have the lower body of a goldfish, began to skulk amongst the men. Ani had died in a fire. At least he assumed so, based on the charred remains of her family's convenience store. He told her to leave. He'd even told her to leave the city, the day after the students were shot in the street. But she dawdled. Froze. As if she wanted it to end this way. Ani did talk fatalistically about the fate of the nation, after the IMF deal was made and parliament re-elected the general for the seventh time. "Nothing ever changes," she said, but then they suddenly, violently did. Fiery beams fell between them and smoke filled his lungs and he couldn't wait any longer. What was he supposed to do? And why did she have to raise her eyes and look at him just before he turned his face toward his jacket, as if finally waking up from a deep sleep? Down in his gullet, amidst the muddy guilt and the true deep sadness that Allah knew he felt for the loss of Ani's life, lived the deep-seated fear that Ani's last moments on earth were drowned in the sort of bitterness that left a permanent stain.

Something was shaking beside him. He looked first at the dancers—the demon-king had emerged from behind a brick wall and caught sight of the princess, eyes on fire—and then at Melissa, who was the source of the tremors. Dimas thought at first that she was shivering, but when he saw her chin warbling and her eyes rolling back into the gulf of her skull and a small trail of saliva running down her chin, he knew this was worse. Then she slipped off her chair, falling onto a group of French tourists in the next row.

For a spare second in the desperate, dark moment that followed—Josh trying to control his seizing wife, Rose screaming at everyone to give the woman space, and the other tourists and all the dancers paying them no mind at all, *cak-kecak-kecak-kecak*, creating the unnerving sensation that the four of them had somehow fallen through a trap door past their waking world and into the next—Melissa's blue eyes focused. Those eyes looked at Dimas, and Rose, and maybe Josh as well, and it was not Melissa looking out. No, it was not. Their ears plugged, like passengers of a falling airplane, and then they were alone with it.

But ten seconds later, her eyes had rolled back again. The world righted itself, and now there was a German doctor on holiday holding up two fingers, and a woman in a hijab offering a dripping bottle of water with an unbroken seal, and a possum-eyed kecak dancer leaning down and asking, "She's on drugs, yeah?"

"TELL ANOTHER GHOST STORY," SAID Josh. "The scariest one you know."

Melissa put her head in her hands and whined, "I'm tired of ghost stories." But Josh didn't even look at her, and Rose just pushed a glass of ice water in her direction, telling her she should stay hydrated. Melissa pushed it back so forcefully that Dimas reached his hand out to catch it. "Jesus Christ, Rose," she snapped. "I'm not your kid."

Rose looked at her sourly.

Josh took another tortured sip of Bintang beer and raised his eyebrows at Dimas. "Well? You got one that'll make me shit my pants or what?"

"I have a story," said Dimas. Melissa started making a strange animal noise, between a growl and a whinny. Before Ani died, she used to say that she would haunt him if one of his stupid adventures got her killed—they were never all that dangerous, just rope bridges and speeding motorbikes and haunted hallways, but they liked to play pretend. And Ani would lean in and say *If I don't make it, I'll come back to get you.* Melissa, who was supposedly all better now, sat like a limp doll on the bench beside him, her jaw slightly slack as she stared ahead into the street, at the humming mass of travelers moving slowly in the half-light.

"A pregnant woman," Dimas started, then took a deep breath and began again. "A pregnant woman is tossing and turning in her bedroom in the middle of the night. She's been sick. She doesn't know what time it is, just that it's dark and she should be sleeping. But the lights to the living room are still on, and her mother-in-law asks her through the door if she's hungry. 'No thank you,' she says. What about some water? No, she doesn't want water either. How is she feeling, is she cold? And the pregnant woman finally says, loudly this time, 'I don't need anything!' So then her husband comes in the room, and wants to know who she's shouting at. Because his mother's not due to arrive until the next morning. So now the woman knows that she's being chased by a kuntilanak. That's the name of the ghost. Everyone here knows what it is. She's the ghost of a woman who died in childbirth and is searching for babies and blood in the afterlife."

A group of sunburned, middle-aged Australians burst out laughing, or crying, next to them—hard to tell which. They had their own tragedies. Their own demons to run from. Dimas looked back at his own cohort, but only Rose met his gaze. Melissa was humming along to "Hotel California," which had started playing over the Club Lizard speaker system for the sixth time that night. Josh was finally looking at Melissa, scorn mixed with longing.

"So the woman gets a pair of scissors from the bathroom and goes back to bed with the scissors clenched in her hand. She goes to sleep. It's still dark when she wakes up again, and there's a shape leaning down over her. And because she's a brave woman, she stabs it, right where she's supposed to—in the back of the head. The creature falls and she turns on the light and realizes it's her husband. And not only has she killed him . . . her beloved, the father of her child . . . but now she's alone with the kuntilanak."

Rose stared at him in hurt and shock. Out of the corner of his eye, he saw that Melissa had struck up a conversation with a man in snakeskin sitting next to her—he didn't seem to be part of the Australian group. "I'm sorry," Dimas whispered. "I don't know why I picked that story."

"I have an idea for a scary story," said Josh, "How about if you talk about what's going to happen to this country once it splits into twenty-seven pieces? How about that? What happens when all these fucking people . . ." He waved his beer around, even though two-thirds of the people in Club Lizard were tourists, ". . . realize that they don't have to worry about the military reining them in anymore? Why don't you give us a prediction for how fast things are going to burn down once the inmates are running the asylum?"

Dimas wondered if Josh had perhaps forgotten that he could speak English. He thought of Gatot's defiance—*We'll just see who dies first*—and forced himself to smile at Josh. He could see Melissa getting up and walking away with her new friend. Rose sitting in the dark, slowly opening and closing a pair of scissors. Ben eaten alive by mosquitoes in the hospital. And he saw himself in his sordid and bloody hometown, running through empty streets toward what used to be *Chinatown*, toward the burning building where he knew Ani would be waiting.

"Hopefully, by the time the world ends, you'll be gone," he told Josh, who didn't respond because he'd just now realized that the woman he'd walked through customs with, walked down the aisle with, was slipping quietly away into slippery anonymity. Fallen down a crevasse in the known world. It happens all the time.

———◇———

No ONE KNEW WHAT DIM, damp alley Melissa had disappeared into, and Josh was too angry to care. "Fuck her," he said, "She does this all the time. Remember Rio? She'll come back when she runs out of cash, the bitch." He kicked at a stop sign, covered in missing persons flyers for tourists who had largely lost themselves at will. *We Love You We Miss You Please Come Home.*

As they ambled back to the hotel, Rose tried again. "Please help me talk to my son," she begged. "I know you can. I know you know how."

Dimas glanced at her, and thought he saw something scuttle in the gutter behind her, something that cast an uneven, shuddering shadow on the heavily graffitied wall. "Bad idea, ma'am," he said again, staring at the glittering sidewalk—coated with dew and vomit. "I told you."

"He died so fast," Rose said. "Ben was driving. County road. We were coming back from a baseball game. Something happened, I don't . . ." She stared at a glowing red sun sign ahead of them for Bounty Discotheque. "There was something in the road. They said he didn't suffer, but . . . I didn't have a chance to say goodbye. I'm sure he's scared. He was such a little scaredy-cat."

Dimas spun around, cutting her off. "Mr. Josh!" His voice came out sounding very weak, very raw. The one thing Gatot always pressed, beyond comfort and satisfaction and legality, was liability: *keep your group together.* He had been thoroughly scarred by a recent incident in which an Australian dive boat had left two divers behind to be eaten by sharks at the Great Barrier Reef. And here Dimas had already lost Melissa. "Mr. Josh, I think we should hurry back to the hotel!"

But Josh had stopped near a clump of skinny teenagers huddled on the stoop of a shuttered scuba store. He had his wallet out and was very conspicuously taking out stacks of weathered rupiah. "Blo'on," Dimas whispered, but didn't step in. Why risk it? He wasn't going to end up in Hotel Kerobokan for anyone, especially not a fucking tourist. He counted to ten, trying to still his nerves and the sense that something besides motorcycle exhaust and patchouli was swirling around them, until Josh stuffed a little plastic baggie into his back pocket and sullenly resumed walking.

"He could never sleep in the dark," said Rose. "But neither can I. Shapes look different . . ."

A local call girl in garish theater make-up stumbled out of Bounty, followed by an anxious-looking man three times her age. "Melissa!" Josh screamed at the call girl, who looked over her shoulder at him and sneered. "*Go home you wanker*," her companion shouted. Josh slapped his hand on the hood of a nearby car—thank God, no alarm—and shouted back, "Come make me!"

It was a bad idea from the start. Cops were never very far from Bounty, and these days they—like everyone else in the country—were teetering on a knife's edge. Too many stories about docile village mobs decapitating bus drivers who ran over small children could make a policeman twitchy. Even the Dayaks, supposedly beaten into submission decades ago, had come out of the jungle and set logging equipment on fire. *Ya Allah!* What's a cop to do? Couldn't trust anybody anymore—not even two drunk Westerners who would have been sent home to their hotels in the good old days. The British man and the call girl eventually teetered away down Jalan Legian, but when the cops found ecstasy in Josh's pocket, that was it. Some chlorine-stained kids in sporty beachwear came out of Bounty to point and laugh, but Dimas hurried Rose away to the growling sound of what Dimas could only hope was thunder rolling down from the highlands.

◆

"TELL ME A GHOST STORY. A real one, this time."

He wanted to tell her that they had all been real, or might as well have been. He could have told a thousand other anecdotes, about mysterious lights and strange coincidences and unexplained illnesses and visions of dead passengers seen by only half the bus—but they had wanted *stories*, hadn't they? Stories with a set-up and an escalation and a terrible, brutal denouement.

"This is the last one," he said, and meant that, because there was a more than decent possibility that he would not make it to the final Day 5. He had seen another humanoid shadow while brushing his teeth the night before, and then found the window to his third-floor apartment open and the drapes dancing, and he knew they were being hunted. Correction: *he* was being hunted, and Allah had sent ghost-seeker Rose to Gatot's Tropical Adventure Tours in order to let him know that it was time for him to buck up and stop running from his fate, soldier.

Dimas was driving this time. He'd told Nyoman where they were going—the huge, unfinished Bali Grand Hotel—and Nyoman had laughed in his face and demanded double a day's pay to make the drive, which Dimas didn't feel like asking Rose about. Rose was cradling the hodgepodge shopping bag of a jelangkung's component parts—two broomsticks, half-a-coconut, permanent marker, incense, twine, a Superman shirt because her son's favorite character was Superman, paper stolen from the hotel room—on her lap as if they were the very bones of her child.

"My friend, my best friend, died in a fire. Along with her father and grandmother. Some people . . ." He shook his head. What to call them? Psychopaths, murderers?

He'd run the streets alongside them, silent while they yelled. "Some very angry people set fire to their store. I was in there with them, trying to convince them to leave the city because I could see it coming—not the fire, of course, or the riots. But once the fires started, I knew what would be burned." His lip quivered. "I got out. Because I didn't wait. I was scared, you know. I thought I was going to die. I convinced myself that she'd follow, if she saw me running. I thought she'd make it out. I stood outside the building for ten minutes, I think, waiting for her. And . . ."

"And she didn't make it."

He glanced back at Rose through the rear view mirror. "She didn't make it. And ever since, I've been afraid of seeing her. Around campus. On the street. Even in a room full of people, I can't look at faces too closely. Because I left her, you see. Because that sort of betrayal leaves a . . . a *mark* in the world. Like a cigarette burn. I got so scared that I couldn't leave my house, but even then, I could feel *someone* sitting on the couch and just looking at me. That's why I decided to leave Jakarta. Just being near those buildings, I couldn't . . . I could feel her spirit. Her energy."

There was a small white mass in the road ahead that he realized in a few moments was a goat. He slowed to a stop, hoping the engine roar would scare it into moving, but its milky eyes barely registered the vehicle. Sighing, he kept his foot on the brake. He contemplated telling her that after a few lonely months, Ani had apparently found him again—bringing with her the shadows, the whispers, the cold sensation of being under someone's eye, the hazy cloud of a spirit's hug, the sick-in-the-gut *feeling* of hovering by a bungee cord over the gaping maw of the great unseen world—but when he opened his mouth, he was too afraid to say the words out loud.

Rose's voice had softened when she spoke next. "I know what that's like."

"After your son died?"

"Even before that. It got stronger after Connor died, but . . . I'd felt it for a long time. A *presence*. That feeling like even when you're alone in a locked room, you're never alone." Then she chuckled and wiped a tear out of the corner of her eye. "Ben always called it my guardian angel. I think he was just trying to make me feel better. But I've been thinking that maybe he's right. Who's to say it's not a guardian angel? Who's to say your friend's angry at you? Maybe she's just watching over you."

The goat's minder, an old man with a long beard, came out of the bushes and pushed the goat along with a few swats of a small stick. The old man flashed a black-toothed smile at their van—no, not quite at the guilt-eaten man at the wheel nor the mournful woman in the backseat, but at something just behind them, something that must have been beautiful.

"*I'd* be angry," was all Dimas said.

THE BALI GRAND WOULD HAVE been horrific, had it been allowed to live. It was gaudy, too heavy and too white and far too marbled for the gentle green hills it was nestled in. The general's son had signed off on the final design after an extended stay at the casino-hotels of Las Vegas. Thankfully, the project ran out of money during the financial crisis, leaving the hotel unfinished with its very bones exposed, like the broken-open jaws of a long-dead giant. Rumor was that the general's son still lurked somewhere amongst the pillars and arches, but that was bullshit. Everyone knew he was hiding in Europe, in a premium suite of a hotel he hadn't designed.

The Bali Grand was still horrific now, but for different reasons—under the flapping tarps and abandoned construction equipment it was undoubtedly haunted, if not by dead workers then by the ghosts of offshore private loans and weakly-regulated banks.

Dimas and Rose went to the partially-constructed lobby, where tile floors had been laid and a patchwork roof had been erected, to build their conduit. The jelangkung. Then they leaned the doll against the wall to watch them eat their martabak and wait for night to fall.

Nothing happened the last time Dimas played this game, with Ani and a couple other jokers at school. No one had been expecting anything, of course—they were just bored and trying to take their minds off exams. They gave the coconut-shell a googly face and asked the oxygen molecules and cigarette smoke whether they would pass their tests. Nothing tuned into their antenna. But this time, as Dimas led Rose in a shaky overture to the spirit world—*we're having a little party*—he felt that he was practically inviting Ani—whatever was left of Ani—to come forward.

Dimas saw Rose holding the wooden creature, turning the broomstick body gently in her hands like one of those hunchbacked beach-women who traverse the littered coastline hawking umbrellas and massages and temporary tattoos, and closed his eyes. Imagined the peace of the sea. He only opened them after he felt the pressure in the room plummet, as if an anchor had dragged him and Rose and the Bali Grand Hotel ten meters below the surface. With tensed muscles and an aching top row of teeth, he expected to see Ani levitating above the jelangkung, with peeling skin and denouncing eyes. But though the darkness had grown touchably thick beyond their struggling candlelight, he saw nothing. Just Rose . . . gagging on something lodged in her throat.

"Miss Rose? Are you all right?"

Rose was not fine. At that moment Rose was a broken vase, and someone—something—that wasn't Rose came spilling out of her like a gush of tar and slithered across the floor. No, not Rose. Also not Ani. And he was willing to bet the value of Rose's all-inclusive tour package that no matter how badly Rose wanted it to be, that it wasn't Rose's little boy Connor either.

The oily shadow crawled across the floor, wrapped itself around the jelangkung, and held it upright when Rose's grasp failed. It drenched the Superman shirt and twirled the permanent marker dangling from one broomstick arm. Rose whispered, "Connor? Sweetie, is that you?"

The jelangkung was supposed to tip and use the pen to mark a Yes or a No on the paper. It did lean in, at first—and then it started shaking. Violently. It was almost like a headshake, *NO NO NO*, but then with a terrifying bang and a howl from the ends of the earth, the wooden body flew apart. One broomstick nearly hit Dimas in the temple, and a shredded piece of the Superman shirt landed in Rose's lap. Like a taunt. Meanwhile, the shadow spread. Covered the ceiling beams and dripped down the unpainted walls. Occasionally, its edges would curl together and form the shape of a man or a cow or a tiger—*shapes look different*, wasn't that what Rose said?—and then it would flatten out and seep to another corner of the room. Though it had hitched a ride with Rose, this shadow didn't know sadness. It was more primitive than that: it was just hungry. It lay so oppressive on their fragile human souls simply because it wasn't human, and never had been.

By then, Dimas had slid over to Rose so he could quietly urge her to say goodbye, to end the ritual. She was feverishly muttering something—about Connor, and a number of other things Dimas couldn't identify—and he had to lean in close: "Miss Rose, you have to close the door."

This only made her whisper more frantically, clenching the Superman rag to her chest.

"Miss Rose, close the door so we can drive away. We can go to Kuta. See your husband . . ."

"Can't leave it . . ." Did she mean *the presence?* "I can't leave."

Every human cell in his body wanted to leave, because it knew this feeling and wanted to survive. This thing had come to this country wrapped around Rose's skeleton—it wouldn't have chased him. He'd have gotten away. Yet he helplessly sank to his knees as if his feet were lodged in mud. Ani's legacy, he supposed. Because that was when he finally felt her outside of her normal Jakartan habitat: the same electric seizure he'd feel when pedaling past her blackened building or the empty, tortured malls where they used to fantasize about a Someday Life of large televisions and luxury brands. He imagined her putting her arms around him, pulling him down, saying, *Stay.* Not meanly, not hatefully. But honestly. *Keep your eyes open this time, scaredy-cat. Here it comes.*

—◦—

A RED-AND-BLACK CENTIPEDE CRAWLED ACROSS Dimas's hand, down into the dark concrete valley, and then onto the denim of Rose's jeans. Dimas, who'd woken up to the sound of rain, nudged her; Rose didn't react. He could feel the chill emanating from her body. He shifted to get a better look at her and confirmed the sick feeling in his stomach. She was dead. Eyes open, jaw slightly slack. Heart attack? Theft of the soul? He didn't want to touch her, but knew if he didn't close her eyes now then she would definitely roam the earth forever.

Very cautiously, he crossed the empty expanse of the hotel lobby, watching for shadows or drops in atmospheric pressure or noises of any kind. Nothing but the rain gave him goosebumps. He ran to the van, not bothering to shield his head.

He told the first cops he could find, two boys who probably should have been guarding a mall in Denpasar. For some reason—conditioning?—they believed his story, and promised to go up to the Bali Grand just as soon as the rain cleared up. Then Dimas drove back to Kuta. He thought about checking on Ben at the hospital, or Josh at the prison, but decided not to do either, not yet. He didn't even know where he'd find Melissa, if he'd find Melissa—probably in the Crime & Punishment section of the Bali Post. So instead he went to see Freddy, a tattoo artist who specialized in painting visions of the bug-eyed, toothy Barong, the good spirit-king.

Freddy welcomed him in and sat him down in front of the television. On the table were video cases of Freddy's favorite horror movies: a plastic mess of red eyes and long black hair and frightened, stupid teens. Dimas thought of *The Forgotten*— the legendary ghost story that the censorship board locked up years ago on account of being cursed. Rumor had it that a real ghost had been caught on camera during filming, and that a critic had died of a heart attack during an early screening at Pondok Indah Mall. He didn't remember what it was about anymore—something about a dead witch, and a secret room. *Tell me a ghost story.*

"Hey, did you ever track down *The Forgotten?* You know, the cursed movie?"

Freddy laughed. "Why? You want to watch it? I did find it, my friend. But it was nothing special. Turns out it was banned because the movie didn't have any kiai come in to beat up the evil spirit by the grace of Allah." He handed Dimas a bowl of cup noodles. "Can you believe it? So stupid. But at least we can watch all the shitty movies we want now, after Reformasi."

Dimas wasn't convinced that the little vice president currently on television would change the rules of the censorship board, but he had been wrong before. Right now, the little vice president was forbidding the sort of language that had gotten Ani killed for being Chinese, for not being a true daughter of the land—so there was that. Freddy sat down on the couch with his own cup noodles and switched to the jittery black of channel 4, where a movie was already playing. A lady-ghost in a white shift was moving without weight through a foggy cemetery. If it started with her, it would end with her. She'd been terribly wronged. She'd be avenged.

"I think I did something terrible," Dimas said.

Freddy sighed. "You need to forgive yourself, 'Mas. She's not going to come all the way back here just to forgive you. She has better things to do now, right? She's at peace. Let her go."

A stray memory flickered, of Ani snorting iced tea out her nose at something he'd said about a teacher. "I don't mean that . . ."

"So what now? You left a tourist somewhere?"

"I think I let something loose. Something they were carrying with them."

"What, like heroin?"

"No, something worse." He imagined the shadow loping through the forest, flying among the bodiless leyak, feasting upon the grievers and the guilty and the human guides who so delicately threaded the needle-eye balance—a spirit-monster out of its ecosystem, devouring all in its path like a bulldozer on autopilot. "I'm so sorry. I never should have come to Bali."

He felt Freddy slow turn to look at him as an uncomfortable, unmistakable tension started to clog up the room. On television, the ghost swept aside her long black hair to reveal a gaping, pulsing wound. Rotten and squirming and infested and yet, somehow, very much alive.

———

Nadia Bulkin writes scary stories about the scary world we live in. Her stories have recently appeared in the *Aickman's Heirs, Autumn Cthulhu, Cassilda's Song, She Walks in Shadows,* and *The Mammoth Book of Cthulhu* anthologies, with others forthcoming in *The Madness of Dr. Caligari* collection and *The Dark* magazine. She is also a three-time Shirley Jackson Award nominee. She lived in Jakarta until shortly after Indonesia's violent transition to democracy in 1998, with her Javanese father and American mother. She now works inside the Beltway in Washington, D.C., and remains a true believer in Reformasi. She can be found online at nadiabulkin.wordpress.com.

NONE OF THIS EVER HAPPENED

GABRIELA SANTIAGO

I SAW THE ROCK THAT I didn't take into my apartment when I was going through the dumpster. People move out of our apartment complex in an awful hurry. One time, I found a wok with the noodles not even washed off it.

I picked up the rock that I didn't take into my apartment because I was thinking about giving it to my mom. My mom might have become a geologist if she had taken a geology class when she was in college instead of 20 years later. The story of my life would be very different if she'd become a geologist. The rock that I didn't take into my apartment looked like some kind of sandstone, iron orange, with shiny bits of quartz and a few little fossils, the ones that look like screws.

But I didn't take the rock into my apartment, because when I looked more closely, I saw that someone had scratched the word EAT into one side.

I put the rock back into the cardboard box in the dumpster with the camera and the sock puppet and the book-light partly because it seemed suddenly very personal, like an angry letter or a pair of panties. It had been a part of the story of the person or people who were moving away, a story with hunger etched in thin lines, and as a part of their move they had decided to edit it out. It wasn't theirs anymore, but it had been so much theirs that it could no longer become anyone else's.

Mostly, though, I put the rock back because I have read a lot of books and seen a lot of movies. When you have read a lot of books and seen a lot of movies, you reach a certain level of genre-savvy that you cannot turn off even though you know that you yourself are not in a book or movie and are almost certainly a real person. I am genre-savvy enough to know that you do not take a rock with the word EAT scratched into it in jagged letters into your apartment and expect anything good to happen.

I was not genre-savvy enough, however, to avoid taking the stuffed baby alligator. This was a real actual used-to-be-alive baby alligator. Its eyes were gone. Its skin was brown and sewn down the center of its stomach. I took the stuffed baby alligator because my avoid-the-classic-mistakes-of-horror-story-protagonists drive was overwhelmed by my protect-the-small-inaminate-object-that-resembles-a-larger-animate-object drive. The latter drive is the same reason I collect action figures. They are so small and still in my hands. They feel like they need me to protect them. I feel like I can protect them, that I can protect a small part of the characters and actors that they represent, that I love.

Anyway, it was about the time that I was taking the stuffed baby alligator but not the rock into my apartment that I started thinking about making this into a story.

I admit, I pilfer details of my life for my stories. I am trying to write as many words a day as I can, to finish my stories as quickly as I can, to edit and submit them as quickly as I can, to receive the rejection letters as quickly as I can. I could spend a lot of time thinking up new minor life details, or instead my characters could also have almost drowned when they were five and have met the same creepy people on the 21 bus line.

Of course, in the story that I would write about the person who found a strange rock and a stuffed baby alligator in the dumpster, the protagonist would not be too much like me. It would be necessary to make them at least a little bit less genre-savvy so that they would take the rock that I did not take into my apartment, into their apartment. Perhaps they could be interested in geology like my mother. Or perhaps they could be intrigued by the unknown story of the rock and its disposal: an eating disorder, maybe?

I would also not make the protagonist a writer. Making the protagonist a writer never ends well.

By this point in my ponderings I was indoors with the stuffed baby alligator but not the rock. If I had taken the rock into my apartment like the protagonist of my story, this would be the place where I would look around my apartment and observe several objects to help set the scene. Maybe I could take inspiration for the décor from the other items left in the trash; maybe some sort of doubling/multiplying/doppelganger theme could be wrung out of the six X-Acto knives and four spiked hammers? Those at least made sense, but how many dismembered pianos did anyone really need? Judging by the instrumental innards stacked against the wall, the answer was three.

It had not escaped my attention that a great majority of the items left in the dumpster would make excellent murder weapons. This was both a potential avenue for the story to go down, as well as an alarming clue about the nature of the people whose dumpster I had been sharing before they moved out in such a considerable rush that they left behind a leather satchel with sixteen perfectly good drill bits in various sizes, a stuffed baby alligator, and a rock with the word EAT scratched into it in jagged letters that I did not take into my apartment.

My regrettably un-genre-savvy protagonist, having taken the rock with EAT scratched on it into her apartment, and having gazed around her apartment for a good paragraph or two's worth of time, would now doubtless be overcome by the urge to eat. It would be necessary to do this subtly, especially since there is very little that is subtle about a rock with the word EAT scratched into it. Perhaps she could have a problem with stress-eating, as I do. The problem with stress-eating, of course, is that fairly soon you have eaten everything in the apartment, and you have to leave. I do not do well with leaving my apartment. I do well enough to go outside and look through the dumpster and find a rock with EAT scratched into it and not take it inside, and going to the grocery store is all right on a good day, but less all right on a bad day, though of course today is not a bad day; I am doing just fine, thank you. The thing about leaving the apartment on a bad day is that the floor and walls will seem to flicker and pulse and bulge in time with my heart. The thing about leaving the apartment on a bad day, which this isn't, is that the back of my body will suddenly grow quite heavy, as though coated in a layer of lead, lead all down the back of my head and neck and shoulder blades and buttocks and thighs and calves and heels, and I will have to lie down on the cold wooden floor and stare at the white, white, white ceiling until the back of my body stops being so heavy and I am breathing normally and my mind is putting words on objects again, which makes the world easier to carry, which makes me able to stand up. In certain respects, the white, white, white of a blank Word document is the same as that of the ceiling, yet the effect is completely different, a paralysis like a deer looking into the eyes of a wolf. In order to keep from being devoured, you must march the black typeface from left to right, keep moving so that the predator cannot get a lock on you. Perhaps my protagonist, instead of being soothed by the white walls, could envision them as a great white mouth closing over her mind, erasing her. Perhaps the mouth could whisper the word "eat" over and over as she types—but she would not type, because I would not make her a writer.

I confess that I have gotten away from my original idea of stress-eating in order to underline the thematic appropriateness of the rock with EAT scratched into it that I did not take into my apartment but will be putting into my story. Let me be completely honest, however: I will probably never explain this rock. I will tell myself that I choose not to explain because life does not follow the rules of narrative causality: dismembered pianos just appear in dumpsters with no explanation, and people disappear with no satisfactory build-up or resolution, as if they were swallowed up by the walls.

But probably I am just lazy. I distract from my laziness by incorporating as many elements as possible into a narrative. For instance, if I felt like stopping typing, I might go look up the text of Hansel and Gretel, or firsthand accounts of the Donner party, or the German Craigslist ad looking for someone willing to be devoured. I don't feel like stopping typing at the moment, but these are all potentially promising elements for a story about a rock with the word EAT scratched into it.

And of course, it is also important to avoid getting too married to real life details when choosing story elements. For instance, right now I am sitting at a nice wooden table with a cup of iced chai, whereas my protagonist will almost certainly be sitting at a nice wooden table with a cup of iced chai that suddenly turns to warm blood in their mouth. The nice wooden table will suddenly be covered in scratches: scrawled mouths and entrails, and over and over again in jagged letters, the word EAT. The protagonist will be engaged in some artistic activity that is definitely not typing—again, writers as the protagonist never work out, it's so embarrassing and obviously a self-insert—and be trying to desperately ignore the scrawled mouths and entrails and the word EAT with their jagged fanglike lines all up and down the walls, because despite her previous, almost unforgivable, lack of genre-savvy, there will be an ice-cold certainty coiled in her gut and jammed through her spine to her lower brain, that certainty that never quite left us when we scampered off the savannah to take shelter in the caves with our fires and our tools and our wonderfully distracting and distancing paintings: the certainty that we are being watched and that to look is to be devoured, that as long as we can't see them then they can't see us. We were right all along as children: if we cover our eyes with blankets, the monsters will stay away. And if you see the monsters, oh, pretend you never did, keep looking at something else, keep making something else to look at, or the monsters will know you see them and they will look back and see you.

If the story of my life had been different—if, for example, my mother had become a geologist—I might have become the kind of character who would tell a story bereft of monsters.

Speaking of monsters, it is rapidly becoming clear to me that I will have to get rid of the stuffed baby alligator that I brought into the apartment. I will have to get rid of it both in the story and real life. In real life, it may be small but it is still an alligator, with that prehistoric coldness in the eyes, which is made worse by the fact that its eyes are only empty sockets. My avoid-the-classic-mistakes-of-horror-story-protagonists drive insists that instead of negating the possibility of surveillance, this only heightens the number of entities that could take advantage.

And the stuffed baby alligator cannot be kept in the story either, as the stuffed baby alligator can do nothing in the story but stare, and who would read a story where a stuffed baby alligator does nothing but stare and tell you with its eyes to lift your eyes up and look back at it, look back at those empty eyes and those small teeth and at the white, white, white wall beyond it where its mother lies waiting in the blank spaces where you have no ideas, where there is no mental parade with a brass band blaring words to keep it at bay, where it can wait forever before sooner or later you have to stop doing whatever-artistic-pursuit-I-decide-on-that-is-not-typing because you have nothing left to type or whatever else I decide on instead and it surges forward out of the wall in the split second when the words stop marching left to right across the page? I am just now remembering the real life mystery of Mary Lynch; Dr. John Stockton Hough cutting the skin from her thighs and tanning it to bind his books. Her skin looked like soft leather, brown with age, bits flaking off at the corners where the binding was handled roughly; it looks just like the skin of the alligator. It is cold and my skin is cracking along my knuckles, along each joint, the cold blanches my skin a shade lighter than the alligator skin, and then of course there is the red.

Conventional wisdom is that liars embroider, adding unnecessary details, but this is only true for inexperienced liars, children finding an alibi for the empty cookie jar. Experienced writers—I meant to type liars—know that they may be tripped up in a forgotten detail, so they stick to broad outlines, refuse to embellish when asked point-blank. They use fewer words and fewer different words. A machine can analyze transcripts and predict with an eighty percent success rate who is speaking the truth, a percentage that detectives and profilers can only dream of.

"Tangent!" my older sister would say if I were to switch subjects so rapidly in conversation as I have in the last two paragraphs. My older sister is a biochemist who has qualified for a civilian mission to Mars. Does that sound like a lie? The trick in Two Truths and a Lie is always to pick the most outlandish truths and one slightly less outlandish lie, and perhaps that is an idea for the story, that the rock with the word EAT scratched into it in jagged letters that I did not bring into my apartment has something to do with the lies we tell ourselves, and the truths, and the way they build up inside you and bloat you up like a fattened lamb until the true words and the untrue words left unsaid call through the rocks with the word EAT scratched deep into them that you don't bring into your apartment, call and call and call and oh that sizzle-fat smell of bacon frying in its own grease, it leaves your apartment even when you don't leave your apartment and it travels past Mars into places where there is only a blankness whiter than looming walls or a blank screen and the blankness draws in a deep breath, smells the soured fermented stink of the words inside you, silence like sugar and salt and warm blood on what it has instead of a tongue, and it comes for you and it's always been there but now it's closer and the words will run out soon, language is a discrete combinatorial system and you can type a sentence that has never been spoken before and it can be a "colorless green ideas sleep furiously" bit of grammatical nonsense but don't type "colorless green ideas sleep furiously" because the thing that is not inside the apartment right now moves closer because the sentence "colorless green ideas sleep furiously" is a sentence that has been spoken before and it doesn't create the rattle-bang noise that keeps it away but don't stop typing to think of a new sentence because if you pause for a moment then it is not just closer, it is there. But look, I have been typing "typing" and we have already settled the issue that the protagonist will not be a writer, even if she is a liar.

I can only tell the truth by lying. That is why monsters are necessary, and spaceships and fairies and aliens and things under the bed. The accoutrements of the real world do not convey sufficient emotional impact to properly explain the actions and reactions of the real world. Being a seventeen-year-old girl falling in love with another girl did not feel like being a seventeen-year-old girl falling in love with another girl. Being a seventeen-year-old girl falling in love with another girl felt like being a gruff, self-loathing gelatinous metamorph raised during a brutal occupation by a scientist who named him "Nothing," falling in love with a fiery Bajoran whom he felt would instinctively reject and be repulsed by the unalterable fact of his biology. Thanks, *Star Trek: Deep Space Nine!*

The best episode of *Deep Space Nine* is "Far Beyond the Stars," in which Captain Sisko is suddenly and without explanation catapulted into the life of Benny Russell, a black science fiction writer in the 1950s. The great tragedy of *Deep Space Nine* is that you cannot immediately show this episode to any potential acolytes of the show, because in order to understand why it is the best episode you must have seen every episode leading up to it, so that you will love every character and understand every trope associated with them and weep in the final scene when Benny Russell insists that he has made a world, that knowledge alone can make a world, that the space station with a black commander really exists, it's real, it's real, it's real!

I said without explanation, but there is of course eventually some explanation; Star Trek is in love with explanations. Even when its explanations do not make sense, Star Trek is founded on the belief that explanations exist, and can be hunted down with the scientific method and stuck into place with a pin. Star Trek is a series of endless corridors without a hint of white empty walls, because all the walls are filled with butterfly cases and all the explanations are labeled so neatly. You can walk along the corridors and read all the labels and the labels keep the whiteness out, keep your head filled up with words with the weight of a comforting blanket, and if you keep walking you can keep alive that little flame of hope in your heart that you will understand it all someday, if you just keep walking, keep reading, keep catching butterflies and pinning them oh-so-neatly in place until the walls are a mosaic testament to the scientific method and ether and butterfly nets.

For this reason, I could not make the story about the rock with the word EAT scratched into it that I did not take into my apartment into a Star Trek episode.

I could make it into Star Trek fanfiction. This is not to say anything about the respective quality of writing in either potential piece, only that a Star Trek episode is part of the mainstream media and therefore must follow a conventional narrative arc with a beginning and middle and end, with a clear source of conflict and a clear set of complications that arise as a result of actions taken or not taken by the characters, and with a clear resolution. There will probably not be a clear resolution when I write this story, as I will certainly do any minute now, once I have finished typing. There is no reason why I should not finish typing anytime soon.

Star Trek fanfiction, on the other hand, could employ these traditional narrative tools, but often prefers to focus on interstitial moments instead. The through line of the story has already been so carefully charted; why craft another when you could delve into the little nooks and crannies that took place off-screen? Someone has to write Uhura looking out the window and dreaming of home. Uhura dreams of home regardless, but without the anchoring words she may be forgotten, may go drifting off into the blank whiteness of the pages without typewritten words, until there is no trace of her anywhere, not even far, far beyond the stars. You have to write Uhura over and over again because she was there and she was real, and you're here and you're real, you're real, you're real! You exist and you are made of more things than blood and the food in your stomach and the words you're typing out on the page; you have to be more than the words because otherwise the thing will come out of the walls where it always is and out of the place it always is and it will always have been inside you and you were never there.

Maybe I could put H.P. Lovecraft in this story. My writer friend Marie does not like H.P. Lovecraft. Who does? He was a racist asshole. But Marie also does not like his writing. She says he uses too many words, and he never uses them to actually describe anything, only to explain over and over again how indescribable the horror is. But if I put H.P. Lovecraft into the story of the rock with the word EAT scratched into it that I did not take into my apartment, then something like an explanation emerges about the thing that lived under the streets of Providence and shifted and stretched and looked for the true and untrue unspoken words; and a lonely, cruel man sat and wrote about the world that was changing in ways he could not understand, about the people that were coming to his town who he did not understand, and called it the same thing. And he never looked in their eyes because what if the thing was there? Or worse, what if it wasn't there, which would mean it might be somewhere else, might be close by, might be inside—

I am thinking specifically of a poem H.P. Lovecraft wrote about a black cleaning woman. H.P. Lovecraft's poetry is truly laughable, and everyone should read a collection of it at least once to feel better about themselves. But that poem was terrifying; not because of the cleaning woman, but because of the way H.P. Lovecraft abducted her in words to make a point. Because he was so afraid. Always, always so afraid of things touching and mixing and becoming something that was not clear-cut, so afraid and yet he couldn't look away. He had to keep describing.

My writing is probably more influenced by H.P. Lovecraft than I would like to admit. It comes back to the explanations again, and the lack thereof in my magical systems. Perhaps this is because I do not believe in magic. I once flippantly told another writer friend, Kodiak, that everything I have ever written has been an anguished scream of realization that magic is not real. I didn't realize it at the time, but that was already a lie. That had been the reason I wrote, all through high

ORIGINAL SHORT FICTION · 24

school and college when all the expectations and lists of steps to be checked off to transform into a successful adult had weighed down on me like chains. But when there was suddenly no more carefully structured syllabus of life, I started writing because of all the little places where the possibilities live. The in-between moments of an everyday life, the liminal thresholds and barriers and slightly broken chain-link fences on the edge of the railroad by Fairview where true-crime shows film their episodes. I still do not believe in magic, but I write because it is not necessary to believe in magic in order to love magic and fear magic and see all the places where magic could lurk, all the little ragged edges, ragged like fingers beckoning you to come closer, closer, come closer and see and maybe you will go mad or maybe you will die or maybe you will go to a secondary school with a curse on the position of Defense Against the Dark Arts professor, but something will happen, you will see something and not nothing.

Also, I write because the words taste nice when I read them. If this were a story it would be far too late in the narrative to introduce the fact that I have mild synesthesia, but since this is the truth it does not matter at what point the facts are disclosed. My synesthesia used to be more limited, but four years of college reading heavy tomes and poorly photocopied excerpts over sandwiches and yogurt means that I now taste words in addition to picturing them in different colors. My own words taste like tomato soup with toasted cheese, like hot black tea with a spoonful of honey and lots of whole milk. Temple Grandin has one of the best tastes, like Ritz crackers and milk but with an entirely different texture, crisper and less crumbly, more like iceberg lettuce. I have to read and read and read or I cannot write; there is nothing for me to make my writing out of. Please try not to follow this metaphor to its logical conclusion.

I might give my protagonist an exaggerated version of my synesthesia. Then when she has finished stress-eating all the food in her house, when she has finished eating all the furniture and the sheets and the blankets and the books and her own flesh as much as she can before the pain gets too much, the red running over the dry skin—she'll eat everything she can reach except her fingers, she'll need her fingers for her artistic pursuit that isn't typing—she'll try to eat the words inside her head. She'll start with other languages, Hmong—I have a community education class in Hmong tonight and it's going to kick my ass assuming I can leave the house, all those tones and those consonant clusters blurring together in my brain—and then Japanese and then Spanish, or maybe Spanish first, since even though it's closer linguistically to English I learned it almost ten years after I learned Japanese when I lived in Yokosuka. And finally she'll have to eat English, starting with the words she won't use, racist and homophobic slurs, then ones like "moist" that no one likes, then snobby performance theory terms—until finally she has to eat them all, her jaw curving around in non-Euclidean space to carve them out of her brain, grey matter spattering on her keyboard; the jaws in the white walls around her curving into something that would be a laugh if it could be described, because anticipation heightens the pleasure, because it is fun watching the lamb delay by fattening itself up further for the slaughter. "Anticipation heightens the pleasure" is a cliché and it is a mask over the true thoughts of the thing in the walls, and a truer mask would be teeth, would be blood, would be a rock with the word EAT scratched deep into it in jagged letters that I did not take into my apartment.

But they would all be masks, because some things cannot be described, because to describe is to consume, and to be indescribable is to be the consumer, the consuming, eternally consuming like a black hole. Eternity does away with the problem of endings, which are always difficult. Happy endings are the most difficult of all. But endings are necessary, because there is a point at which we must stop typing—I meant to type "she," I meant to type something besides "typing"—must sit up and look around, because we have eaten the table and bitten chunks of flesh out of our forearms and our laptop is being cradled in the bloody remains of our lap and we ate the power cord a half hour ago, the plastic and wire snagging and breaking between our teeth, because the rock with the word EAT scratched deep into it in jagged letters that I did not take into my apartment will not stop looking at me from across the table where I did not put it because I did not take it into my apartment. There is a point at which the battery icon has a thin red line and the passive-aggressive message pops up that you may want to plug in your computer, but there is no way to plug in your computer, and the story must be saved and you must write the words THE END and stop typing in order to hit Save and leave your scrawling on the cave wall where maybe someday someone will read it besides the thing in the walls because if no one will read it then what was the point? What was the point of all the truths I told and all the lies? It's all very well to say "write for yourself" and that helps with submissions and keeping a stiff upper lip after the fiftieth form rejection. But I am frightened to end this, I confess, I am telling the truth now, I really am: I am frightened. My heart is beating in my chest and every beat is a moment I am alive and I am myself and I am in the world and what if this is the only record I have of myself in the world and if I can't hit Save quickly enough then it will wink out as quickly as I wink out? But the battery icon is now saying 7% and so I have to. I have to type the last thing and stop typing. I will, any second now. I will commit to one version of reality, the real one, the one where I did not take the rock with the word EAT scratched into it in jagged letters into my apartment. Any second now I will stop typing and hit Save, and then I will go outside and I will walk to Whole Foods and I will spend money I do not have on chips and mango salsa and peach-apple sparkling cider, and I will call my girlfriend and we will go the Hmong community education class. Look, I did it! A happy ending.

This is what will happen.

Gabriela Santiago grew up in Illinois, Montana, Florida, and Yokosuka, Japan; these days she lives in St. Paul, where she spends her days professionally playing with kids at the Minnesota Children's Museum. She is a graduate of Macalester College and the Clarion writing workshop, as well as a proud member of Team Tiny Bonesaw. Her fiction has appeared in *People of Colo(u)r Destroy Science Fiction*, *Betwixt*, and *Black Candies – Surveillance: A Journal of Literary Horror*; her Black Candies story is also available in audio form on Episode #16 of the *GlitterShip* podcast. In addition, she has a story forthcoming in *States of Terror, Volume 3*. You can find her online at writing-relatedactivities.tumblr.com or @LifeOnEarth89 on Twitter.

A DIET OF WORMS

VALERIE VALDES

YOU'RE NOT THE KIND OF person who shows up late to work, but today was a piece of shit, so it's seven thirty and your mom is finally dropping you off at the movie theater. It's a weeknight, only one person in the box office selling tickets, so you shame-walk past a line of your fellow high school grads enjoying their last summer break before college. You hope you can sneak in without anyone noticing and grab some popcorn, because you missed dinner and you're starving. Nope.

The floor manager is Yamilet, and she stares you down from concession while you creep into the break room to clock in. You turn to go and there she is, smiling with her big shark teeth like you're a little fish.

"Your shift started at six."

"Yeah," you mumble. "My mom's car wouldn't start, and—"

"I already wrote you up," she says. "You can sign it later. Go clean 1 and 16."

"It wasn't my—"

"Did I stutter? Go. Now."

You go. She doesn't need to be such a bitch, you tell yourself. You can't wait to get the hell out of there and see your girlfriend. You can't wait to quit and get a real job. Maybe tonight. You'll finish your shift and tell Yamilet to eat shit and die. The more you think about it, the better you like the idea. You'll get through this one last night, and that's it.

Now you're the one smiling.

Old Man Lemuel is at the doorman's stand, tearing tickets. You grab a walkie-talkie and your copy of the schedule, folding it so you only see the start and end times and the theater numbers.

"Who's in projection?" you ask Lemuel.

"Is Peter, you know," he says. "Mister Leon is in the office."

Worst threesome of managers ever: Yamilet the hardass, Peter the comemierda and Mister Leon, general manager, king of rules. If he's here, it also means you'll have to play his stupid theater-checking game all night.

"Who's closing?" you ask, your stomach suddenly tight with horror.

"Is Yamilet and you," Lemuel says.

Yeah, that's what you thought.

You flip to the end of the schedule and see the last movie starts at 12:45 and ends at . . . 3:25. *The Queen in Red*, one of those history movies schools come to see on field trips, but no school means no one watching so it's in the smallest theater, 12. You want to kill whoever made the schedule this week. Probably Mister Leon.

First you have to clean theaters 1 and 16, and they are absolute clusterfucks, both of them playing big dumb summer fun movies: *Time Riders Versus the Nitro Bears* for kids, and *Capital Vices* for kids whose parents didn't give a shit if they watch rated R movies. Yamilet takes over at the door and sends Lemuel in to help, but he's so slow you might as well be alone.

It's like someone set off a popcorn and soda bomb with candy shrapnel. You use your broom to scrape a million crushed pieces of chocolate off the sticky floor, sometimes smearing them into a shit-brown mess you have to clean on your hands and knees with paper towels. Four soda spills means a trip to the supply closet for the mop and bucket, bleach burning your nose until everything smells like a swimming pool. Yamilet radios you once a minute to ask if you're finished yet, which of course makes it take twice as long.

On the plus side, you find an unopened box of sour gummy worms and slip it in your pocket for later. It's like winning a sweet three-dollar lottery.

Finally you're finished, so it's time to start checking theaters. People used to lie about having done it, so Mister Leon goes into every house and hides a keychain by the emergency exit, way on the opposite side of the room. You have to collect all the keychains like some kind of shitty video game and bring them to the office so he can hide them again for the next rush.

You will never, ever level up.

You fall into a rhythm, wandering up and down the dark halls with their cosmic carpets, blue and purple and abstract yellow stars. Cardboard standees lurk in corners and posters for the movies line the walls, back lit and begging for attention.

Customers pass you on the way to the bathroom or concession, but they don't see you because they don't have any problems to bitch about. You go in and out of theaters like an annoying ghost, shining your flashlight around the exit until you find the stupid keychain, glancing up to see if anything is on fire, then leaving.

You walk into the last theater on the schedule, number 12. *The Queen in Red.* It's hot as balls, like the inside of your mom's car after you and your girlfriend make out. AC must be busted again.

You grab your walkie-talkie. "Projection," you say. No answer. Who knows what Peter is doing. Smoking on the fire escape, probably.

You watch the picture on the screen, a lady's face in profile, zoomed in so close you can only see the bottom of her nose, her mouth, her chin. Perfect red lips drink from a wine glass, drink and drink like the wine is never going to run out, and you stand there staring until a burst of static from your walkie-talkie wakes you up.

You see Lemuel sitting front row center, shadows hanging on his face like in an old vampire movie.

"Did you go on break already?" you ask.

He doesn't answer, just stares at the screen. Probably can't hear you, he's so old.

Great. Now you won't get to eat anything until after eleven, except maybe that candy you found. You bet Yamilet did this to spite you for being late, and you still have to sign that stupid write-up. You are so going to enjoy quitting later.

As soon as you leave the theater, something feels off, but you can't figure it out. You drag your dustpan along the carpet so it scoops up stray popcorn while you walk. The standee in one corner catches your eye, and you stop. *Capital Vices 2: Escape from Hell.*

That can't be right. The first movie just came out, it was in theater 16 . . . You unfold your schedule and stare at the movie titles, and sure enough, there it is. CV 2 ESCAPE HELL. So what's in theater 1? TIME RIDERS GHOST. You stagger over and see the poster outside, NOW PLAYING, and sure enough it's *Time Riders Versus the Ghost Ninjas.*

The world seems to tilt ten degrees left, like you took a shot of aguardiente and it just hit. Your mind races through three years of memories like a reel of film unraveling onto a dark floor.

"Shut your mouth, flies will get in." Yamilet is at the doorman's stand with her cartoon shark smile. She takes your wad of keychains and waves you away. "Go check the bathrooms. And you better sign that write-up before we close or you'll get another."

The write-up. You almost forgot. You were late because your daughter was sick, and you didn't want to leave your girlfriend alone at the urgent care, and no one would trade shifts with you, and you were closing so they wouldn't let you call out. Stupid shitty job. You can't wait to quit at the end of the night. Yamilet can shove that write-up directly in her stinky asshole.

"I tried," you say, but your throat is so dry you start to cough.

"Spit it out," Yamilet says.

"I tried to tell projection that the AC in 12 isn't working, but he didn't answer."

She whips her walkie-talkie out. "Projection," she says. "Can you check the AC in 12?"

"Yeah, sure," is the immediate reply.

Yamilet looks at your walkie-talkie. "Let me see that," she says, yanking it off your belt before you can respond. She fiddles with it and hmmphs. "Battery's dead. Go get a new radio from box."

You cross the lobby, wishing you could take a break to play one of the fighting games blasting its music at no one, and knock on the back door to the box office. Whoever's inside doesn't answer, so you head for the exit to bug them from the front. Except the door is locked for some reason, so you can't get out. You rattle the bar but nothing happens. Outside, a line of teenagers stares at you like you've gone crazy. Your cheeks get hot.

"What?" Now the girl in box has opened up, and for a moment you have no idea who she is. Your stomach twists. It's Claudia, she started a few weeks ago, grabbed your ass once until you told her you had a kid.

Then she tried to grab your crotch.

"I need a new radio," you say.

She points at two of them sitting on their chargers and goes back to selling tickets. You take one and hurry out; her last body spray bath wasn't enough to cover up the vinegar of her sweat. You probably smell like bleach, so who are you to judge.

The bathrooms are the usual gross mess of toilet paper on the floor and piss on the seats, but the men's bathroom near the front does one better. The toilet in the handicap stall is clogged by shit and something else you can't identify, and plunging it doesn't help.

"Usher, where are you?" says Yamilet through the radio.

"Men's bathroom," you answer.

"Hurry up and go clean the theaters letting out."

"One of the toilets isn't working. Just send Lemuel and I'll catch up." But as soon as you say it, your mouth sours. Old Man Lemuel died a year ago, heart attack. He lived alone in an efficiency, and they didn't find him until he missed work and someone called the cops. Tonight the other usher was Jeff, who's underage so he already went home.

"Are you high?" Yamilet asks.

You don't answer.

Out of frustration, you stab the wood end of the plunger into the toilet and poke around, touching something sort of soft, squishy. Carefully, nose wrinkling from the smell, you fish out a pair of disgusting underwear. Not even dude ones; these are lady panties, kind of like shorts but lacy and possibly silk. You toss them in the garbage and try not to barf, not that you have anything in your stomach since you haven't eaten in forever.

You wipe up the drips as best you can with paper towels and wash your hands, avoiding your reflection so you don't have to see what a fucking shit-cleaning loser looks like.

Yamilet gives you the stink-eye when you pass her at door. "What was up with the toilet?"

"Somebody tried to flush underwear," you say. "It was covered in sh—crap." No cursing. That's automatic dismissal. You'll save it for the end of the night when you quit.

She laughs in your face. "Aw, poor little baby, playing with caca." Her scowl returns in a flash. "Don't worry about 5, 9, and 12. We didn't sell any tickets for those."

Once you finish, you think maybe Yamilet will let you go on break, but she laughs again and tells you to check the theaters first. You don't even remember seeing Mister Leon hide the stupid keychains again; he must have been right behind you while you worked. Probably checking up on you, too, making sure you did a good job cleaning. What a dick.

So you take your trusty flashlight and check theaters. You wonder if they're ever going to change the peeling purple wallpaper in the hallways, or scrape up the old gum crusting the space carpets like tiny black holes. Your sneakers make soft snick-snick sounds on the tile floors in the dark even though you try to move quietly. As you grab another keychain, you think maybe you could duck out for a minute, run next door to order food and be back before anyone noticed.

Instead, you pull the sour worms out of your pocket; you can eat them while you walk. Your memory lurches again, but it can't seem to right itself this time, and you're left with a feeling like mental vertigo. The box you hold is still wrapped in plastic, but the color is a bit off, not as bright and shiny as you expected. The expiration date is a year ago.

Why would you be carrying around expired candy? You remember finding it while cleaning, and then . . . What? It doesn't make any sense.

You feel a strong urge to throw it away, but instead you put it back in your pocket.

One more theater before you can go on break: 12, *The Queen in Red*. Some kind of art film, blah blah teenager hooking up with an old guy, totally not your thing. Or anyone else's, apparently, since it isn't selling any tickets. But the rules say check every theater, so Mister Leon puts keychains in all of them, even the empty ones.

It's still hot as balls, like when you steamed up the bathroom at your apartment earlier to help your kid breathe. You go straight for the keychain so you can get the hell out already, but there's this sucking noise everywhere, like surround sound, only it's inside your head and you feel like you're going to barf if it doesn't stop soon.

You look up at the screen and it's a close-up of a face from the nose down, bright red lips pursed around a straw, drinking soda from a glass bottle. The never-ending soda. It's probably supposed to be sexy. Your urge to barf rises.

There's a different sound, a counter-suck that pulls you out of your thoughts. Claudia from box sits in the middle of the theater, drinking a soda of her own out of a plastic cup she probably brought from home. She's not so bad looking, you think. You could sit with her for a minute, share her drink, see what happens. She looks down at you and winks before going back to watching the movie.

What the hell are you doing, idiot, you tell yourself. Get the keychains and go on break already. You've still got like five hours left on this stupid shift and you need to eat.

The door sticks as you try to exit but you get it open after a few shoves. You head straight for door, not even bothering to sweep up the few stray kernels of popcorn on the worn-out carpet. Not like it makes a difference. Fewer people coming here since the new theater opened a few miles away. You're amazed this place is still around.

"I've been calling you," Yamilet says when you pass her. She's wearing enough makeup to scare little kids, but it doesn't make her look any younger.

You check your radio. Dead again. With a sigh, she hands you a spare.

"I'm going on break," you say.

"You can't," she says. "You have to do the closing chores while I cover box."

"But what about—" You swallow the name Claudia like a mouthful of vomit as your head spins. Funny you'd remember her all of a sudden. She died, what, twenty years ago? Car accident, freak thing where a stray piece of rebar went right through her eye. Game over.

"Did I stutter?" Yamilet asks. You shake your head. You can't wait to tell her off at the end of the night when you quit. "Start with bathrooms," she says. "You can do walls last."

Walls. What the shit. You gripe about it under your breath while you sweep up the bathrooms one last time. You gripe while you clean the thirty glass doors and windows in the lobby. You gripe while you grab the big rolling dumpster and start collecting all the trash in the building. Such a stupid waste of time, cleaning all the walls in the lobby and hallways to get some extra life out of the shitty wallpaper. It's going to completely screw up your knees and back, which already hurt all the time, even when you take enough ibuprofen to aggravate your ulcer. Being old is hot garbage, but what are you gonna do? It is what it is.

That's the kind of thing your mom says, drives you crazy, and look at you now. Sounding more like her every day. Since she retired, she won't stop complaining about how she thinks she has Alzheimer's, not since your grandmother died of it last year.

You're the one starting to worry about your memory, though. You keep having these moments where it's like you forget what year it is, like your life passed in a blink but your brain is still processing what happened even though it's long over.

And yet nothing changes, not really. You're still at the same stupid job, cleaning the same shitty theaters, listening to the same ads on loop in the lobby every twenty minutes. Even the movies are repeating, remakes of the stuff that came out when you were just out of high school. You eyeball the standee for *Capital Vices* ("Sin Is Always In") and wonder why you never quit and got a real job.

And you still have to clean all the damn walls.

You grab a roll of paper towels and some degreaser and get started. Up and down, back and forth, from the concession stand all around the lobby. Your shoulders ache before you've even finished that single room. Your legs shake from squatting over and over. There is no end to the number of walls, and you still have to go through all the hallways.

You could leave early, you think. You haven't torn a single ticket, anyway. The movies run on timers since they switched to digital projectors, so if you don't sell, they won't play. You can tell Yamilet to suck it, and maybe you can catch the last bus home so your daughter doesn't have to put more miles on her car picking you up. And eat something; you feel like you've never been so hungry in your life.

You remember you have some sour worms in your pocket, and you pull them out.

You're not sure whether it's the exhaustion or the degreaser fumes, but you feel incredibly dizzy all of a sudden. The candy in your hand fades like an old Polaroid, until the color is washed out and wrong. The logo seems to warp as you stare at it, stretching and rippling, as if it's trying to become something else.

Yamilet pokes her head out of box. "Go turn on the house lights in all the theaters. I'm locking the doors. And don't forget to come back and sign that write-up."

She can eat that write-up for all you care. This is it. You're almost free. You put the candy back in your pocket; you'll figure that out later.

You grab your walkie-talkie and start back at theater 18, flipping the overhead lights on for the cleaning people and to make sure no one is hiding inside. The switch from dark to light makes you wince as your eyes adjust, but it also feels good, like your soul is getting brighter. You go from theater to theater, bringing that light with you, like a god using your power to drive out the shadows lurking in dingy old corners.

You come to the last theater. Good old number 12. *The Queen in Red.* It's a horror movie that takes place in a spaceship, with the crew either being hunted by aliens or going crazy thinking there are aliens when it's just one of them killing the others. You kind of wanted to see it, actually, but you haven't had the time, and the last thing you want to do when you're not working is come back to the theater.

As soon as you walk in, a wave of heat hits you, like when your mom tries to save money by turning off the AC. You realize the movie is running, which is weird because you don't think any tickets were sold. Must have happened while you were checking the other theaters, and Yamilet forgot to radio you. Now you'll have to stay until the end of the night. Damn it.

Your shoulders sag and you feel so, so tired.

Might as well see if that stupid keychain is in here, though you didn't notice Mister Leon pass you at any point to hide it. Didn't he retire? You're not sure anymore. You don't have your flashlight because you didn't think you'd need it, so you follow the dim floor lights into the house.

Hell, maybe you'll even stay and watch the movie.

The picture is so black that even with the light from the projector, you can barely see where you're going. The emergency exit light is out, too. Sweat starts to drip down your forehead, wetting your armpits and back, as the air fills with the sound of heavy breathing. Yours? No, this is a horror movie. A good one, because you're certainly scared.

You look up at the seats and you could swear they're full, every seat in the house, dark figures sitting up straight as statues. Ridiculous. One of them flashes the barest glint of white teeth like a shark smelling blood, like Yamilet.

You turn to face forward and there's nothing; it almost looks like a hole, a doorway, the blackness in the center somehow thicker than in the theater where you stand. You take a step toward where you think the exit is.

Then the sucking sound starts.

You freeze, panic squeezing your chest. You start to back away, back toward the floor lights and the ramp that takes you out of number 12. You want to run but your legs are tired, your joints popping and throbbing, your heart banging like your landlord's fist on your apartment door.

You finally make it to the exit, and for the longest moment of your life, it doesn't open.

Then you're out, into the hallway where the old cosmic carpets have been ripped up, leaving only bare concrete until the new floors are installed. Your breath comes in gasps, and you almost lean against a wall for support until you remember they're covered in a wallpaper-stripping chemical. For the renovations, now that the theater is under new ownership.

"Hey, you okay?" someone asks, grabbing your arm. You nod. You feel cold, so cold, but you're still covered in sweat. Your vision blurs.

In moments, someone's brought you a chair and a glass of water, and someone else barks orders into a walkie-talkie. Young people you don't recognize, until you do, but you still can't remember their names. On the tip of your tongue.

"I'll be fine," you insist. "I just need to call my daughter to pick me up."

She can't, though, because she doesn't live here anymore. She and her wife moved years ago, with your sweet little grandson that you only get to see when they visit. Little? No, he's a teenager now, isn't he? And you, you live a few blocks away so you can walk to work.

Why is it so hard to remember anything?

"I'll drive you," says a nice looking girl who could be about your daughter's age. You think she might be a manager. "Come on, let's go."

You shake your head. There's something you have to do first. "I have to sign my write-up," you say. "Yamilet wrote me up and I can't leave until I sign it."

Your three saviors share a look. "Who?" the manager asks.

"I think she used to work here," another person says.

"Are you sure you don't want to go to the hospital?" the third person asks.

"No," you say. "I just want to go home. I'm so hungry."

Then you remember: you have a box of sour gummy worms. You're not supposed to eat candy—bad teeth—but you're old and who gives a shit. You wriggle the box out of your pocket and stare at it. They don't even make this candy anymore. Where did you get this? It expired ages ago.

You start to laugh, and it turns into a cough and you keep laughing anyway, until your lungs feel like wet paper bags. With trembling fingers, you claw open the plastic wrap.

The smell of decay fills your nose, sweet and vile like overripe fruit, and you open the box you've carried your whole miserable, brief life.

The worms inside writhe like living things, but they're not, not really. You slide one out and take a bite, and to your delight it shrieks as it dies in your mouth. It feels like a kind of victory, though you're not sure why.

Despite the horrified protests of the people around you, you eat every single one, smiling like a shark.

———

Valerie Valdes copy edits, moonlights as a muse and occasionally plays video games if her son and husband are distracted by Transformers. Once upon a time, she attended the University of Miami, where she majored in English literature with minors in creative writing and motion pictures. She currently teaches for The Brainery, which offers online writing workshops focusing on speculative fiction. Her latest work is published in *She Walks In Shadows*, the first all-women Lovecraft anthology by Innsmouth Free Press. Join her in opining about books, BioWare games and robots in disguise on Twitter @valerievaldes.

THE TAMING OF THE TONGUE

RUSSELL NICHOLS

PERSON COUNTY, NORTH CAROLINA (1868)

Under the ghostly wisps of moonlight, way out there on the farthest edge of Foster Plantation, the white boy puts his hand over your mouth and whispers: "You have to be quiet."

"Why?" Your voice comes out muffled. His palm smells like dirt and tobacco.

"Because . . ." His blue eyes scan the forest like he's expecting someone or something. But you see nothing. You hear nothing. It's just you and Mr. Foster's youngest son, alone, creeping deeper into the dark. But the next word out his mouth makes you stop dead in your tracks: "Zwelgen."

A wind grasps at your exposed, bony brown legs, like hairy fingers crawling under the tawny dress your grandmother stitched up last Christmas. And you shiver, but not from the cold.

You've heard the horror stories since back when you were a slave girl. How the zwelgen roam in the shadows beyond every plantation. How they scream out into the dead of night. How, before the freedom war, they used to catch and eat any runaway slaves, every body part but the heart, which they spat back out, you reckon, 'cause black hearts don't go down so easy.

You don't know what this boy wants you to see way out here, but ain't nothing worth getting eaten alive for. You look over your shoulder. "Uh . . . I best be getting home."

He turns to hide a smirk and motions for you to follow. "This way."

The boy's name is John. John is a blacksmith. He's fifteen, like you, and your grandmother told you to never mind him because "he ain't nothing but a trickster." But he's always been kind to you, made you feel like a person and not his father's property, and that felt good, tell the truth. He even confessed one time that he dreams about you at night and wishes to make you his wife, but Mr. Foster forbade him, saying only filthy boys had relations with slave girls.

John the blacksmith grabs your hand and pulls you toward a big bush covered in thorny vines. The crickets seem to be getting quieter the farther you go. He holds up a branch for you to scurry under. Crack, crack, go the twigs under your bare feet. Thorns get caught in your hair. You emerge on the other side and what you see there makes you nearly choke.

"That . . ." You couldn't coax the words out with a hoe.

"Shhh," he goes, "don't give it a fright."

Lying there before you is a real-life zwelgen. You've never seen one before, and seeing one right here, right now makes your stomach knot up tighter than that black oak over by the whipping post. John holds out his hand for you to stay put as he circles the beast. It's big, like an elephant, and covered in a wrinkly ashy skin. You count five limbs, until others start sliding in and out from under its belly. The zwelgen's got eyes all over, most of them closed. The open ones glow. But what stands out most is the mouth. It's big and wide and shut tight right now, but the sight alone makes your soul shake, remembering everybody you knew who disappeared in a mouth just like this one.

Words finally take shape in your dry throat, enough to mutter out loud: "You ... did this?"

John gives a curt nod as he makes his approach with caution. Each step he takes is a beat your heart misses out on. But he gets in good and close and puts his hand on the beast's swollen side. "I set a trap." Then speaks calm to the monster like it's a child lost. "There, it's okay, it's okay, shhhhh."

You wonder, what kind of trap if zwelgen only eat runaway slaves? Or are you the trap? You want to ask him, but you cover your mouth instead, in fear. You can't believe he's not scared. You're terrified. Of Mr. Foster coming from town and catching you. Of your grandmother finding out you're out here instead of helping clean up with your dumb, pregnant sister. But mostly of the zwelgen.

The zwelgen aren't human. The zwelgen got no idea about the freedom war. The zwelgen don't know you're free. In their glowing eyes, you're still a slave girl and you'll always be one, and that makes you forever a target, live bait, just because of your color.

So when John smiles and says, "How's it go?" you back up, shaking your head so hard, it could've snapped off.

"No way," you say.

"It won't eat you, I promise. I got her under control, see?" And it does seem so, as he pets the ugly thing. "What's the rhyme? C'mon, tell me. I just wanna see if it works."

The rhyme. Long ago, Pappy said he learned it from slaves he met on other plantations. He said if you whisper it to a zwelgen at nighttime, the beast will open its big mouth and you can crawl inside. That was how Pappy got away. But you dare not go beyond the plantation fence. If the zwelgen didn't chew you up, your devout grandmother surely would. "You think I'm a fool or something?"

"What? No, of course not, Cat." He looks hurt by your question. "I was just thinking, if you can't be my wife, at least you can be free."

"I am free."

"Then maybe you could use her to, you know, go after your father," he says, pointing out into the shadows. "Isn't that what you want?"

More eyes open while others close. More limbs snake out while others slurp in.

John the blacksmith reaches out to you with his free hand. But you back away slowly, feeling the clay dirt clump between your toes as twigs keep cracking. You don't realize you've stopped breathing until you start running. You run and you run and you keep running away from the beast, fast as your bony, brown legs can take you.

—◦—

Slave-eater! Slave-eater! Open up wide!
Hold yo' tongue, lemme git inside.
I's too much'a sinner to make for good dinner,
a nigger jes needa safe place to hide.[1]

—◦—

YOUR BODY'S STILL SHAKING FROM the zwelgen when you reach home. Home is a shack with dirt floors and a stick chimney. Not much else. You've lived here long as you can remember, since before the freedom war. Mr. Foster lets your family stay on his land in exchange for half of what y'all grow. Mostly corn, but also some pumpkins and peas. But he still has you do other work, too. Your grandmother still works in the tobacco field, and Brenda still cooks in the big house, and you still wait on the ole mistress, Mrs. Foster, and the younguns. Tell the truth, not much has changed since the freedom war, except you're free now and not a slave anymore.

Around the house, you find your grandmother out back in the garden. She looks so frail in that pale light, down on her knees in the earth, singing low to herself like always:

Oh father, let's go down, let's go down, let's go down
Oh father, let's go down, down in the valley to pray
As I went down in the valley to pray
Studyin' about that good ole way
Who shall wear that starry crown
Good Lord show me the way

You try to sneak by without her noticing. But she stops singing, not even looking up to say: "Thought I told you 'bout running round with young massa."

Her words catch you off guard. "I . . . I wasn't."

But she sees right through you, doesn't she? Your grandmother glares at you, then puts a hand on a rail, lifting herself up. "You telling me the truth?"

"I was with mistress, I was helping mistress . . ."

Your grandmother is small, but only in stature. She's got a presence about her, a quiet demeanor that either awes or scares you, depending on the hour. She's always been slow to anger, but when she does anger, you don't want to be nowhere near.

She steps towards you, taking her time, giving you a chance to confess. But you keep your mouth shut, remembering the scripture she's always quoting. Proverbs 21:23: *Whoso keepeth his mouth and his tongue keepeth his soul from troubles.* Telling her about the zwelgen is out of the question. She would scold you all night, growling and grumbling on about how your grandfather got eaten and Uncle Francis got eaten and your two brothers, Jonah and James, got eaten too. It made not a lick of sense trying to flee, let her tell it. Especially now that you have your freedom and a piece of farmland to call your own and a loving family.

---

1. This rhyme with translation can be found in *Lost Rhymes from Slave Times* by J.F. Rucker (1922).

"Catherine . . ." She grabs your face, pinching your cheeks together so hard, they nearly touch inside your mouth. "I swear I'll slap the black off you till Jesus comes back if I find out you lying. Now. I'll ask you one last time: Was. You. With. Young. Massa?"

Before you get a word out, her backhand flies up so fast, next thing you know you're on the ground in your dress with the pumpkins.

"Get up!" she says and grabs you up.

You try to reason with her. "But I mighta found a way out. The zwelgen—"

"Child, if you don't hush up . . ."

And she starts swinging away, blow after blow against your backside. You squirm to break free, but she's got too tight a grip on your arm, so you only run in circles.

"I told you . . ." She spins right around with you. ". . . to hush up, didn't I?"

You pull away with all the force you can muster. And get free. Your grandmother nearly falls over, trying to snatch you back. But you dart toward the shack.

<hr>

Slave-eater! Slave-eater! Open up wide!
Hold yo' tongue, lemme git inside.
I's too much'a sinner to make for good dinner,
a nigger jes needa safe place to hide.

<hr>

YOUR BODY'S STILL STINGING AS you run inside. Your sister's there, pregnant and kneeling over the tin wash bucket. She's scrubbing dishes from supper—kush, peas and leftover catfish, stewed with onions—and you pray she might save you from your grandmother's wrath.

"Brenda, help me, please."

But Brenda doesn't budge. You don't know why you thought she would. Your sister is a year older than you, but she's nothing like you. You asked your grandmother one time why she stopped speaking, and she told you Mr. Foster took her voice. You knew other girls on the plantation who got their voices stolen by Mr. Foster, but they all got sold away before the freedom war.

Brenda is still scrubbing when the door opens. Your grandmother rushes in, looking to finish what you done started. You move round the small wooden table, where your grandmother's big old Bible lies.

She stands there a moment, then finally says: "Come here."

You've never pulled away from her before now. You don't know what kind of hell to expect. "Okay, wait, just . . . please listen, okay? I wasn't . . . I didn't . . ." The words are there, but you can't calm your nerves enough to order them. You take a breath. "I was . . . I knew you'd be mad, so that's why . . . but I think there's a way outta here, because John, he trapped a zwelgen—he showed me, and I think we could go in it and go away from here. Like Pappy did."

A long silence hangs in the space like a clean dress on a clothesline.

Your grandmother just stares like she does when you bring up Pappy. You don't know why. Pappy is a legend, the only slave to ever escape in the mouth of a zwelgen. Uncle Francis told you the story, how Pappy snuck out one night, went over the fence and into the dark forest. When the zwelgen saw him, Pappy went right up to that beast, said the rhyme and the zwelgen opened its mouth for him to get inside. And Pappy rode all the way to the North, where he got spat out, a free man.

You were seven at the time, so you don't remember much of that night. All you remember is Pappy kissing you on your cheek, and whispering in your ear: "Shh. Don't you fret none, little girl. I'll be back for you. I promise." And you've been waiting ever since, but now you're done waiting.

"Come here," says your grandmother, her voice like molasses.

You know better. "Unh-uh."

More silence.

"I'm getting outta here."

"Riding in a zwelgen, huh? Like your pappy?"

"Uh-huh, that's right. If he could do it, I can do it too."

Your grandmother starts coughing and her coughing turns into laughter. "You know how foolish you sound right now? 'The zwelgen won't eat me, I swear, I'll just go inside his mouth,'" she mocks. "What kind of sense do that make, huh? But here you go, talking all kind of crazy, believing everything you hear. Your father didn't escape. He got eaten up real good, just like the rest of them."

You feel your eyes burning. "That's not true."

"Young massa's trying to trap you, child. Don't you know nothing?"

You shake your head. You feel like there's a rock stuck in your throat and you want to cry and you want to yell out: *You're the one trapped! That's what I know. You and Brenda both. The freedom war done been over, but you doing the same ole thing you did before, like ain't nothing changed. You always saying the Good Lord got a plan, well, I got plans of my own.*

You fix your lips to say this, but nothing comes out.

"You's a ignorant somebody, you know that?" says your grandmother. "I work sunup to sundown to keep you in meat and clothes. You got a roof over your head—" walking towards you "—you think you gonna do better out there? What you thinking you gonna find, huh? Your pappy?" You move round the table with nowhere to go. "You think you gonna find a husband out there? Huh? Who gonna marry a skinny, little slave girl?!"

Nobody moves. The shack falls silent once again.

Then, a knock on the door breaks the silence. Your grandmother's eyes go wide and she waves at you and mouths out: "Hide." But you stay put, frozen by your grandmother's harsh words.

Another knock.

Your grandmother calls out: "Yes? Who's there?"

The door opens and in comes Mr. Foster's frantic wife, whose skin looks like it ain't never seen a sunray in its life. Her eyes are all swollen like she's been crying for days on end.

"What's all that racket I hear?" she asks.

"Sorry to disturb you, ma'am," says your grandmother. "Just sorting out some things is all, but I got it under control."

Mrs. Foster walks past your grandmother, and you think she's confronting Brenda like she used to. She hates Brenda because of how close her and Mr. Foster are. And how Brenda's babies, the three who got sold off, were too fair-skinned to belong to Uncle Francis. Whenever Mr. Foster left the plantation, she used to beat on Brenda in the basement of the big house. Tell the truth, if Mr. Foster wasn't around, your mistress would've killed your sister. But she isn't coming for Brenda this time.

"Where were you this evening, Catherine?"

You can tell by her tone that any answer would be the wrong answer. You don't say a word.

"Did you not hear me? I asked you a question, Catherine. Where were you?"

Whoso keepeth his mouth and his tongue keepeth his soul from troubles.
Whoso keepeth his mouth and his tongue keepeth his soul from troubles.
Whoso keepeth his mouth and his tongue keepeth his soul from troubles.

Your grandmother's voice comes out of nowhere. "She was here. With me in the garden."

Mrs. Foster turns and pinches your grandmother by her cheeks. "Let the child speak for herself." Mrs. Foster then picks a thorn out of your hair. "You can speak, can't you, girl?" The tone of her question is familiar. Like the one she used with Brenda back when. "You weren't here, were you? You were with my husband."

You shake your head. "No, no, ma'am. No, I wasn't. I was with John—"

"Don't you deceive me."

"I'm not. You can ask him, he'll tell you."

"I just spoke with my son. He was by himself in the blacksmith shop all night."

You don't believe what you're hearing. "That's not true—"

Mrs. Foster backhands you on the same cheek that your grandmother did. But her wedding ring cuts a piece of flesh. Blood oozes out. You taste salt. She grabs the big old Bible off the table and commands you to: "Kiss this holy book and swear before God you were nowhere near your master—"

You weren't with Mr. Foster, and he's not your master anymore, and you want to say these things out loud, but she presses the Bible against your lips. "Kiss the book!!"

And then you hear a voice you haven't heard in years. "Leave her be!" Your big sister gets up on her feet and pushes Mrs. Foster, who goes stumbling into the wall. Her wig falls off.

All is quiet.

Brenda stares with tears streaming down her face, watching as Mrs. Foster picks up her wig. Before she puts her hair back on, you notice purple blotches around her neck, bruises of some kind. Was that Mr. Foster's doing? You don't have time to think because, right then, your grandmother grabs you by the arm and throws you out of the shack.

"Go, child," she whispers. "Go now."

Then your grandmother shuts the door, locking you out. You don't know what's about to happen in there. And you don't know where to go. But you go. Running. Fast as your bony, brown legs can take you, past the whipping post and the knotted oak tree, away from the big house, through the crop fields and into the forest, into the shadows beyond the Foster Plantation.

You've been running for God knows how long when you sense something chasing after you. Don't turn back, you tell yourself. You keep on, pretending it's not there, that thing behind you with its ugly mouth wide open, good and ready to gobble you up. Don't think about your bones snapping between its jaw. Don't think about your skin melting off as you slide down its nasty throat. How long will it hurt, you wonder. How long before your body goes numb? Before you pass out? No! Don't think, just run. But you know good and well you can't outrun no zwelgen.

So you stop.

And turn around to face the beast head-on.

The zwelgen stops about ten steps back waiting for your next move.

Out there in the darkness, you stare at those slithering limbs. Those bubbling eyes. That mouth. You're standing there, hearing nothing. It's just you and the zwelgen. All alone. But your mind's racing every whichway. You think about your grandmother and how she survived working sunup to sundown, sacrificing her body to save her family. You think about your big sister and how she survived Mr. Foster sticking his sick, nasty old arm deep down her throat to steal her precious voice. You've got survivor's blood in you, and if they could do it, you could do it too.

You feel your bare feet in the dirt, one cracked twig at a time, as you move toward the zwelgen. You can't swallow. Your heart's beating, beating so bad, trying to break through your breastbone.

You stop breathing. You get close, then closer, then closer still.

You're within eating range now.

One of its long, slimy limbs brushes up against your ankle. Feels cold. You shiver. And every ever-loving fiber in your being is telling you to run back home, but you keep on. You look the zwelgen right in all those eyes and fix your lips to say:

———◦———

Slave-eater! Slave-eater! Open up wide!
Hold yo' tongue, lemme git inside.
I's too much'a sinner to make for good dinner,
a nigger jes needa safe place to hide.

———◦———

YOUR BODY'S STILL ACHING AS you climb into the beast's big mouth. Its tongue is all slick and black, you reckon, from spitting all those hearts out. But still, you slide on in and kneel down at the tip, and the zwelgen traps you inside.

The roof of its mouth presses your hair. The damp walls of its cheeks graze your elbows. Behind you, its throat, a narrow tunnel, throbs with pus. You've been holding your breath, but you can't hold your breath forever. So you inhale. And your nostrils burn with a stench of old pea soup and black flesh, freshly branded. You gag. Hot vomit bubbles up in your throat, but you swallow it back down with blood from your cut lip and tears from your leaky eyes.

You ride. You're looking out between the gaps in its teeth as you go through the forest, where big dark trees look like big black arms, silently reaching to the heavens for mercy. Up the grassy hills that roll on and on. Across rivers that slither like headless snakes. You're thirsty. How long have you been in here? Feels like days, but you've yet to see the sun.

Is this how Pappy felt? Riding his way to freedom? You think about Pappy, a true legend. But where is he now? And how come he didn't come back like he said he would?

You can't tell if it's the question or the motion that's making you feel sick all of a sudden. Light-headed. Weak. Sweat covers your face. You're so thirsty. Whatever you do, don't faint, you tell yourself. Don't faint. You know if you faint, you'll fall back into the beast's throat, swallowed up like your grandfather, like Uncle Francis, like your two brothers, Jonah and James. Are they down there now? Down in this beast's belly? With their bones snapped and black skin half-melted?

And what about Pappy? Where the hell's Pappy?!!

But deep down you already know the truth: there is no truth. Maybe he escaped. Maybe not. You can only go by what's been told to you. And tongues got a way of doing what they got to do to survive, be it keeping quiet or telling tales.

You're so, so thirsty. You wipe your palm across the inside of the zwelgen's cheek, then lick whatever liquid that is. Tastes bitter and horrible. You gulp it down, trying to pretend it's well water, but you realize you can't pretend. Not anymore.

You squint out into the wilderness. Everything looks all blurry. Trees look familiar. The rolling hills too. Like you're going round in circles. Going nowhere. Stray winds whisper like spirits lost.

Shh. Don't you fret none, little girl. I'll be back for you. I promise.

But you're not a little girl anymore. You're not a slave anymore. You're done living lies. You refuse to remain silent. You're alive and you're free and you want everybody on God's Green Earth to know, so you take the deepest breath you ever took in your life to lift your voice like never before and right here, right now in the mouth of the monster, you scream out into the dead of night.

———

Russell Nichols is a speculative fiction writer, poet and endangered journalist. Raised in Richmond, CA, he writes about race and other man-made myths. His story about a black vampire on trial in Boston was included in the *Best of Apex Magazine: Volume 1*. His short science fiction play about police brutality will premiere at Houston's Fade to Black festival. In 2011, he and his wife left the States to wander the world indefinitely, vagabonding from desert villages in India and the Himalayas to Panama and the Caribbean during hurricane season (current location: Puerto Rico). Look for him @russellnichols and russellnichols.com.

REPRINT FICTION

EDITED BY

TANANARIVE DUE

CRUEL SISTAH

NISI SHAWL

"You and Neville goin out again?"

"I think so. He asked could he call me Thursday after class."

Calliope looked down at her sister's long, straight, silky hair. It fanned out over Calliope's knees and fell almost to the floor, a black river drying up just short of its destined end. "Why don't you let me wash this for you?"

"It takes too long to dry. Just braid it up like you said, okay?"

"Your head all fulla dandruff," Calliope lied. "And ain't you ever heard of a hair dryer? Mary Lockett lent me her portable."

"Mama says those things bad for your hair." Dory shifted uncomfortably on the sofa cushion laid on the hardwood floor where she sat. Dory (short for Dorcas) was the darker-skinned of the two girls, darker by far than their mama or their daddy. "Some kinda throwback," the aunts called her.

Mama doted on Dory's hair, though, acting sometimes as if it was her own. Not too surprising, seeing how good it was. Also, a nervous breakdown eight years back had made Mama completely bald. Alopecia was the doctor's word for it, and there was no cure. So Mama made sure both her daughters took care of their crowning glories. But especially Dory.

"All right, no dryer," Calliope conceded. "We can go out in the back garden and let the sun help dry it. 'Cause in fact, I was gonna rinse it with rainwater. Save us haulin it inside."

Daddy had installed a flexible hose on the kitchen sink. Calliope wet her sister's hair down with warm jets of water, then massaged in sweet-smelling shampoo. White suds covered the gleaming black masses, gathering out of nowhere like clouds.

Dory stretched her neck and sighed. "That feels nice."

"Nice as when Neville kisses you back there?"

"Ow!"

"Or over here?"

"OW! Callie, what you doin?"

"Sorry. My fingers slipped. Need to trim my nails, hunh? Let's go rinse off."

Blood from the cuts on her neck and ear streaked the shampoo clouds with pink stains. Unaware of this, Dory let her sister lead her across the red and white linoleum to the back porch and the creaky wooden steps down to the garden. She sat on the curved cement bench by the cistern, gingerly at first. It was surprisingly warm for spring. The sun shone, standing well clear of the box elders crowding against the retaining wall at the back of the lot. A silver jet flew high overhead, bound for Sea-Tac. The low grumble of its engines lagged behind it, obscuring Calliope's words.

"What?"

"I said 'Quit sittin pretty and help me move this lid.'"

The cistern's cover came off with a hollow, grating sound. A slice of water, a crescent like the waning moon, reflected the sun's brightness. Ripples of light ran up the damp stone walls. Most of the water lay in darkness, though. Cold smells seeped up from it: mud, moss. Mystery.

As children, Dory, Calliope and their cousins had been fascinated by the cistern. Daddy and Mama had forbidden them to play there, of course, which only increased their interest. When their parents opened it to haul up water for the garden, the girls hovered close by, snatching glimpses inside.

"Goddam if that no good Byron ain't lost the bucket!" Calliope cursed the empty end of the rope she'd retrieved from her side of the cistern. It was still curled where it had been tied to the handle of the beige plastic bucket.

Byron, their fourteen year old cousin, liked to soak sticks and strips of wood in water to use in his craft projects. He only lived a block away, so he was always in and out of the basement workshop. "You think he took it home again?" Dory asked.

"No, I remember now I saw it downstairs, fulla some trash a his, tree branches or somethin."

"Yeah? Well, that's all right, we don't wanna—"

"I'll go get it and wipe it out good. Wait for me behind the garage."

"Oh, but he's always so upset when you mess with his stuff!"

"It ain't his anyhow, is it?" Calliope took the porch steps two at a time. She was a heavy girl, but light on her feet. Never grew out of her baby fat. Still, she could hold her own in a fight.

The basement stairs, narrow and uneven, slowed her down a bit. Daddy had run a string from the bare-bulb fixture at their bottom, looping it along the wooden wall of the stairwell. She pulled, and the chain at its other end slithered obediently against porcelain, clicked and snapped back. Brightness flooded the lowering floor joists.

Calliope ignored the beige bucket full of soaking willow wands. Daddy's tool bench, that's where she'd find what she wanted. Nothing too heavy, though. She had to be able to lift it. And not too sharp. She didn't want to have to clean up a whole lot of blood.

Hammer? Pipe wrench? What if Mama got home early and found Calliope carrying one of those out of the house? What would she think?

It came to her with the same sort of slide and snap that had turned the light on. Daddy was about to tear out the railroad ties in the retaining wall. They were rotten; they needed replacing. It was this week's project. The new ones were piled up at the end of the driveway.

Smiling, Calliope selected a medium-sized mallet, its handle as long as her forearm. And added a crowbar for show.

Outside, Dory wondered what was taking her sister so long. A clump of shampoo slipped down her forehead and along one eyebrow. She wiped it off, annoyed. She stood up from the weeds where she'd been waiting, then quickly knelt down again at the sound of footsteps on the paving bricks.

"Bend forward." Calliope's voice cracked. Dory began twisting her head to see why. The mallet came down hard on her right temple. It left a black dent in the suds, a hollow. She made a mewing sound, fell forward. Eyes open, but blind. Another blow, well-centered, this time, drove her face into the soft soil. One more. Then Calliope took control of herself.

"You dead," she murmured, satisfied.

A towel over her sister's head disguised the damage. Hoisting her up into a sitting position and leaning her against the garage, Calliope hunkered back to look at her and think. No one was due home within the next couple of hours. For that long, her secret would be safe. Even then she'd be all right as long as they didn't look out the kitchen windows. The retaining wall was visible from there, but if she had one of the new ties tamped in place, and the dirt filled back in . . .

A moment more she pondered. Fast-moving clouds flickered across the sun, and her skin bumped up. There was no real reason to hang back. Waiting wouldn't change what she'd done.

The first tie came down easily. Giant splinters sprung off as Calliope kicked it to one side. The second one, she had to dig the ends out, and the third was cemented in place its full length by dried clay. Ants boiled out of the hundreds of holes that had been hidden behind it, and the phone rang.

She wasn't going to answer it. But it stopped, and started again, and she knew she'd better.

Sweat had made mud of the dirt on her hands. She cradled the pale blue princess phone against one shoulder, trying to rub the mess clean on her shirt as she listened to Mama asking what was in the refrigerator. The cord barely stretched that far. Were they out of eggs? Butter? Lunch meat? Did Calliope think there was enough cornmeal to make hush puppies? Even with Byron coming over? And what were she and Dory up to that it took them so long to answer the phone?

"Dory ain't come home yet. No, I don't know why; she ain't tole me. I was out in back, tearin down the retaining wall."

Her mother's disapproving silence lasted two full seconds. "Why you always wanna act so mannish, Calliope?"

There wasn't any answer to that. She promised to change her clothes for supper.

Outside again, ants crawled on her dead sister's skin.

Dory didn't feel them. She saw them, though, from far off. Far up? What was going on didn't make regular sense. Why couldn't she hear the shovel digging? Whoever was lying there on the ground in Dory's culottes with a towel over her head, it was someone else. Not her.

She headed for the house. She should be hungry. It must be supper time by now. The kitchen windows were suddenly shining through the dusk. And sure enough, Calliope was inside already, cooking.

In the downstairs bathroom, Daddy washed his hands with his sleeves rolled up. She kissed him. She did; on his cheek, she couldn't have missed it.

The food look good, good enough to eat. Fried chicken, the crisp ridges and golden valleys of its skin glowing under the ceiling light. Why didn't she want it? Her plate was empty.

Nobody talked much. Nobody talked to her at all. There were a lot of leftovers. Cousin Byron helped Calliope clear the table. Daddy made phone calls, with Mama listening in on the extension. She could see them both at the same time, in the kitchen and in their bedroom upstairs. She couldn't hear anything.

Then the moon came out. It was bedtime, a school night. Everyone stayed up though, and the police sat in the living room and moved their mouths till she got tired of watching them. She went in the backyard again, where all this weird stuff had started happening.

The lid was still off the cistern. She looked down inside. The moon's reflection shone up at her, a full circle, uninterrupted by shadow. Not smooth, though. Waves ran through it, long, like swirls actually. Closer, she saw them clearly: hairs. Her hairs, supple and fine.

Suddenly, the world was in daylight again. Instead of the moon's circle, a face covered the water's surface. Her sister's face. Calliope's. Different, and at first Dory couldn't understand why. Then she realized it was her hair, *her* hair, Dory's own. A thin fringe of it hung around her big sister's face as if it belonged there. But it didn't. Several loose strands fell drifting towards Dory. And again, it was night.

And day. And night. Time didn't stay still. Mostly, it seemed to move in one direction. Mama kept crying; Daddy too. Dory decided she must be dead. But what about heaven? What about the funeral?

Byron moved into Dory's old room. It wasn't spooky; it was better than his mom's house. There, he could never tell who was going to show up for drinks. Or breakfast. He never knew who was going to start yelling and throwing things in the middle of the night: his mom, or some man she had invited over, or someone else she hadn't.

Even before he brought his clothes, Byron had kept his instruments and other projects here. Uncle Marv's workshop was wonderful, and he let him use all his tools.

His thing now was gimbris, elegant North African ancestors of the cigar-box banjos he'd built two years ago when he was just beginning, just a kid. He sat on the retaining wall in the last, lingering light of the autumn afternoon, considering the face, neck, and frame of his latest effort, a variant like a violin, meant to be bowed. He'd pieced it together from the thin trunk of an elder tree blown down in an August storm, sister to the leafless ones still upright behind him.

The basic structure looked good, but it was kind of plain. It needed some sort of decoration. An inlay, ivory or mother of pearl or something. The hide backing was important, obviously, but that could wait; it'd be easier to take care of the inlay first.

Of course, real ivory would be too expensive. Herb David, who let him work in his guitar shop, said people used bone as a substitute. And he knew where some was. Small bits, probably from some dead dog or rabbit. They'd been entangled in the tree roots. He planned to make tuning pegs out of them. There'd be plenty, though.

He stood up, and the world whited out. It had been doing that a lot since he moved here. The school nurse said he had low blood pressure. He just had to stand still a minute and he'd be okay. The singing in his ears, that would stop, too. But it was still going when he got to the stairs.

Stubbornly, he climbed, hanging onto the handrail. Dory's—his—bedroom was at the back of the house, overlooking the garden. His mom kept her dope in an orange juice can hung under the heat vent. He used the same system for his bones. No one knew he had them; so why was he afraid they'd take them away?

He held them in his cupped palms. They were warm, and light. The shimmering whiteness had condensed down to one corner of his vision. Sometimes that meant he was going to get a headache. He hoped not. He wanted to work on this now, while he was alone.

When he left his room, though, he crossed the hall into Calliope's instead of heading downstairs to Uncle Marv's workshop. Without knowing why, he gazed around him. The walls were turquoise, the throw rugs and bedspread pale pink. Nothing in here interested him, except—that poster of Wilt Chamberlain her new boyfriend, Neville, had given her . . .

It was signed, worth maybe one hundred dollars. He stepped closer. He could never get Calliope to let him anywhere near the thing when she was around, but she took terrible care of it. It was taped to the wall all crooked, sort of sagging in the middle.

He touched the slick surface—slick, but not smooth—something soft and lumpy lay between the poster and the wall. What? White light pulsed up around the edges of his vision as he lifted one creased corner.

Something black slithered to the floor. He knelt. With the whiteness, his vision had narrowed, but he could still see it was nothing alive. He picked it up.

A wig! Or at least part of one. Byron tried to laugh. It was funny, wasn't it? Calliope wearing a wig like some old bald lady? Only . . . only it was so weird. The bones. This—hair. The way Dory had disappeared.

He had to think. This was not the place. He smoothed down the poster's tape, taking the wig with him to the basement.

He put the smallest bone in a clamp. It was about as big around as his middle finger. He sawed it into oblong disks.

The wig hair was long and straight. Like Dory's. It was held together by shriveled-up skin, the way he imagined an Indian's scalp would be.

What if Calliope had killed her little sister? It was crazy, but what if she had? Did that mean she'd kill him if he told on her? Or if she thought he knew?

And if he was wrong, he'd be causing trouble for her, and Uncle Marv, and Aunt Cookie, and he might have to go live at home again.

Gradually, his work absorbed him, as it always did. When Calliope came in, he had a pile of bone disks on the bench, ready for polishing. Beside them, in a sultry heap, lay the wig, which he'd forgotten to put back.

Byron looked up at his cousin, unable to say anything. The musty basement was suddenly too small. She was three years older than him, and at least 30 pounds heavier. And she saw it, she had to see it. After a moment, he managed a sickly smirk, but his mouth stayed shut.

"Whatchoodoon?" She didn't smile back. "You been in my room?"

"I—I didn't—"

She picked it up. "Pretty, ain't it?" She stroked the straight hair, smoothing it out. "You want it?"

No clue in Calliope's bland expression as to what she meant. He tried to formulate an answer just to her words, to what she'd actually said. Did he want the wig? "For the bow I'm makin, yeah, sure, thanks."

"Awright then."

He wished she'd go away. "Neville be here tonight?"

She beamed. It was the right question to ask. "I guess. Don't know what he sees in me, but the boy can't keep away."

Byron didn't know what Neville saw in her either. "Neville's smart," he said diplomatically. It was true.

So was he.

There was more hair than he needed, even if he saved a bunch for restringing. He coiled it up and left it in his juice can. There was no way he could prove it was Dory's. If he dug up the backyard where the tree fell, where he found the bones, would the rest of the skeleton be there?

The police. He should call the police, but he'd seen Dragnet, and Perry Mason. When he accepted the wig, the hair, he'd become an accessory after the fact. Maybe he was one even before that, because of the bones.

It was odd, but really the only time he wasn't worried about all this was when he worked on the gimbri. By Thanksgiving, it was ready to play.

He brought it out to show to Neville after dinner. "That is a seriously fine piece of work," said Neville, cradling the gimbri's round leather back. "Smaller than the other one, isn't it?" His big hands could practically cover a basketball. With one long thumb he caressed the strings. They whispered dryly.

"You play it with this." Byron handed him the bow.

He held it awkwardly. Keyboards, reeds, guitar, drums, flute, even accordion:

he'd fooled around with plenty of instruments, but nothing resembling a violin. "You sure you want me to?"

It was half-time on the TV, and dark outside already. Through the living room window, yellow light from a street lamp coated the grainy, grey sidewalk, dissolving at its edges like a pointillist's reverie. A night just like this, he'd first seen how pretty Dory was: the little drops of rain in her hair shining, and it stayed nice as a white girl's.

Not like Calliope's. Hers was as naturally nappy as his, worse between her legs. He sneaked a look at her while Byron was showing him how to position the gimbri upright. She was looking straight back at him, her eyes hot and still. Not as pretty as Dory, no, but she let him do things he would never have dreamed of asking of her little sister.

Mr. Moore stood up from the sofa and called to his wife. "Mama, you wanna come see our resident genius's latest invention in action?"

The gimbri screamed, choked, and sighed. "What on earth?" said Mrs. Moore from the kitchen doorway. She shut her eyes and clamped her lips together as if the awful noise was trying to get in through other ways besides her ears.

Neville hung his head and bit his lower lip. He wasn't sure whether he was trying to keep from laughing or crying.

"It spozed to sound like that, Byron?" asked Calliope.

"No," Neville told her. "My fault." He picked up the bow from his lap, frowning. His older brother had taken him to a Charles Mingus concert once. He searched his memory for an image of the man embracing his big bass, and mimicked it the best he could.

A sweeter sound emerged. Sweeter, and so much sadder. One singing note, which he raised and lowered slowly. High and yearning. Soft and questioning. With its voice.

With its words.

I know you mama, miss me since I'm gone;
I know you mama, miss me since I'm gone;
One more thing before I journey on.

Neville turned his head to see if anyone else heard what he was hearing. His hand slipped, and the gimbri sobbed. He turned back to it.

Lover man, why won't you be true?
Lover man, why won't you ever be true?
She murdered me, and she just might murder you.

He wanted to stop now, but his hands kept moving. He recognized that voice, that tricky hesitance, the tone smooth as smoke. He'd never expected to hear it again.

I know you daddy, miss me since I'm gone;
I know you daddy, miss me since I'm gone;
One more thing before I journey on.

I know you cousin, miss me since I'm gone;
I know you cousin, miss me since I'm gone;
It's cause of you I come to sing this song.

Cruel, cruel sistah, black and white and red;
Cruel, cruel sistah, black and white and red;
You hated me, you had to see me dead.

Cruel, cruel sistah, red and white and black;
Cruel, cruel sistah, red and white and black;
You killed me and you buried me out back.

Cruel, cruel sistah, red and black and white;
Cruel, cruel sistah, red and black and white;
You'll be dead yourself before tomorrow night.

Finally, the song was finished. The bow slithered off the gimbri's strings with a sound like a snake leaving. They all looked at one another warily.

Calliope was the first to speak. "It ain't true," she said. Which meant admitting that something had actually happened.

But they didn't have to believe what the song had said.

Calliope's suicide early the next morning, that they had to believe: her body floating front down in the cistern, her short, rough hair soft as a wet burlap bag. That, and the skeleton the police found behind the retaining wall, with its smashed skull.

It was a double funeral. There was no music.

———

Nisi Shawl's story collection *Filter House* co-won the 2009 James Tiptree, Jr. Award. With Cynthia Ward she coauthored *Writing the Other: A Practical Approach*, recipient of a Tiptree Honorable Mention. She edited *WisCon Chronicles 5: Writing and Racial Identity* and *Bloodchildren: Stories by the Octavia E. Butler Scholars*, and she currently edits reviews for the literary quarterly *Cascadia Subduction Zone*. Shawl coedited the 2014 Aqueduct Press anthology *Strange Matings: Science Fiction, Feminism, African American Voices, and Octavia E. Butler*, and Rosarium Publishing's August 2015 anthology *Stories for Chip: A Tribute to Samuel R. Delany*. Shawl's Belgian Congo steampunk novel *Everfair* was released by Tor Books September 2016. She serves on the boards of the Clarion West Writers Workshop and the Carl Brandon Society. She's fairly active on Twitter and Facebook, and promises to update her homepage soon.

THE SHOW

PRIYA SHARMA

THE CAMERA CREW STRUGGLED WITH the twisting, narrow stairs. Their kit was portable, Steadicams being all the rage. They were lucky that the nature of their work did not require more light. Shadows added atmosphere. Dark corners added depth. It was cold down in the cellar. It turned their breath to mist, which gathered in the stark white pools shed by the bare bulbs overhead.

Martha smiled. It was sublime. Television gold.

Tonight there'd been a crowd. Word had got out. She'd have to find out who blabbed. There had been only a few fans at the start but now they needed security to keep them back.

She'd joined the presenter, Pippa, and her producer-husband Greg at the barrier. The three of them had posed for photographs and signed autographs. Pip had been strict about that. Be nice to the public. The audience would make or break the show, not studio executives.

Martha laughed out loud when a woman produced a photo of Pip and Greg in their previous incarnation as chat show hosts.

"Nice haircuts," she said as they both signed it. Their fashionable styles dated this period of fame, but Martha was careful when she joked about their pasts. It was Pippa's new idea that had reinvented their careers.

Pippa was popular, but it was really Martha the crowd wanted. She recognised the faithful amid the curious locals. The ones who wanted to touch her hand, as if it were a blessing. To ask her help to reach the dead, to say what they'd left unsaid.

A man reached out as Martha tried to leave, snatching at her coat sleeve.

"Good luck," he said. "May God keep you through the night."

⎯⎯◆⎯⎯

MARTHA LEANT AGAINST THE CELLAR wall to watch Pippa in discussion with the team. She could tell Pippa was well pleased. The first part of the show comprised of interviews. The bar staff had been verbose in their remembering. The tall tales of the spooked. The cellar had fallen fallow. Too many broken beer bottles. Boxes overturned, alcopops leaking on the floor. Too many barmaids emerging with bruises flowering on their arms. Too many accusations. Too many resignations.

Yes, it was horrible down here. Its history appalled. The chill seeped from the floor, through her boot soles and crept into her feet. She fastened up her coat. Red cashmere. She'd decided to live a vivid life. She wouldn't exist in shades of grey. She'd no longer bow or obey. She'd promised herself good money. In the bank. Not tatty fivers from someone's housekeeping, like the ones her mother would take with embarrassment and stuff into the chipped teapot on the dresser. Iris never asked for more. Only barely enough. *You can't abuse the gift.* Cheap meat on Sundays as a treat. For Martha and her sister Suki, white knee socks gone grey, but still too good to throw away.

The second part of the show was a vigil. The team were busy setting up thermometers and motion sensors to add the illusion of science, but it was Martha that added the something special to the mix.

"Don't forget," Pippa would say, face tight into the lens, "Martha, our psychic, doesn't know our destination. She'll be brought here and do a reading, blind."

Martha stamped her feet to expel the cold. Pippa was busy with her preparations. Vocal exercises. Shaking her limbs. If Martha channelled spirits, then Pippa channelled the audience. With the cameras on, Pippa (like Martha) became a true believer. Her range spanned from nervous to hysterical. Her tears of fear turned her heavy eye makeup to muddy pools. Her performance heightened suggestibility and atmosphere.

"Have you destroyed them?" Greg sidled up to Martha. He was talking about the copy of his research notes that he always gave her.

"Don't treat me like I'm an amateur. You know I learn them and then burn them."

These were hot readings, as they were called within the trade, when a medium was already primed. Martha would reveal the memorised histories of suicidal serving girls, murdered travellers and Victorian serial killers.

Martha's key was subtlety. She was frugal with the facts. Too direct and the show would be a pantomime. Too detailed and she'd be reciting by rote. And what couldn't be confirmed couldn't be denied, which was useful when the truth wasn't juicy enough to appeal. All Martha needed was a name, a date, a hard fact around which to embroider her yarns. Greg, who also played on-screen researcher, would fake surprise with widened eyes, saying such as, "Yes, Martha, there was a third son here by the name of Walter, but we can't corroborate there was a maid by the name Elaine whom he killed on Midsummer's Day."

"New coat?" Greg's fingers stroked her collar.

"Keep your paws off."

"Watch it. Pippa will think we're paying you too much."

Greg was clumsy where Pippa's angling had been more oblique. Martha had chosen to ignore her jibes and hints, having stuck to the deal made when they were all green and keen. She'd not allow Greg to change the terms.

"You're not and I'm worth every penny."

Worth a better time slot and channel. Worth another series.

"How many personal clients do you have now? How much for your last tour?"

A lot. The world was ripe. She'd weighed it in her palm.

"None of your business."

Martha was brisk. Even with her clients she was sharp. She'd not pander to their fantasies that mediums were soft and ethereal.

"Take care. We built you up and we can pull you down."

Her laughter echoed around the empty cellar. Pip turned and stared at them.

"You won't. You can't."

To reveal Martha as a fraud was to expose them all. The true believers would be incensed. Most viewers though were sceptics, they would already suspect, but the fun lay in the possibility of doubt. The chance that Martha might be real. So, not perjury, not a lie to shatter worlds, but was it one to shatter careers?

"We can find someone new. You'd be easy to replace."

"Don't threaten me. I'll send you all to hell."

"Keep it down," Pippa stalked over. "Do you want everyone to hear? We'll talk about this later. Do you understand, Martha? There are things to be addressed. Now get ready, it's time to start the show."

<hr />

MARTHA HAD LEARNT FROM WATCHING Iris and Suki. Both had reigned at Lamp Street, lumpish in their muddy-coloured cardigans, giving readings to anyone who called. Muttering thanks to spirit guides. Turning tatty Tarot cards.

Martha had no claim to special gifts. She learnt to read the hands and face, the gestures that betrayed need and greed. The skill of deciphering a tic, interpreting a pause. Martha studied hard and learnt how to put on a show.

"Yes, David. Thanks."

Made-up-David helped Martha to the other side. A fictional spirit guide to help usher in an imaginary spectral presence or fake demonic possession. David was a friar. Shaman. Priest. Rabbi. Denomination was irrelevant. People seemed to find religious men more comforting in the afterlife than in the flesh. David was based on an engraving that Iris kept by her bed. A monk with his hands folded in prayer.

"What do you make of it?" Pippa asked, now in character.

"It's a big place." Martha sniffed. "It smells bad. Like something's rotted down here."

The low ceiling pressed down on them, while the walls stretched out into shadow. Martha rubbed her temples, where pain had started to gather. She walked to the opposite wall, as if in search of something. It was her trick. The camera was forced to follow and the others had to orbit her to stay in shot.

"Brother David, help me." Martha gained momentum. She covered her ears with flat hands. "Make them stop. They're deafening me."

"What is it?"

"Clanging. Fit to wake the dead. The sound of banging metal." She winced as if uncomfortable. Tonight had to be special. She had a point to prove. "It's claustrophobic. Too many souls in too small a space. A strong sense of punishment."

Pippa made a display of her excitement, trying to reclaim screen time for her and Greg. "Greg, can you tell us more?"

"It's a fascinating place. A gruesome history. It was a prison in the eighteenth century."

His eyes shone in the viewfinder.

"What about the clanging?" Pippa asked. More professional than Greg, she'd not prove a point at the show's expense.

"An inmate, Samuel Greenwood, was questioned by the prison board. One of them, shocked, recorded the interview in his diary. The main gates were locked but down here the doors were all open. New arrivals were greeted by the banging of the cell doors." He mimed a man clutching bars and rattling them. "An unholy din, by all accounts."

Martha took off her gloves and trailed her fingers along the crumbling mortar of the wall, talking continually to David as she went. Her eyes closed in concentration. The camera loved the gesture.

"Of course. I see it now." She stopped and the spotlight overshot her. "There's so much misery here. Pain. Searing. Physical."

The cameraman tripped up on an empty crate. The world was upended as an explosion of panicked feathers went off in his face. Too stunned to scream, Pippa did it for him. The bird, in its eagerness to escape incarceration in the upturned crate, sprang up and hit the ceiling. It landed with a dull thud upon the floor. It jerked and flapped, a reflex of the freshly dead, until finally it came to rest. Martha knelt and picked it up. It was a scrawny thing, its feet deformed, head lolling on its broken neck.

Pippa had stopped screaming, looking over Martha's shoulder.

"I wonder how it got down here. And how long ago."

Martha laid the carcass back on the crate. She shook her head in disbelief. Sickened by this small, crushed life, her headache was suddenly much worse. She'd never experienced a full-blown migraine but recognised the signs. Lights danced at the periphery of her vision. Strange patterns hovered in the air. It interfered with coherent thought. She tried to reassert herself.

"This is no ordinary prison, is it, Greg? All these voices cry out, but no-one comes. No-one keeps the peace."

"Samuel Greenwood said the inmates ran the place. The authorities didn't get in their way."

Martha tasted bile rising in her throat. *I'll not be sick. I'll not be sick.* Not a mantra but a command. She'd last vomited in childhood. Its associations were too painful to encounter. Not like this. Not here. Martha fought it back.

"There's uncontrolled rage within these walls. Frenzy. Violation." She turned on Greg as if he were to blame. "Men, women, children, all mixed in together."

"Yes," Greg's voice was serious and low. "Murderers and thieves," he savoured the words, "cheats and fraudsters."

Martha wasn't listening. The lingering odour of decay she'd noted was getting worse. It was rotting flowers, fungi and burnt sugar. The pain in her head was punctuated by explosions. Monstrous white blooms contracted and expanded before her eyes. She clutched the wall with one hand, bent double, and threw her stomach contents upon the floor.

The sensation of muscles moving in her throat, of acid burning in her nose, evoked the shock and grief of that distant summer her father died. Passed over was the term they used at home. Martha despised this euphemism, even though it was part of her work's vocabulary. Not long after her father's sudden death, she had been burnt up by a fever. She'd vomited without relief. She had the same sensations now as then, like she'd died and was floating out of reach.

"Where's Daddy?" Hot and hallucinating, Martha was emphatic. She wanted her father, not her mother's comforts.

"Daddy's here," Iris replied. "He's in the room. He's telling you he loves you. Can't you hear?"

"No," Martha whimpered. Had there been a time when the world was full of voices? She couldn't recall.

"Oh, my sweetheart," and under her breath, Iris spoke the damaging, damning words that separated Martha from her tribe, "you used to be like us. You used to see but now you're blind."

So Martha was left in darkness, Iris and Suki in the light.

Martha dabbed her mouth, vomit dripping on her coat. Greg motioned for the filming to continue. Pippa ladled on concern.

"Are you okay?"

"I'm sorry. It's the smell."

"It's bad, isn't it? Maybe there's a dead bird or rat that's rotting." Then, because Martha's pallor couldn't be feigned, "Do you want us to stop?"

Martha clutched a crumpled tissue to her mouth to stem the swelling tide. She recognised the smell now. It was death. Bedridden Iris, nursed by her girls in the front parlour, had been rank with it. Devoured by a cancer in her breast that had ulcerated and wept pus throughout her long slide towards a terrible demise.

People still came, even at the end. To see her. Just for a minute. Just to ask advice. Women whose daughters followed Suki and Martha home from school. Hair pullers, name callers, shin kickers who loved to plague the pair of witches. These same mothers would sit and wait, watching the girls no older than their own move around the unclean kitchen, washing their mother's soiled sheet in the sink. Not a single one offered aid.

Suki started reading to give Iris peace. So this wall-eyed girl who was clumsy at PE and hated school inherited her mother's mantle and the regulars. She stayed at home and read the cards, while Martha passed her exams and got into fights with anyone who looked at her askew.

"I'm dying, a little more each day. There's no need to be afraid." Iris had beckoned Martha over. "They're waiting for me on the other side. Suki will be just fine. She has the gift but what will become of you, Martha? What will you do?"

Yes, Martha was familiar with the smell. It was enough to make her turn and vomit once again before the floor rose up to meet her. She felt her bones crunch with the impact.

"Martha, can you hear me?"

She was shaken back to consciousness by rough, frightened hands. The pain had gone and left her empty headed, her brain replaced by cotton wool, her mouth with acid and sand.

"Thank God. What happened?" Greg motioned for the crew to stand back and give her air. She tried to sit.

"Just a faint."

In the seconds she was away, the cellar had reassembled itself. She could see anew. The investigators were still there. The bare bulbs still shed their light, but there was a whole world superimposed upon their own. A past that occupied the present, which shared their time and space. Figures moved around them, weak imprints on here and now. She had peeled back the skin of the world and was looking underneath. When one of these shadow prisoners walked through Martha, she shuddered. It felt like cobwebs were being brushed against her skin.

"There's a lot of residual energy here." The stock phrase had been given shape. Martha wanted to cry. Something locked away was liberated. Was this how Iris saw the world? She realised it had been six years since she last spoke with Suki. How much they had to share. "This place was a health hazard. They're all filthy."

Ragged figures milled around or else they squatted in huddles. Food was piled in troughs as though for swine. There was a gentle buzz. They were too afraid to speak up.

A group of convicts emerged from the far end of the prison, the overlords of this peculiar hell. These self-tattooed, beribboned demons strutted with such swagger that Martha quailed with fear. They singled out a shadow-boy for sport. They hauled him up and took their time at play. One swung his knife about and it passed through Martha's chest, making her gasp, even though it was only a projection of things past. Another one unfolded his razor and the boy's face was devastated. The crime he suffered for most was his prettiness.

"Martha, what is it?"

"A gang ran this place." She found her voice. She talked too loudly so she could hear herself above the shrieks and jeers.

"They kept the peace," Greg said.

"Not peace. I wouldn't call it that."

Martha struggled to her feet. She tipped and tilted until the horizon righted.

"Jimmy Bailey, Michael O'Connor, Kit Williams, Simeon Weaver . . ." Martha repeated the names as they were shouted at roll call.

"I don't have it here but there is a ledger . . ." Greg fumbled with his notes.

"Check if you want. They'll all be there."

Greg twitched. This was unexpected. She had raised the stakes. He hadn't thought she'd do her own research.

"Emma Parker," Martha's eyes were horrified. Emma lay on the floor. Slit from pubic bone to ribcage, her blood sprayed upon the walls. "They were animals. When she fell pregnant they opened her up with a knife. They cut out her womb and watched her bleed to death."

Greg frowned at her nasty embellishments. After all, this was a family show.

"The smell. It's death."

She walked back towards the twisted stairs. She had been shocked, but now she was afraid. Something was missing from this nether, neither world. Someone was missing.

"There's something about this spot." She strained to listen to the henchman who stood beside the steps like a lackey at some royal court making proclamations. "Thomas the Knife, that's his name."

It sparked of recognition. The name in Greg's notes was Thomas Filcher. Where was he?

"Close. Thomas the Blade." Greg was glad of her return to the script. "He sat waiting for new inmates to be brought down. Tapping on his boot heel with a knife."

Martha pushed her fists against her eyes. Where was the architect of this regime? Why could she not see him?

The clearing of a throat. It was a quiet sound.

"Did you hear that?" Pip piped up. "Who's there? We mean no harm. Give us a sign."

It came again. This time between a chuckle and a growl.

"Did you hear it?"

Greg was normally subtle in the projections of his voice, but in for a penny, in for a pound.

Cold trickled down Martha's spine. What did it mean that the others could hear him too? There came a laugh, cruel and amused. Martha held up a hand to silence Pip. "Come out. Show yourself. Or else leave us well alone."

He rose to her challenge, stepping from shadow into light. Thomas the Knife stood before her, denser than the other shades. There was enough of him to trip a movement sensor. It called out in alarm.

"What is it?" Pippa hissed.

They can hear him, Martha thought, but they can't see him.

"Everyone, step back towards the stairs."

"Why?"

"Just do it." Martha could smell her own stale vomit and fear. "This isn't residual energy. It's active. He's here."

The crew started to retreat but Pip hovered by her side. She'd not be upstaged.

"Martha, tell us what you see."

"He's tall. Handsome." Thomas smirked at that. "Well dressed and fed compared to the rest. A dandy in a blood splattered shirt."

He was a gentleman butcher, linen stained by the evidence of his industry. Long hair tied back and boots up to his thighs. Even dead, he bristled with an energy

Martha rarely saw in men. She watched him like he was a predator. Magnificent and unpredictable. Her eyes were fixed on him in retreat. She clasped Pippa's elbow but the presenter shook her off.

"He's King down here. He thrived. He sniffed out the proudest and the most delicate. Broke their spirit as if it were a game." Martha looked up, a line of girls crucified upon the bars, their modesty and disfigurements on display. "He's full of hate and it's women that he hates the most."

Martha knew the cleansing rituals, protective circles and holy chants. Iris had been most insistent that they learn, even if Martha wasn't blessed with special sight. Arrogant and adamant in her disbelief, she'd come down here totally unarmed.

"We have to get out now."

Too late. Too late. Thomas the Knife wanted company. His boots fell heavily on stone. Surprisingly loud, considering he was a ghost.

All the lights went out, leaving only sounds. Pip's screaming and struggling. Greg shouting for her. The metallic crunch as a camera hit the ground. One of the bulbs shattered overhead, showering them in glass. Tiny fragments lodged in Martha's face. A dozen tiny stings.

"Leave her alone." Martha tried to help, calling over muffled cries. "Please stop. Don't hurt her."

He did stop. Eventually. Then the movement sensors were set off one by one, marking Thomas' progress around the room. Martha found the wall and groped along it in the direction of the stairs. Greg shouted out, a single cry of pain.

The lights came on and the carnage was revealed. Greg was within Martha's reach, lying on the floor. She crouched beside him, dabbing at his wound. A neat line joined his ear to the corner of his mouth, blood oozing from the deep wedge of red flesh revealed.

"Where's Pip?" Greg, dizzy and disorientated, struggled to lift his head.

They followed the soft sobbing to the corner. This was not Pippa's TV histrionics but the heartbreak of the truly wounded. Thomas stood back, well satisfied with his work.

Pip was revealed in the dim circle of the lamp. She was curled against the wall, bare torso revealed. Thomas had remade her. When the blood crusted and the scabs fell off, she would be a work of art. That a single, common blade could carve such detail was remarkable. She was etched with arcane calligraphy. Profane flourishes. No plastic surgeon could eradicate his dirty graffiti. But that would be for later. For now she was slick and slippery with snot and tears and blood. Martha slipped her coat off to cover her. Greg moved to enclose her in his arms. Nothing could diminish her distress until the paramedics arrived and she slipped into the dreams of deep sedation.

◆

THE TRAFFIC WAS STREAKS OF light. Neon discoloured the night. The police kept the crowds at bay. Greg went to where Martha stood alone. Her hair, soaked with perspiration, stuck to her head in unflattering curls.

"You did this, didn't you? When I find out how, I'll kill you."

A policeman came over, casting them a warning look.

"Miss Palmer. We're taking everyone in for questioning. It's time for you to come along with me."

"Greg, he says you got it wrong." Her last words to him. "It's Thomas the Knife. Not Thomas the Blade."

Martha settled into the slippery car seat. Her new travelling companion by her side. They stared at one another, neither speaking. Iris' lessons came to mind.

A medium must take care. The opening of consciousness is a special time in a girl's life. When a spirit guide is acquired, don't be scared. I'll be here to keep you safe.

Suki had smirked when it was her time. The advent of Martha's menstruation seemed paltry by comparison.

You'll never want for company.

You'll never be alone.

For all those years, I believed all the things you said, Martha thought. *You're not the gifted one. You're not gifted.* It was always you and Suki, talking to voices I couldn't hear.

Talking to Dad.

If only you could see me now, Iris. If only you could see me now.

———

Priya Sharma's fiction has appeared in *Interzone*, *Black Static*, *Albedo One* and on *Tor.com*. She's been anthologised in several of Ellen Datlow's *Best Horror of the Year* series, Paula Guran's *Year's Best Dark Fantasy & Horror* series, Jonathan Strahan's *The Best Science Fiction & Fantasy 2014*, Steve Haynes' *Best British Fantasy 2014* and Johnny Main's *Best British Horror 2015*. She's also been on previous *Locus'* Recommended Reading Lists (2010, 2012, 2013 & 2015). She is a Shirley Jackson Award Nominee and British Fantasy Award nominee for her story "Fabulous Beasts", which appeared on *Tor.com* in 2015. Find her online at priyasharmafiction.wordpress.com.

WET PAIN

TERENCE TAYLOR

I ONCE SAW A SIGN on a pillar in a New York City subway station, "WET PAIN," written in bright red block letters on glossy white card stock. Back then I thought it was a joke or mistake, meant to read "WET PAINT," but maybe I was wrong; maybe it was a warning of a different kind and I just missed the point, because I didn't know enough to understand what I was reading.

That's how I feel about what happened to my good buddy, Dean; that I saw the danger signs all along but never realized what they meant, what they really warned me about. Not until he opened my eyes and I saw a side of the world I never wanted to see.

It all started when Dean moved back to New Orleans.

⬦

WE MET ALMOST FIVE YEARS ago, on a job.

Dean was master electrician and I was tech director for a live multimedia press conference announcing the UPN Network's new fall season. The client reps for the ad agency handling it were assholes, cut corners in all the wrong places, so we had to cover each other to survive. We worked together on floor plans for his lighting and my video equipment to do what they wanted with what they gave us, and made it through a two-week job from Hell without killing each other or anyone else.

We stayed in touch. No one expected a white reformed redneck from New Orleans and a black gay geek from Park Slope like me to become best friends, least of all us, but we did. We were opposites in taste, education, upbringing, everything but how we saw the world and thought it should work; Dean called us "Twin brothers of different mothers . . ."

I made regular treks out to New Jersey for dinner with the family, but didn't know his wife, Lynn, was a black girl from the Bronx until my first visit almost a year after meeting Dean. I must have looked surprised when a stylish black woman opened the door instead of the suburban southern belle I'd expected. A short Afro crowned a dark pretty face, big gold hoops hung on either side of her broad smile. She feigned shock when she saw me, raised her eyebrows and widened her eyes as she turned back to yell at her husband.

"Omigod, Dean! You didn't tell me he was a NEGRO!"

I loved her immediately.

After dinner we discussed Dean's colorblindness over beers on the back porch while their three-year-old, Milton, an only child then, ran around the yard in circles. Dean was built like a truck; six-foot tall capped with a military-style crew cut. Lynn was small, compact; she nestled under Dean's free arm on the couch while we sipped beer and the two of us talked about her husband like he wasn't there.

"Dean says since he doesn't care about race he sees no reason to bring it up. I think it's passive-aggressive. You just know he only married me to see if it would kill his cracker family . . ."

"Worth it, even if I am stuck with her," Dean said with a grin. She smacked him lightly. He winked at me, took a deep swig of beer.

"Anyway. I say ignoring color implies something's wrong, when difference should be recognized and celebrated," finished Lynn.

"Just sounds like a cheap way for them to get off the hook to me," I said. "'Black people? What black people? Everybody looks the same to me!'"

"Yeah, I get it." Lynn slapped Dean on the thigh with a grin. "No black people, no reparations! 'Slavery? What slavery? We don't owe you shit!'" We laughed like co-conspirators, while Dean waggled his empty bottle until Lynn passed him another beer.

"Y'all need to keep me on your side," he said as he twisted off the cap. "We remember not the words of our enemies, but the silence of our friends . . ."

"Smartass," said Lynn. "He quotes King, but doesn't fool me. Shakespeare said even the devil can cite Scripture for his purpose . . ."

"Never marry a teacher," laughed Dean. Lynn kissed him hard, and he kissed her back; they kissed a lot, had an easy affection for each other I envied.

Between jobs I'd hang with Dean at his place or mine, kick back, knock down tequilas and take apart the world. Most of the time we talked by telephone. I had a headset that let me chat with both hands free while I drew floor plans at home on my Mac. He'd call on his Bluetooth earpiece from location while his crew set up lights and we'd burn up free long distance by the hour while we both worked.

Lately more conversations were in person, less about Dean's dreams than nightmares about the war and a looming recession. A downturn in New York's economy after the Twin Tower bombings cut back on jobs for both of us; a few years of the Iraq war hadn't made things any better. I was single with low expenses in a rent-controlled Brooklyn apartment, but Dean had a family to support in Jersey, a wife and two kids.

Debts grew and no work was in sight; his wife's teaching salary wasn't enough to pay the bills. They'd already gone through their savings and started cashing out their IRAs, no matter how much they lost in early withdrawal.

"Freelance sucks, bruh. You know what they say," he said with a sigh. "Sometimes ya gotta chew off a leg to set yourself free . . ."

Then his mother died.

—◦—

I HEARD THE PHONE RING as I walked upstairs with my grocery bags, but couldn't get inside my third floor apartment in time to answer before it went to voicemail. There was a short message when I checked, no name, but I knew it was Dean.

"Greg, give me a call on cell, will ya? No big, bruh. Just need an ear, okay?"

He was down in New Orleans with the movers, getting furniture and boxes unloaded and into his mother's house before the wife and kids arrived from New Jersey to help unpack. I called him back on my headset phone while I put away groceries.

"Dean! How's life in the Big Easy?"

"Nothin' easy 'bout it, bruh." He paused. I heard a ring top pop, followed by what sounded like a long swallow from a tall cold beer. "Got everything in, so I'm takin' time off with my ol' pal Sam Sixpack. Don't think he's long for this world."

"How's the place look?"

"Like Hell, but always did. Still can't believe what this dump is worth. Glad now I didn't burn it down as a kid. Lord knows I tried."

He grew up in New Orleans, a short walk from the main tourist drag of the French Quarter. Dean and his generation moved out first chance they got, but his widowed mother stayed in the family house until the end, in a quiet neighborhood called Marigny.

"Named after Bernard Marigny. His only piece of history's bringing craps to America in the 1800s and sellin' off the land we live on to pay his debts."

"From losing at craps?" I asked.

"My roots have cursed me, bruh; it's why my fortunes rise and fall." Dean had been out of work for over a year, had a family to support. "You know what houses in the French Quarter sellin' for now? Shit. Had no choice but to move back, and cash out ma's place to stake a new start."

The move to New Orleans was only temporary. Lynn made that clear. Even in the early twenty-first century, she didn't look forward to being the black half of an interracial couple in what she still considered the Deep South, no matter how "New" everyone said it was.

I finished unpacking groceries and started making lunch, commiserated with Dean about the twin nightmares of a major move and low cash flow. He sounded more down than usual; I wrote it off to the stress of moving. It was only later I'd look back and see it as the start of something more. By the time I made a sandwich and heated a bowl of soup, he'd finished three beers and was opening his fourth. I signed off to eat, but couldn't get the last thing he said out of my head.

"They say you can't go home again, bruh, but they're wrong. It's not that you can't, only that you shouldn't. Sometimes leaving home's the best thing to do, and you should stay away like you had sense."

"Too many memories?"

"Too many ghosts."

I laughed as I sat at the table to eat.

"Don't tell me you believe in ghosts."

"Don't matter, bruh," he said, "They just have to believe in you." That was the phrase that struck me.

They just have to believe in you.

———◦———

DEAN CALLED BACK A FEW days later.

His mother had lived on the ground floor of her worn yellow clapboard corner house and kept everything else stored in the small narrow rooms upstairs, packed so full over the years, Dean could barely get in to clean. He'd dug in, found things he'd forgotten and others he never knew about. Old family photos, even a few original daguerreotypes, trunks of antique clothes, books, family papers. Some he packed in garbage bags to throw out, some he put aside to be appraised.

"Might be sumpin' worth a few bucks. Maybe I'll give it all to some local museum. The Dean Duvall Collection."

"Yeah, they could name a wing after you."

"Be some 'preciation, bruh. More'n I get round here."

Dean's speech was slurred, his accent the bad cliché movie redneck he always affected when drunk. It sounded like he'd been sitting with Sam Sixpack again, plus a few of his pals. I looked at the clock. It seemed a little early even for Dean to be in the tank.

"What do you mean?"

"Damn wife, f'true. Don't matter what you do, never enough."

"It's just the move. She'll settle down once you get the place cleared out."

"That's what they say."

I tried to lighten the mood. "Hey, how's the famous food down there? You have a chance to go out and check some of your old haunts?"

"Only haunts I seen been up here, bruh. No time or money for fun. Wife makes sure of that."

"You're upstairs now?" For some reason the news startled me, sent a shudder through my body, like some childhood fear was triggered by the thought of him crouched in a long, low dust-filled upper room while we talked, sunlight streaming through small windows to cast long shadows while he labored late into the afternoon, alone with me . . . and the ghosts.

"Where else I gon' be, bruh? Takin' care of business while we talk. All I do's take care of business . . ."

We talked a while longer, but conversation never strayed far from complaints about his wife and kids weighing him down, giving him a hard time. I wanted to be supportive, but felt drowned in his self-pity. When it was clear I couldn't pull him out of it I had to escape before I sank, told him I needed to get to a store before it closed, the best excuse I could think of to get off the phone.

"No problem, bruh. Catch ya later. Oh, and keep an eye out. Got a little surprise headed your way . . ."

He wouldn't say what it was, no matter how hard I pressed. The way he'd been talking, I wasn't sure what to expect. I hung up and poured a drink, stared at my computer screen instead of working or going out and wondered what was happening to the man I'd known in New York.

❖

A FEW DAYS LATER MY present arrived.

The bell rang and the mailman called me downstairs to sign for an oversized delivery sent Priority Mail. It was a long flat package wrapped in taped together brown paper bags, thickly padded inside with cardboard for protection, "Do Not Bend!" and "Fragile! PLEASE Do Not Fold!" scrawled all over it in Dean's blocky print. I carried my gift upstairs and opened it on the dining table where I had room to lay it out flat.

I unwrapped it and carefully removed the packing.

Inside was an old panoramic photograph over three feet long; brittle, cracked, the black and white image gently faded to sepia browns on thick, yellowed paper. It was a huge crowd at the base of the Washington Monument, ghostly pale women and children in the foreground, scattered in a semi-circle around the edges of an open clearing.

Outnumbering them many times was a multitude of men that extended back to the horizon as far as the eye could see, dressed in dark street clothes or light robes, with and without hoods, many with left arms outstretched in a salute to the monument, to their fellow Ku Klux Klansmen, to their families, their country, and their God.

In the middle of the photo, Klansmen and their women stood around the edges of a massive American flag, long enough to take twenty to hold aloft at chest level, displayed proudly as if at a patriotic event, and on that day it was. I felt a chill despite Brooklyn's late summer heat.

The casual audacity of it scared me the most, the easy social exchanges among people in the crowd, that the photographer had snapped the picture and labeled it in precise handwritten text at the bottom, as if it were a quaint scene of any other approved public assembly:

"Gathering of the Klans"

Virginia Klans arrive at Sylvan Theatre

Potomac Park * Washington, D.C. * Aug. 8th 1925

I went to my computer, did a quick Google and confirmed that there had been a big meeting in Washington that year and read some history of the first Klan, founded in 1865 by Masons. They donned masks to inspire terror in their enemies; the white robes and masks were either to imitate the Knights Templar who fought in the Crusades or to pose as avenging spirits of Confederate dead come back as ghouls.

One site said by 1925, the Klan numbered four million, its members unlikely to be convicted by local Southern juries even if arrested. I stopped reading and called Dean on the phone. He picked up after one ring, knew it was me without asking.

"Bruh! Guess you got my little package."

"Pretty big package for a white man," I joked.

"Yeah, well, saw it and thought of you." He laughed, long and loud.

"Not sure how to take that, but thanks. I'm touched. It's probably a collectible."

"Don't say I never give yuh nuthin."

"Did Lynn see it?" She'd marched in demonstrations against Bush and the Iraq war, organized petitions for feminist and civil rights issues; I could only imagine what she had to say when he brought it downstairs.

Dean laughed. "Yeah, took one look and said if I wanted to live with it, I could move my picture and fat white ass into the garage . . ."

"No surprise there."

"Guess not. Nearly told the bitch where she could put it, but like they say, you gotta pick your battles."

I paused. Despite their differences, Dean and Lynn were one of the most functional couples I knew. "Since when are you two fighting?"

"Ain't no fight, bruh. Just me layin' down law on who's boss around here. You know what they say, give 'em an inch and they'll take your balls!" He guffawed.

I tried to laugh it off, but was disturbed by the force of his cracks about Lynn. Dean made the usual guy jokes about his wife in the past, but never anything this hostile. I asked to speak to her later and he either didn't hear, or ignored me.

"Me, bruh, I think it's a piece of history. Real Americana."

"I'm with you. What's the story? You related to any of these guys?"

"Hell, probably all of 'em. You know how inbred those old bastards were." He laughed and coughed.

"Did you know you had Klan fans in the family?"

"Bruh, I'm learning more than I need to know. You'd never believe the shit I found. Scrapbooks of lynching photos, newspaper and magazine clippings of hangings and burnings, a fuckin' museum of the misbegotten. My roots. 'Fraid some's worth somethin', or I'd burn it all." He started to drift. "Need cash now. Never get this place cleared in time . . ." When I asked again to talk to Lynn, Dean made an excuse and rambled on until he ran down like a spent windup toy. While I considered ways to get past him to talk to her, I got off the phone and rewrapped the photograph.

I took it to a local frame shop in Park Slope. The teenaged white clerk behind the counter did a double take when he realized what it was, smiled slyly while he took my order as if in on some secret joke between us. His manager came in from lunch as we finished up, a professional looking young woman, styled with current fashion magazine cover perfection. She glanced at the photo with a polite smile of feigned interest that dropped as soon she read the caption.

"Is this for a museum or gallery?" she asked, pushed back frosted blonde hair for a better look.

"It was a gift. A friend found it in his mother's house in New Orleans."

She arched her eyebrows, as if wondering what kind of friend he really was. "Well. I wouldn't want to live with it."

"Sometimes it's good to remember it wasn't so long ago."

"I suppose . . ." She looked unconvinced. "I know my grandparents don't keep postcards of Auschwitz."

"They were there. The rest of us need reminders."

"I suppose," she repeated, smiled professionally but failed to conceal a scowl as she turned to walk away. I pictured her coming back that night, turning off the alarm, unlocking the door and tearing the picture to pieces with her well-manicured nails, savaging it with the sharp stiletto heels of her designer shoes, then dismissed the image. This was the civilized Slope where we publicly aired our differences in the light of day, not Dean's inscrutable South that sent me souvenirs of a time when they were settled under cover of darkness.

I GOT BUSY ON LOCATION for a job and lost touch with Dean. After a few more calls like the last one, I was glad for the break. We traded messages on voicemail, but by the time my job was over, I was too tired to deal with one of his repetitious rants, so I put off calling back until I'd regained my strength. Hopefully by then things would have improved.

The phone rang one night after I fell asleep on the couch watching TV. It woke me enough to fumble for the phone without thinking to check caller ID, and I caught it just before it went to voicemail.

"Yah?" I said.

"'Bout time! Who do I kill to hear back from you, bruh?"

"Dean." I stretched, carried the phone to the kitchen to get coffee and a drink. A double. "Sorry, I got tied up on a gig. Had to spend more time on site than I thought. You always say beggars can't be choosy."

"I ain't mad at you. Do what you gotta, I'll do the same."

He was so drunk I could barely understand him. It was exactly the call I'd been trying to avoid. "How's Lynn?"

He snorted, blew his nose and laughed. "You know what they say, the darker the berry, the sweeter the juice . . . Bitch is fine, boy, why, you want some of that?"

"Boy? Excuse me?" My voice went up like a Richard Pryor routine. "Don't call me boy, asshole. And stop calling Lynn a bitch. I don't like it and I doubt she does." I'd had arguments with Dean over politics and art, but never really been mad at him until now.

His voice came back low and deep, dead serious. "I'll call you whatever I want to, boy. You ain't got no right ta tell me what to do, no more'n that black bitch downstairs."

There was a moment when I was going to respond with an easy retort, tell his cracker ass what I thought as usual, but there was something in his voice that stopped me. When he said those words, it hadn't been the slurred accents of the drunk who called me. It was a voice of authority, clear and decisive, stating the truth. I wouldn't be challenging Dean, but everything he thought and believed in. I wasn't sure enough of what that was anymore to start a fight. Not without knowing what I was up against.

"We'll talk later. When you sober up."

"Ain't drunk, boy. I'm high on life." He laughed like that was some kind of joke. "Yeah, that's it. High on . . ." He started to cough again, from a chest thick with phlegm.

"Enough with this boy shit, okay?"

Dean wheezed as he chuckled into the phone.

"High on lives, boy. We high on lives . . ."

I disconnected, turned up the TV to drown my thoughts.

I'd never been called "boy" by anyone before, and to have a good friend be the first made it all the worse. I felt trapped in the apartment, the scene of the crime, and needed to get out, so I called a nearby friend and asked him to meet me at Excelsior, a local gay bar only a few blocks from us.

Winston was tall, dark and dressed to kill as always, already posed cocktail in hand at the long curved wooden bar when I arrived. He'd just had his shoulder-length dreadlocks done, still moist and glistening with fresh oils, and toyed with them while we talked.

It was a quiet night at the bar, still early, and the jukebox played soft music instead of blasting dance hits. Excelsior was like any neighborhood bar, only gay, one of the few bars I'd ever felt comfortable hanging in. I'd met Winston there when he'd introduced himself to one of my friends that appealed to him. They lasted one night, but Winston and I ended up friends for years.

"What can I say, honey?" he said after I told him about my grim conversations with Dean, raved and ranted the rage out of my system. "I'm from Louisiana. White folk down there can be that way. Friends for years until you hit a rough patch that shows you who they really are. He's just getting back to his racist roots."

"I can't believe that."

"I tell you true. It's pack nature; when the choice is between you and their own . . ." He waved a hand to finish the rest of the thought while he downed the last of his drink.

I told him he was crazy. I told him he was wrong. I told myself to stay calm and give Dean time to redeem himself.

"Sometimes friends need a vacation from each other, boo. Let it go," Winston said as I finished my beer. "Forget it and him."

We walked out the door and hugged as we said goodbye. There was a crash of breaking glass against the sidewalk behind us as we heard voices yell, "Faggots!" from the street, then the roar of an engine.

People ran out of the bar before Winston and I understood what had happened and described it to us. A car full of teenagers was passing when one of the kids threw a bottle while the others jeered and cheered him on, then they took off through a red light. Regulars made sure broken glass hadn't hit us while the owner, ordinarily a quiet gentle man, ran out with a cell phone in his hand, snapped out orders to his burly partner behind him.

"I'm on hold with the local precinct. Did anyone get a plate number?" Someone waved, and he went to talk to her while I checked out Winston. He was furious.

"Goddamn them! How dare they! Goddamn motherfuckers!" He stamped back and forth in front of the bar, cursed while people tried to console him, or encouraged him to let it out. The owner came back over to me.

"Lord, Greg, I am so sorry. The cops are on their way. I don't know what to say. We've been open for years and that's never happened. Never. Come in if you need a drink while you wait. On the house." Winston headed back inside before I could answer for either of us. He turned at the door and gestured to the street, in the direction the car had sped off.

"Pack nature," he said, and disappeared inside.

<hr/>

OVER THE NEXT WEEK I noticed a rise in news stories about hate crimes; synagogues and cars vandalized with swastikas, fires in Baptist churches, Hassidic Jews attacked by Latin teens, black men beaten with bats by a white gang in Howard Beach, a turbaned Sikh assaulted for the Twin Towers. I was extra watchful on the subway after a news story about an outpatient off his meds who'd pushed a girl onto the tracks, stopped wearing my MP3 player so I could keep my ears open for suspicious sounds behind me on the street. I couldn't tell if the surge was real or if what happened outside the bar made me pay more attention to stories that were always there. It was as if whatever shadow Dean was living under had made its way up here to look for me.

I picked up a voicemail message that my picture was ready, and stopped on my way back from the city to pick it up. When I got it home I saw they'd done a great job, despite the manager's reservations. The matte was a narrow strip of ivory with a thin blood red border on the inside. The frame was rounded, high gloss blood red to match the border. The best place to put it seemed to be over my desk, so the long dead Klansmen could watch over me while I worked at my computer.

When I was done hanging it I sat in my chair with a shot of tequila to take a look. Smoldering eyes stared down in disapproval, an allied assembly of racists who would gladly have lynched me for being the free nigger cocksucker I was. I was everything they'd tried to prevent; I thought trapped in framed glass their world was harmless, frozen in the past, too far away to hurt me, but Dean had proved me wrong.

I stared up at the panorama, examined faces and details while I tried to forget my last conversation with him, tried to let the anger die down, but drink only fueled my fury. The rest of the night was spent brooding, as I gulped tequila and smoked weed, tried not to call Dean and start a new fight, used all my years in therapy to try to understand what made him change. I'd picked a bad combination; the tequila broke down my defenses, left me open to paranoid fantasies inspired by the weed. They came all too easily and all made sense when I was stoned.

There were only two explanations, internal or external.

If the answer was internal, Dean was having a mental breakdown. The expenses and pressure of the move had been too much, even for him. He was striking out at the only ones in reach, his family and me. If it was external . . .

All I needed to spur my stoned fantasy was the photograph in front of me. The crowd of Klansmen swarmed in a ring like white blood cells gathered to engulf invaders, a mass of individuals united to think and act as one killing organism. What if evil wasn't born of any single thought but was the product of a group mind, spread through the body of society like a virus that ate into healthy heads and converted them, made them its own?

What if there was an evil infecting America, demons, haunts, call them hungry ghosts. Something that followed us from the old world and made its home in the heartland where it grew and nourished itself on lynchings, serial killings, race riots and state executions. It could have started in Spain during the Crusades, accidentally unleashed by the same Knights Templar that inspired early Klan leaders, crusaders foolish enough to test powers they didn't understand and couldn't control.

Maybe alchemy or incantations woke an ancient hunger that followed them to inspire the tortures of the Inquisition, the violence of the French Revolution, sent somber pilgrims across the sea to murder natives for their land, advised judges to hold witch hunts in Salem, donned hoods of the Ku Klux Klan to spread terror through the South, ordered officials to intern Japanese-Americans and drop the atomic bomb, while its forebears in Europe bred the Holocaust, traveled with soldiers to My Lai and Abu Ghraib, pushed misfortune into disaster, whenever, wherever it could to make things worse, fed our fear of each other to nourish itself. I didn't know what it was, what form it took; maybe it was hidden in all our hearts, passed down from generation to generation like a congenital disease.

So here was Dean, freshly infected by the Old South he'd fled. Whatever it was had slept buried in boxes of his family's racist memorabilia, waited for the right host and woke when it found Dean in its reach, weak, afraid and alone, sank in its fangs, fed on his soul and regurgitated what was left back into his brain like poison.

That was the hate I heard, not Dean's, but the raw fury of the hungry ghosts of America, speaking through Dean's mouth like ventriloquists through a dummy.

I fell asleep on the couch in front of the photo, sure I had it all figured out, and was going to let Dean know first thing in the morning.

I WOKE WITH MY WORST hangover since high school.

There'd been some major epiphany the night before, but the details escaped me, scraped away with the rest of my memories of the night by pain. I cleaned up as well as I could, put dishes and glasses in the sink before I made coffee. There were scribbles on a pad on the desk, a map or diagram like a family tree with roots in Jerusalem ending in New Orleans, branches through Europe and North America, "Knights Templar" and "Ku Klux Klan" scrawled at either end. I remembered something about evil as organic or viral, that the photo had seemed significant; all that really remained was a churning in my stomach, a sense of foreboding, that there was something very wrong with Dean and not just a drinking problem.

I decided to call Lynn later and ask her how she felt. It was possible I was only overreacting to Dean blowing off more steam than usual. It was a tense time for them; I had to remember that when I brought up the subject with her.

In the living room I turned on the T.V. After 9/11, the biggest change in my life was that I turned on local news as soon as I woke up, to see what had happened overnight. It looked like a quiet morning until they got to the weather.

While I sipped coffee and washed down a handful of aspirin for my head, the forecast went from New York's heat wave to a hurricane off the coast of Florida called Katrina. I didn't pay attention at first, but when they started talking evacuation and New Orleans I turned it up, heard enough to make me swallow my pride and call Dean.

The phone rang for a while. No machine or voicemail picked up. I imagined the sound ringing through the worn yellow house, echoing off bare cracked walls. I got ready to hang up. Maybe they'd left already. The ringing stopped. There was silence, then Dean's voice, rough, as if he'd been sleeping. Or drinking.

"Yeah?"

"It's me. I've been hearing bad weather reports . . ."

"Bruh, wassup . . ." He dropped the phone. I heard it rustle as he picked it up and put it back in his ear. "I'm busy here."

"Yeah, look, there's a class four hurricane coming in, they're talking about evacuating New Orleans . . ."

"S'what damn bitch downstairs says. Not leavin' my home, boy. Don't need damn niggers tellin' me what to do. Niggers and illegals why I ain't got no work, why decent God-fearin' white men can't find jobs no more . . ." His breathing was heavy, labored. I knew Dean had a temper; I'd seen him reduce teamsters to near tears, but he'd never lashed out at me.

"Slow down. Stop." I held it together, kept myself from launching into a speech. "This isn't like you."

"Maybe you don't know me good as you thought."

"No. I know you. Something's wrong. It's like something down there . . ."

Dean laughed it off.

"What, boy? Go ahead and say it."

I couldn't.

A flash went off in my head and I saw the photograph.

I remembered everything I'd thought sitting in front of it the night before, as insane as it all seemed now. The infectious pack nature of ancient evil accidentally unleashed by the Knights Templar and carried to the new world like a plague. Dean taunted me as if he knew exactly what was in my head, dared me to say the words and hear how ridiculous they sounded out loud.

"Say what's on your mind, boy."

It was as impossible for me to believe Dean was possessed by evil spirits that fed on racism and fear, as it was to believe he'd always been like this, that his easy smile and our long hours of conversation had been a mask, a pretense. That was more terrifying than believing in monsters.

"What is it, boy? You think I been bit by a hungry ghost? Superstitious enough to believe in nigger crap like that?" He started humming, some old rock relic I couldn't quite make out. I heard things move in the background, like he was pushing boxes around, or digging through them like he'd lost something.

"You have to get out of there. Forget this fight. Go downstairs, pack some bags, lock up and get the family out of town for a few days. Just go to the airport, I'll charge tickets, you can fly up here..."

"Can't leave. Got work to do, boy. Maybe your kind don't get that, but down here we take care of business..."

"Let me talk to Lynn."

I heard dial tone and got a busy signal every time I called back. After a few tries I got the message and left for a drink to slow the creeping dread in my gut.

EXCELSIOR WAS HAVING ANOTHER QUIET night.

There were still enough people for me to blend in and be alone in the crowd. I ordered a beer and before I'd half-finished it saw a blond white guy in his late twenties notice me from the end of the bar. I wasn't in the mood for company, but before I could break eye contact he smiled and wandered my way. He wasn't my usual type, small, wiry and a little too friendly, like a terrier, but cute.

"Hey," he said when he reached my side, and signaled the bartender as if he was just there to order.

I nodded.

"I don't usually see many black guys here. Too bad."

"Yeah, well, at these prices, you won't see many more."

He pulled out a twenty and slapped it down on the bar. "Next one's on me, then. Gotta keep you coming back."

"I'm kidding," I said. "It's an old joke, about a bartender and a horse." I let him buy my next beer, anyway.

"Yeah? Comparing yourself to a horse?" He swayed a little, rested his hand on my thigh as his smile broadened. I could tell he was more than a few beers ahead of me. "What's funny about that?"

"What? No . . ." I laughed and started to explain, realized we were past any pretense of intelligent conversation. He leaned closer and I let him kiss me as his fingers explored the front of my pants, found what he was looking for and squeezed. His mouth tasted of beer and cigarettes, but his tongue was warm and wet in my mouth, and his hand was doing a good job of convincing me to let him go further.

I didn't bring guys home from bars often, the few nights I did were like this one, when all I needed was someone warm beside me to pull my mind from whatever bothered me back to my body and its needs. We left our beers unfinished and walked the few blocks to my place.

Outside, back in the real world, we looked like a couple of straight buddies barhopping down Fifth Avenue, while he whispered dirty comments under his breath about what he'd do to me once I got him home.

We raced up the stairs and into my hot apartment, tumbled onto my bed, moist shadows in the dark, undressed each other and twisted on the sheets like snakes tying each other into knots until I heard the words hiss out of his wet lips . . .

"Yeah, that's it. That's my sweet nigger . . ."

I shoved him away, rolled out of bed and turned on the light, stared at him like I'd just walked in on a naked stranger.

"Okay," I said. "I don't need that right now."

"What's wrong?" He looked sincerely baffled as he stood, his pale boner poked up like a raised eyebrow. "Shit, what I said? Everybody says it. No big deal anymore, right? Hip hop made it okay, they say it on MTV and BET all the time, know what I mean, mah niggah?" He said the last with a broad urban accent, laughed as if it was funny, then saw I hadn't joined him.

"Do you know how many black parents and grandparents died to keep me from being called that? I don't care how you spell it. You gots to go. Now. Get the fuck out of my house, faggot." I shook my head, pulled on my pants.

"Damn, bro," he started, but stopped when he caught the new look I gave him and put on his clothes.

"Yeah. Not so funny now, is it, queer? Didn't we make those words okay, too?" I walked him out, silent, as furious at myself as with him for playing his hot black stud long enough for him to think he could say those words and have them excite me. After he left, I double-locked the door behind him, as if that could keep out what I was trying to escape.

Whatever it was.

———————

THE STORM WAS COMING.

They were past warning; it was on its way, tore along the Florida coast. I flipped channels to follow the coverage, stayed whenever I saw long lines of cars leaving New Orleans, the mayor and governor of Louisiana urging citizens to abandon their homes and get to safety.

The hurricane was hyped so hard by the media it was hard to believe they were serious, that it could really be that bad. What they predicted sounded epic, the kind of biblical disaster we were used to seeing in other countries on TV. The idea that New Orleans could be washed out of existence seemed insane despite digital simulations that showed us how and why; how could anyone in power leave levees that unprotected in a city built below sea level? I stopped only to make dinner, watched coverage until I fell asleep on the couch as the sun went down.

The phone rang. I woke in the dark.

"Hey, boy . . ." It was Dean. A bad connection or my imagination made his voice sound distorted, off-pitch, like a horror movie sound effect. "Can you hear it, boy?"

I reached over and turned on the light next to the couch. The room looked the same as always, intact, the clutter I never keep cleared for long still strewn, but it all felt alien. There was an odd air of exploration, like I was in a new world where anything could happen, finding my footing for the first time.

"It'll be here soon."

"What's that? The storm?"

He laughed, the same choked chortle I'd heard before, like he was dying of consumption.

"Ain't no storm. It's the dark that's comin'. Not dark like you, nigger, but real dark, deep dark, deeper than night, blacker than black, so deep nothing gets out. It's calling me, boy, like God called to Abraham. It's awake and hungry and ain't going back to sleep until it's been fed."

I froze; his words echoed the fantasy that haunted me since the night I'd fallen asleep in front of the panorama. I'd never admitted it to him, never spoken the words aloud. There was no way for him to know.

"What are you talking about, buddy? Doesn't sound like you."

"You sure right there, boy . . ."

"What's that supposed to mean?"

"You're so bright. What do you think?"

I looked up at the sepia-toned Klansmen over my desk. Some looked directly into camera like they could see me, made me half afraid Dean could see what they saw, that they were all connected across time and space.

"Cut it out."

"Why? Not so sure there's not somethin' out there can push people past the limit? Put icin' on the cake; turn a simple muggin' into vicious murder, date rape into a weeklong torture session? Not so sure you're always in control?" His voice was soft, seductive, an old time movie country lawyer selling his case to the jury, Daniel Webster defending the Devil for a change.

"You're talking crazy." I was frozen, unable, unwilling to believe what I feared the most.

"You want to hear crazy? Listen to this, nigger." He was on his feet, walked downstairs to the tiled kitchen wearing the headset phone.

"Hey," I started, but he cut me off.

"What?" Dean laughed and coughed at the same time; one rolled into the other, almost a death rattle, dry, but filled with mucous. "You ain't a nigger? Any more'n that nigger bitch asleep in the bedroom?"

"Stop it."

"Stop what, cocksucker? I'm just getting started."

He laughed again and I knew this wasn't some kind of game or sick practical joke. Money stress, the move, something had pushed him too far to come back, over some edge I hadn't seen coming—that or something else. I heard kitchen drawers open and close, silverware rattle.

A butcher knife clanged as it hit a cutting board.

I recognized the sound because I knew the knife, had used it to help make dinner in their Jersey home, sharpened it myself the last time I was there and chastised Dean for not keeping a better edge on the blade. I wondered if he'd taken my advice, wondered how sharp the knife was now as I listened to his footsteps leave the tiled kitchen and walk into silence on the carpeted hall.

"Hey, what's up?" I asked, tried to sound casual.

"Just cleaning house, boy. Got work to do. Some folks don't seem to know their place. But I'll be taking care of business every day, and every way . . ."

He started singing the old Bachman-Turner "Overdrive" song aloud. I recognized it when I heard the lyrics; it was what he'd been humming for weeks upstairs while he talked to me on the phone. The way he chanted the words broke the spell that held me frozen. The only place he could be going was to the bedroom.

With a butcher knife.

I stood up with no idea where to go. To the police? The airport? Even the fastest flight would get me there hours too late. I couldn't hang up as long as I could use the phone to hear what Dean was doing, and I couldn't call his local precinct on my cell without him hearing me.

I started to panic, then stopped. There was still one thing I could do. I went to my computer and searched for the police station nearest the house in Marigny, found the precinct closest to them and an e-mail address, sent a short but explicit note that explained what was happening, where, and that I was on the phone with him now. Then I sent it again a hundred times.

"Dean? What's going on, there, buddy?"

"Gonna put her down, bruh, put the black bitch down like a rabid dog, and take care of her little black bastards. Then we're comin' fer you, boy, every last one of you, until every nigger knows their place . . ."

He kept humming the song, moved to the back of the house a step at a time with a little laugh every now and then. To be sure the police got my message I found their fax number and computer-faxed fifty copies of the note in large type so someone would be sure to notice it pouring out of the machine. For once, I was glad to be a geek.

"Listen to me, Dean . . ."

"Shhh . . . Bitch is still asleep . . ."

In my earpiece I heard the bedroom door creak open, Lynn's sleepy voice in the background, too slurred to make out what she said.

"Hey, baby," whispered Dean. I heard Lynn gasp and try to scream; instead there was the sound of struggle, a punch, and I heard the breath go out of her with a dull thump. I remembered how much bigger Dean was, imagined him throwing Lynn to the bed like a rag doll.

"Damn it! What the fuck are you doing?" I shouted into the phone, helpless to stop him any other way.

"Quiet, boy, got my hands full right now . . ." His voice was strained, breathless. Lynn screamed for the children to run, until he gagged her. I heard sheets rip; Dean's breath came in short bursts as they struggled.

"Jesus Christ!"

"Don't you take the name of our Lord in vain, motherfucker," he snarled. "God don't care what happens to this nigger bitch any more'n he cares about your black ass . . ."

I listened to him hum that damned song as he went about his work. "Still there? What do you think, bruh? Is Dean at work here? Or somethin' else?"

He headed down the hall to the kids' room. I heard them weep as he entered, pictured Dean shoving seven-year-old Milton back down the hall to the master bedroom by the neck, two year old Shana tucked under his other arm like a football. Dean wouldn't need the knife to handle the kids. I heard him throw them to the floor, slap them to shut them up while he bound them.

A new e-mail came in from the police that my messages had been received. "Is this for real? We're in the middle of a citywide evacuation ..."

I typed a fast reply, "I swear to God, I have him on the phone now trying to slow him down, you have my permission to tap into my line if you have to verify," and hit Send, waited until they confirmed to relax. I just had to keep him talking until they got there. I tried to keep the excitement out of my voice.

"Dean? You still there?"

"Yeah, boy."

The children's panicked howls had subsided to sobs; all I could hear from Lynn were moans and muffled cries through her gag as Dean snickered.

"They say beauty's skin deep, don't they, bruh? That true, nigger? Let's take a look ..."

There was a wet rip and new shrieks from Lynn, then she must have passed out from the pain; when I didn't hear her anymore I couldn't hold back tears. I felt helpless, even knowing help was on the way. The only question was if it would be in time.

"In the name of God," I said. "If there's anything of you left in there. Stop this before it's too late."

"You started this, boy. You needed proof. Satisfied? Believe in us now, nigger?"

I must have screamed, and it all poured out, the rage, the fear and pain and I denied him at the top of my lungs, I didn't believe, it wasn't anything but Dean at work and he was going to burn in Hell if there was one, and if there wasn't I would build one to hold him ... I don't know what else I said, it was drowned out by the sound of sirens in the background as the police finally came, close enough that he knew he could either finish his task or flee. I prayed Dean was still sane enough to run. He hissed into the phone.

"You did this, boy. Don't know how, but it was you, you nigger bastard. We comin' fer you, boy. Comin' fer you ..."

And the line went dead.

SOMEONE FROM THE PRECINCT HAD the mercy to call an hour later to let me know Lynn and the kids were safe, the longest hour of my life. They found Lynn tied spread-eagle, tortured, bleeding, the kids hogtied on the floor, forced to face the bed. They couldn't find Dean. He got away before they could get inside. I lost contact with Lynn and the kids until friends told me they'd been safely evacuated after the rescue to her mother's house in the Bronx.

"The kids are fine as they can be," she said when I reached her. "The house sounds like it's still in one piece. Our street wasn't hit bad, no flooding, just lost a few windows and shingles. Neighbors next door rode out the storm, they're keeping me posted when they can." There was a brief almost unnoticeable pause.

"Still no word about Dean," she added, as if he'd wandered off at the mall.

"How are you?"

"Oh, well. Everything works. Thank you for that. If he'd had more time ..." She sighed, tried to laugh it off. "I won't be wearing shorts or sleeveless tops for a while, but didn't much anyway."

I never asked what Dean did to her in the bedroom that night, what the children were forced to watch. All I knew was what I heard; that was bad enough. I was afraid to know any more. Facing what Dean was capable of either meant admitting I hadn't known him at all, or that something else wore my friend like a Halloween costume and tried to destroy everything he loved.

I watched CNN news coverage of the hurricane aftermath with the same mute disbelief I felt witnessing the fall of the Twin Towers. It was hard to believe it was real, happening to us as we'd seen it happen to so many others in the last few years of earthquakes and tsunamis.

As days went by, I couldn't tell if the crisis was under control as the government claimed or if the city had descended into the surreal Hell described on the news. Official reports tried to play down the crime, TV showed waterlogged devastation and hinted at unspeakable acts committed in the stadium, while online blogs painted a worse picture of the troops' behavior. Poor black residents were made to look like animals, patrolling soldiers portrayed as storm troopers; if Dean was host to something that fed on fear, it was feasting now.

I went to a party planned before the hurricane that became a benefit for Katrina victims. I'd planned to skip it, but Winston talked me into it.

"It's a healing thing, baby. Not just for you, but all of us, so you're going. Meet you at your place at seven."

It was at a loft in DUMBO, high under the Brooklyn Bridge, with a view of Manhattan outside factory-sized windows. I saw faces I hadn't seen in ages, heard stories about friends and family in affected areas who were struggling to recover or helping others. The events of the last week started to blur with more drinks, passed joints and mellow music, lulled by human voices exchanging soft consolation.

My cell phone rang, and I opened it. The signal was weak, so I stepped out onto the fire escape to get better reception. The number was blocked; the screen said Unknown Caller. I slipped the earpiece on and pushed the talk button.

"Yeah?"

"Hey, bruh."

"Dean." It wasn't a question, I had no doubt it was Dean's voice, weak as the signal was, even if I knew it couldn't be him.

"O, my nigger," the thing that spoke like Dean breathed into my ear, from a place no calls could come from, would not come for days. "O, nigger, the things we have seen. You would tear your eyes from their sockets to forget them." Then it laughed, a thick sound still filled with phlegm. "But not us, bruh. Not us. We like to watch."

I shivered though the air outside was warm as I listened to the impossible voice, looked back through the window to watch the party still going on. Music played, flickering couples swayed on the dance floor; it looked like a distant world light years away, one I could see but never reach again in my lifetime.

"Where are you?"

"Like to know that, wouldn't you, nigger? Like to know we're not waitin' downstairs for you, in your closet or under your bed. Never know for sure, will yuh, bruh?"

I didn't want to hear the answer but had to ask.

"Who are you?"

"Call us Legion, for we are many."

"You lie," I said. "There are no demons. Just excuses."

"Excuses? Come on, boy," it said, "All people want is a way to blame the bad on someone else, God or the Devil. An easy explanation for why y'all take an eye for an eye instead of turnin' the other cheek, why niggers get dragged to death behind trucks and fags tied up to freeze to death, even now . . .

"So we let you tell yerselves it ain't your fault. It's ours. Don't say we never give yuh nuthin' . . ." I could hear the sounds of female shrieks and deep male laughter in the background. It chuckled again, just like Dean. "Gotta run. Got a date with an angel . . ."

The screams grew louder as the phone approached them and disconnected, after one last laugh from my dead good buddy.

———◇———

THEY FOUND ME ASLEEP ON the fire escape, phone still in my ear, said I told them I dreamed I was on the phone with a long lost friend, and then was in New Orleans looking for him.

I said I stood on dry land under a full moon at night, looked east at a flooded road ahead, water as far as the eye could see. The flood whispered to me like sirens of old; I felt a pull, looked down and saw water rise over my feet and up my shins before I could back out.

Hushed voices rose with the waters as they covered my waist, my shoulders and head. Fully submerged, I could hear them clearly as I watched my last breath bubble up out of my mouth to the surface, now yards away. My ears filled with an infernal chorus of "Dixie" as I struggled to ascend . . .

I looked down and saw the singers drift up from the depths in tattered Confederate gray, white hooded robes, sheriff uniforms, army fatigues, anonymous black suits, faceless men bound only by hate and fear. They sang as one, swung swords, sticks, Billy clubs, pistols, rifles from muskets to AK-47s in rhythm to the steady beat of an unseen drum, like the inhuman sound of a giant heart.

Dean rose to the head of the hellish choir, a noose in one hand; his other gripped my ankle and pulled me back down as I fought my way up towards the light . . .

———◇———

THEY FOUND DEAN A FEW weeks later—what was left—wedged between a Dumpster and the side of a truck someone had loaded with the last of their worldly goods or loot, too late to get out of town. Dean's death went unnoticed in the torrent of news from Katrina, the far greater losses and atrocities; it was a small story worthy of note to only a few, but it was our story and we took it hard. Life quieted down after that; Dean's recovery led to our own.

I went to New Orleans a few months after the waters receded to help Lynn sell the house. The city was like an invalid who'd nearly died, still unsure of its chances for full recovery. It was stronger, saner, had regained some of its old fire, but there was a haunted look behind the eyes, the look of one who'd seen how close the end could be and would never be the same again. It was the same look I saw in Lynn's eyes when she thought no one was looking.

Except for missing roof tiles and broken windows, Dean's old family home was intact and ironically worth even more, as survivors who'd lost homes looked for replacements. It sold for more than enough to move Lynn and the kids back north near her family. I flew back to Brooklyn where I felt at ease, if not entirely safe; it would be hard to feel safe anywhere for a long time.

When I got home, I took down the panorama of the Klan.

I was tempted to burn it, but that would mean I believed it was part of something supernatural, that it held contaminating magic of its own that could somehow influence others or even me. I was too civilized for that. Then I remembered what Dean had said; it doesn't matter whether you believe in ghosts if they believe in you. The rational part of me wrapped the photograph and donated it to the Museum of Intolerance in Dean's name.

No one could tell me if Dean was dead or alive the night of the party. Water and weather conditions made it impossible. He was dead, case closed; they told Lynn she was lucky to get a body, much less an autopsy. She was still in shock over losing him, too distraught to remember or discuss changes in Dean before the end. I was left to find my own answers. There were none.

I don't know what's harder to live with; that Dean went off the deep end and fell back on the only solid ground he could find or that he'd confessed to being consumed by an ancient hunger. I'll never know which was true, whether he needed a shrink or an exorcist, and I'm not sure I want to know.

I once saw a sign on a pillar in a New York City subway station, "WET PAIN," written in bright red block letters on glossy white card stock. Back then, I thought it was a joke or mistake, meant to read "WET PAINT," but I could be wrong; as much as I don't want to believe it, maybe sometimes signs say exactly what they mean.

———

Terence Taylor (terencetaylor.com) is an award-winning children's television writer whose work has appeared on PBS, Nickelodeon, and Disney, among many others. After years of comforting tiny tots with TV, he turned to scaring their parents. In addition to horror and science fiction short stories, Terence is author of the first two books of his *Vampire Testaments* trilogy, *Bite Marks* and *Blood Pressure*, and has returned to work on the conclusion of his trilogy, *Past Life*. He has recently appeared in *Fantastic Stories of the Imagination*, *Lightspeed's People of Colo(u)r Destroy Science Fiction!* and the *What the #@&% Is That?* anthology. Find Terence on Twitter @vamptestaments or walking his neighbor's black Labrador mix along the banks of the Gowanus Canal and surrounding environs.

MONSTRO

JUNOT DÍAz

At first, Negroes thought it *funny*. A disease that could make a Haitian blacker? It was the joke of the year. Everybody in our sector accusing everybody else of having it. You couldn't display a blemish or catch some sun on the street without the jokes starting. Someone would point to a spot on your arm and say, Diablo, haitiano, que te pasó?

La Negrura they called it.

The Darkness.

⊷⬥⊶

These days everybody wants to know what you were doing when the world came to an end. Fools make up all sorts of vainglorious self-serving plep—but me, I tell the truth.

I was chasing a girl.

I was one of the idiots who didn't heed any of the initial reports, who got caught way out there. What can I tell you? My head just wasn't into any mysterious disease—not with my mom sick and all. Not with Mysty.

Motherfuckers used to say culo would be the end of us. Well, for me it really was.

⊷⬥⊶

In the beginning the doctor types couldn't wrap their brains around it, either.

The infection showed up on a small boy in the relocation camps outside Port-au-Prince, in the hottest March in recorded history. The index case was only four years old, and by the time his uncle brought him in his arm looked like an enormous black pustule, so huge it had turned the boy into an appendage of the arm. In the glypts he looked terrified.

Within a month, a couple of thousand more infections were reported. Didn't rip through the pobla like the dengues or the poxes. More of a slow leprous spread. A black mold-fungus-blast that came on like a splotch and then gradually started taking you over, tunneling right through you—though as it turned out it wasn't a mold-fungus-blast at all. It was something else. Something new.

Everybody blamed the heat. Blamed the Calientazo. Shit, a hundred straight days over 105 degrees F. in our region alone, the planet cooking like a chimi and down to its last five trees—something berserk was bound to happen. All sorts of bizarre outbreaks already in play: diseases no one had names for, zoonotics by the pound. This one didn't cause too much panic because it seemed to hit only the sickest of the sick, viktims who had nine kinds of ill already in them. You literally had to be falling to pieces for it to grab you.

It almost always started epidermically and then worked its way up and in. Most of the infected were immobile within a few months, the worst comatose by six. Strangest thing, though: once infected, few viktims died outright; they just seemed to linger on and on. Coral reefs might have been adios on the ocean floor, but they were alive and well on the arms and backs and heads of the infected. Black rotting rugose masses fruiting out of bodies. The medicos formed a ninety-nation consortium, flooded one another with papers and hypotheses, ran every test they could afford, but not even the military enhancers could crack it.

In the early months, there was a big make do, because it was so strange and because no one could identify the route of transmission—that got the bigheads more worked up than the disease itself. There seemed to be no logic to it—spouses in constant contact didn't catch the Negrura, but some unconnected fool on the other side of the camp did. A huge rah-rah, but when the experts determined that it wasn't communicable in the standard ways, and that normal immune systems appeared to be at no kind of risk, the renminbi and the attention and the savvy went elsewhere. And since it was just poor Haitian types getting fucked up—no real margin in that. Once the initial bulla died down, only a couple of underfunded teams stayed on. As for the infected, all the medicos could do was try to keep them nourished and hydrated—and, more important, prevent them from growing together.

That was a serious issue. The blast seemed to have a boner for fusion, respected no kind of boundaries. I remember the first time I saw it on the Whorl. Alex was, like, Mira esta vaina. Almost delighted. A shaky glypt of a pair of naked trembling Haitian brothers sharing a single stained cot, knotted together by horrible mold, their heads slurred into one. About the nastiest thing you ever saw. Mysty saw it and looked away and eventually I did, too.

My tíos were, like, Someone needs to drop a bomb on those people, and even though I was one of the pro-Haitian domos, at the time I was thinking it might have been a mercy.

—◇—

I WAS ACTUALLY ON THE Island when it happened. Front-row fucking seat. How lucky was that?

They call those of us who made it through "time witnesses." I can think of a couple of better terms.

I'd come down to the D.R. because my mother had got super sick. The year before, she'd been bitten by a rupture virus that tore through half her organs before the doctors got savvy to it. No chance she was going to be taken care of back North. Not with what the cheapest nurses charged. So she rented out the Brooklyn house to a bunch of Mexos, took that loot, and came home.

Better that way. Say what you want, but family on the Island was still more reliable for heavy shit, like, say, dying, than family in the North. Medicine was cheaper, too, with the flying territory in Haina, its Chinese factories pumping out pharma like it was romo, growing organ sheets by the mile, and, for somebody as sick as my mother, with only rental income to live off, being there was what made sense.

I was supposed to be helping out, but really I didn't do na for her. My tía Livia had it all under control and if you want the truth I didn't feel comfortable hanging around the house with Mom all sick. The vieja could barely get up to piss, looked like a stick version of herself. Hard to see that. If I stayed an hour with her it was a lot.

What an asshole, right? What a shallow motherfucker.

But I was nineteen—and what is nineteen, if not for shallow? In any case my mother didn't want me around, either. It made her sad to see me so uncomfortable. And what could I do for her besides wring my hands? She had Livia, she had her nurse, she had the muchacha who cooked and cleaned. I was only in the way.

Maybe I'm just saying this to cover my failings as a son.

Maybe I'm saying this because of what happened.

Maybe.

Go, have fun with your friends, she said behind her breathing mask.

Didn't have to tell me twice.

Fact is, I wouldn't have come to the Island that summer if I'd been able to nab a job or an internship, but the droughts that year and the General Economic Collapse meant that nobody was nabbing shit. Even the Sovereign kids were ending up home with their parents. So with the house being rented out from under me and nowhere else to go, not even a girlfriend to mooch off, I figured, Fuck it: might as well spend the hots on the Island. Take in some of that ole-time climate change. Get to know the patria again.

◦—◦—◦

For six, seven months it was just a horrible Haitian disease—who fucking cared, right? A couple of hundred new infections each month in the camps and around Port-au-Prince, pocket change, really, nowhere near what KRIMEA was doing to the Russian hinterlands. For a while it was nothing, nothing at all . . . and then some real eerie plep started happening.

Doctors began reporting a curious change in the behavior of infected patients: they wanted to be together, in close proximity, all the time. They no longer tolerated being separated from other infected, started coming together in the main quarantine zone, just outside Champ de Mars, the largest of the relocation camps. All the viktims seemed to succumb to this ingathering compulsion. Some went because they claimed they felt "safer" in the quarantine zone; others just picked up and left without a word to anyone, trekked halfway across the country as though following a homing beacon. Once viktims got it in their heads to go, no dissuading them. Left family, friends, children behind. Walked out on wedding days, on swell business. Once they were in the zone, nothing could get them to leave. When authorities tried to distribute the infected viktims across a number of centers, they either wouldn't go or made their way quickly back to the main zone.

One doctor from Martinique, his curiosity piqued, isolated an elderly viktim from the other infected and took her to a holding bay some distance outside the main quarantine zone. Within twenty-four hours, this frail septuagenarian had torn off her heavy restraints, broken through a mesh security window, and crawled halfway back to the quarantine zone before she was recovered.

Same doctor performed a second experiment: helicoptered two infected men to a hospital ship offshore. As soon as they were removed from the quarantine zone they went *batshit*, trying everything they could to break free, to return. No sedative or entreaty proved effective, and after four days of battering themselves relentlessly against the doors of their holding cells the men loosed a last high-pitched shriek and died *within minutes of each other*.

Stranger shit was in the offing: eight months into the epidemic, all infected viktims, even the healthiest, abruptly stopped communicating. Just went silent. Nothing abnormal in their bloodwork or in their scans. They just stopped talking—friends, family, doctors, it didn't matter. No stimuli of any form could get them to speak. Watched everything and everyone, clearly understood commands and information—but refused to say anything.

Anything *human*, that is.

Shortly after the Silence, the phenomenon that became known as the Chorus began. The entire infected population simultaneously let out a bizarre shriek— two, three times a day. Starting together, ending together.

Talk about unnerving. Even patients who'd had their faces chewed off by the blast joined in—the vibrations rising out of the excrescence itself. Even the patients who were comatose. Never lasted more than twenty, thirty seconds—eerie siren shit. No uninfected could stand to hear it, but uninfected kids seemed to be the most unsettled. After a week of that wailing, the majority of kids had fled the areas around the quarantine zone, moved to other camps. That should have alerted someone, but who paid attention to camp kids?

Brain scans performed during the outbursts actually detected minute fluctuations in the infected patients' biomagnetic signals, but unfortunately for just about everybody on the planet these anomalies were not pursued. There seemed to be more immediate problems. There were widespread rumors that the infected were devils, even reports of relatives attempting to set their infected family members on fire.

In my sector, my mom and my tía were about the only people paying attention to any of it; everybody else was obsessing over what was happening with KRIMEA. Mom and Tía Livia felt bad for our poor west-coast neighbors. They were churchy like that. When I came back from my outings I'd say, fooling, How are los explotao? And my mother would say, It's not funny, hijo. She's right, Aunt Livia said. That could be us next and then you won't be joking.

—◦—

So WHAT WAS I DOING, if not helping my mom or watching the apocalypse creep in? Like I told you: I was chasing a girl. And I was running around the Island with this hijo de mami y papi I knew from Brown. Living prince because of him, basically.

Classy, right? My mater stuck in Darkness, with the mosquitoes fifty to a finger and the heat like the inside of a tailpipe, and there I was privando en rico inside the Dome, where the bafflers held the scorch to a breezy 82 degrees F. and one mosquito a night was considered an invasion.

———◆———

I HADN'T ACTUALLY PLANNED ON rolling with Alex that summer—it wasn't like we were close friends or anything. We ran in totally different circles back at Brown, him prince, me prole, but we were both from the same little Island that no one else in the world cared about, and that counted for something, even in those days. On top of that we were both art types, which in our world of hyper-capitalism was like having a serious mental disorder. He was already making dough on his photography and I was attracting no one to my writing. But he had always told me, Hit me up the next time you come down. So before I flew in I glypted him, figuring he wasn't going to respond, and he glypted right back.

What's going on, charlatan, cuando vamos a janguiar? And that's basically all we did until the End: janguiar.

I knew nobody in the D.R. outside of my crazy cousins, and they didn't like to do anything but watch the fights, play dominos, and fuck. Which is fine for maybe a week—but for three months? No, hombre. I wasn't *that* Island. For Alex did me a solid by putting me on. More than a solid: saved my ass full. Dude scooped me up from the airport in his father's burner, looking so fit it made me want to drop and do twenty on the spot. Welcome to the country of las maravillas, he said with a snort, waving his hand at all the thousands of non-treaty motos on the road, the banners for the next election punching you in the face everywhere. Took me over to the rooftop apartment his dad had given him in the rebuilt Zona Colonial. The joint was a meta-glass palace that overlooked the Drowned Sectors, full of his photographs and all the bric-a-brac he had collected for props, with an outdoor deck as large as an aircraft carrier.

You live here? I said, and he shrugged lazily: Until Papi decides to sell the building.

One of those moments when you realize exactly how rich some of the kids you go to school with are. Without even thinking about it, he glypted me a six-month V.I.P. pass for the Dome, which cost about a year's tuition. Just in case, he said. He'd been on-Island since before the semester ended. A month here and I'm already aplatanao, he complained. I think I'm losing the ability to read.

We drank some more spike, and some of his too-cool-for-school Dome friends came over, slim, tall, and wealthy, every one doing double takes when they saw the size of me and heard my Dark accent, but Alex introduced me as his Brown classmate. A genius, he said, and that made it a little better. What do you do? they asked and I told them I was trying to be a journalist. Which for that set was like saying I wanted to molest animals. I quickly became part of the furniture, one of Alex's least interesting fotos. Don't you love my friends, Alex said. Son tan amable.

That first night I kinda had been hoping for a go-club or something bananas like that, but it was a talk-and-spike and let's-look-at-Alex's-latest-fotos-type party. What redeemed everything for me was that around midnight one last girl came up the corkscrew staircase. Alex said loudly, Look who's finally here. And the girl shouted, I was at church, coño, which got everybody laughing. Because of the weak light I didn't get a good look at first. Just the hair, and the vampire-stake heels. Then she finally made it over and I saw the cut on her and the immensity of those eyes and I was, like, fuck me.

That girl. With one fucking glance she upended my everything.

So you're the friend? I'm Mysty. Her crafted eyes giving me the once-over. And you're in this country *voluntarily?*

A ridiculously beautiful mina wafting up a metal corkscrew staircase in high heels and offering up her perfect cheek as the light from the Dome was dying out across the city—that I could have withstood. But then she spent the rest of the night ribbing me because I was so Americanized, because my Spanish sucked, because I didn't know any of the Island things they were talking about—and that was it for me. I was lost.

⎯◆⎯

EVERYBODY AT SCHOOL KNEW ALEX. Shit, I think everybody in Providence knew him. Negro was star like that. This flash priv kid who looked more like an Uruguayan fútbal player than a plátano, with short curly Praetorian hair and machine-made cheekbones and about the greenest eyes you ever saw. Six feet eight and super full of himself. Threw the sickest parties, always stepping out with the most rompin girls, drove an Eastwood for fuck's sake. But what I realized on the Island was that Alex was more than just a rico, turned out he was a fucking V—, son of the wealthiest, most priv'ed-up family on the Island. His abuelo like the ninety-ninth-richest man in the Americas, while his abuela had more than nine thousand properties. At Brown, Negro had actually been playing it modest—for good reason, too. Turned out that when homeboy was in middle school he was kidnapped for eight long months, barely got out alive. Never talked about it, not even cryptically, but dude never left the house in D.R. unless he was packing fuego. Always offered me a cannon, too, like it was a piece of fruit or something. Said, Just, you know, in case something happens.

⎯◆⎯

V— OR NOT, I HAD respect for Alex, because he worked hard as a fuck, not one of those upper-class vividors who sat around and blew lakhs. Was doing philosophy at Brown and business at M.I.T., smashed like a 4.0, and still had time to do his photography thing. And unlike a lot of our lakhsters in the States he really loved his Santo Domingo. Never pretended he was Spanish or Italian or gringo. Always claimed dominicano and that ain't nothing, not the way plátanos can be.

For all his pluses Alex could also be extra dickish. Always had to be the center of attention. I couldn't say anything slightly smart without him wanting to argue with me. And when you got him on a point he huffed: Well, I don't know about that. Treated Dominican workers in restaurants and clubs and bars like they were lower than shit. Never left any kind of tip. You have to yell at these people or they'll just walk all over you was his whole thing. Yeah, right, Alex, I told him. And he grimaced: You're just a Naxalite. And you're a come solo, I said, which he hated.

Pretty much on his own. No siblings, and his family was about as checked out as you could get. Had a dad who spent so much time abroad that Alex would have been lucky to pick him out in a lineup—and a mom who'd had more plastic surgery than all of Caracas combined, who flew out to Miami every week just to shop and fuck this Senegalese lawyer that everybody except the dad seemed to know about. Alex had a girlfriend from his social set he'd been dating since they were twelve, Valentina, had cheated on her at least two thousand times, with girls and boys, but because of his lakhs she wasn't going anywhere. Dude told me all about it, too, as soon as he introduced me to her. What do you think of that? he asked me with a serious cheese on his face.

Sounds pretty shitty, I said.

Oh, come on, he said, putting an avuncular arm around me. It ain't that bad.

Alex's big dream? (Of course we all knew it, because he wouldn't shut up about all the plep he was going to do.) He wanted to be either the Dominican Sebastião Salgado or the Dominican João Silva (minus the double amputation, natch). But he also wanted to write novels, make films, drop an album, be the star of a channel on the Whorl—dude wanted to do everything. As long as it was arty and it made him a Name he was into it.

He was also the one who wanted to go to Haiti, to take pictures of all the infected people. Mysty was, like, You can go catch a plague all by your fool self, but he waved her off and recited his motto (which was also on his cards): To represent, to surprise, to cause, to provoke.

To die, she added.

He shrugged, smiled his hundred-crore smile. A photographer has to be willing to risk it all. A photograph can change todo.

You had to hand it to him; he had confidence. And recklessness. I remember this time a farmer in Baní uncovered an unexploded bomb from the civil war in his field—Alex raced us all out there and wanted to take a photo of Mysty sitting on the device in a cheerleading outfit. She was, like, Are you *insane?* So he sat down on it himself while we crouched behind the burner and he snapped his own picture, grinning like a loon, first with a Leica, then with a Polaroid. Got on the front page of *Listin* with that antic. Parents flying in from their respective cities to have a chat with him.

He really did think he could change todo. Me, I didn't want to change nada; I didn't want to be famous. I just wanted to write one book that was worth a damn and I would have happily called it a day.

Mi hermano, that's pathetic to an extreme, Alex said. You have to dream a lot bigger than that.

WELL, I CERTAINLY DREAMED BIG with Mysty.

In those days she was my Wonder Woman, my Queen of Jaragua, but the truth is I don't remember her as well as I used to. Don't have any pictures of her—they were all lost in the Fall when the memory stacks blew, when la Capital was scoured.

One thing a Negro wasn't going to forget, though, one thing that you didn't need fotos for, was how beautiful she was. Tall and copper-colored, with a Stradivarius curve to her back. An ex-volleyball player, studying international law at UNIBE, with a cascade of black hair you could have woven thirty days of nights from. Some modelling when she was thirteen, fourteen, definitely on the receiving end of some skin-crafting and bone-crafting, maybe breasts, definitely ass, and who knows what else—but would rather have died than cop to it.

You better believe I'm pura lemba, she always said and even I had to roll my eyes at that. Don't roll your eyes at me. I *am*.

Spent five years in Québec before her mother finally dumped her asshole Canadian stepfather and dragged her back screaming to la Capital. Something she still held against the vieja, against the whole D.R. Spoke impeccable French and used it every chance she got, always made a show of reading thick-ass French novels like "La Cousine Bette," and that was what she wanted once her studies were over: to move to Paris, work for the U.N., read French books in a café.

Men love me in Paris, she announced, like this might be a revelation.

Men love you here, Alex said.

Shook her head. It's not the same.

Of course it's not the same, I said. Men shower in Santo Domingo. And dance, too. You ever see franceses dance? It's like watching an epileptics Convention.

Mysty spat an ice cube at me. French men are the *best*.

Yes, she liked me well enough. Could even say we were friends. I had my charming in those days, I had a mouth on me like all the swords of the Montagues and Capulets combined, like someone had overdosed me with truth serum. You're Alex's only friend who doesn't take his crap, she once confided. You don't even take my crap.

Yes, she liked me but didn't *like* me, entiendes. But God did I love her. Not that I had any idea how to start with a girl like her. The only "us" time we ever had was when Alex sent her to pick me up and she'd show up either at my house in Villa Con or at the gym. My crazy cousins got so excited. They weren't used to seeing a fresa like her. She knew what she was doing. She'd leave her driver out front and come into the gym to fetch me. Put on a real show. I always knew she'd arrived because the whole gravity of the gym would shift to the entrance and I'd look over from my workout and there she'd be.

Never had any kind of game with her. Best I could do on our rides to where Alex was waiting was ask her about her day and she always said the same thing: Terrible.

◄─●─►

THEY HAD A MIGHTY STRANGE relationship, Alex and Mysty did. She seemed pissed off at him at least eighty per cent of the time, but she was also always with him; and it seemed to me that Alex spent more time with Mysty than he did with Valentina. Mysty helped him with all his little projects, and yet she never seemed happy about it, always acted like it was this massive imposition. Jesus, Alex, she said, will you just make it already. Acted like everything he did bored her. That, I've come to realize, was her protective screen. To always appear bored.

Even when she wasn't bored Mysty wasn't easy; jeva had a temper, always blowing up on Alex because he said something or was late or because she didn't like the way he laughed at her. Blew up on me if I ever sided with him. Called him a mama huevo at least once a day, which in the old D.R. was a pretty serious thing to throw at a guy. Alex didn't care, played it for a goof. You talk so sweet, ma chère. You should say it in French. Which of course she always did.

I asked Alex at least five times that summer if he and Mysty were a thing. He denied it full. Never laid a hand on her, she's like my sister, my girlfriend would kill me, etc.

Never fucked her? That seemed highly unfuckinglikely. Something had happened between them—sex, sure, but something else—though what that was isn't obvious even now that I'm older and dique wiser. Girls like Mysty, of her class, were always orbiting around crore-mongers like Alex, hoping that they would bite. Not that in the D.R. they ever did but still. Once when I was going on about her, wondering why the fuck he hadn't jumped her, he looked around and then pulled me close and said, You know the thing with her, right? Her dad used to fuck her until she was twelve. Can you believe that?

Her dad? I said.

He nodded solemnly. Her dad. Did I believe it? The incest? In the D.R. incest was like the other national pastime. I guess I believed it as much as I believed Alex's whole she's-my-sister coro, which is to say, maybe I did and maybe I didn't, but in the end I also didn't care. It made me feel terrible for her, sure, but it didn't make me want her any less. As for her and Alex, I never saw them touch, never saw anything that you could call calor pass between them; she seemed genuinely uninterested in him romantically and that's why I figured I had a chance.

I don't want a boyfriend, she kept saying. I want a *visa*.

Dear dear Mysty. Beautiful and bitchy and couldn't wait to be away from the D.R. A girl who didn't let anyone push her around, who once grabbed a euro-chick by the hair because the bitch tried to cut her in line. Wasn't really a deep person. I don't think I ever heard her voice an opinion about art or politics or say anything remotely philosophical. I don't think she had any female friends—shit, I don't think she had any friends, just a lot of people she said hi to in the clubs. Chick was as much a loner as I was. She never bought anything for anyone, didn't do community work, and when she saw children she always stayed far away. Ánimales, she called them—and you could tell she wasn't joking.

No, she wasn't anything close to humane, but at nineteen who needed humane? She was buenmosa and impossible and when she laughed it was like this little wilderness. I would watch her dance with Alex, with other guys—never with me, I wasn't good enough—and my heart would break, and that was all that mattered.

Around our third week of hanging out, when the riots were beginning in the camps and the Haitians in the D.R. were getting deported over a freckle, I started talking about maybe staying for a few months extra. Taking a semester off Brown to keep my mom company, maybe volunteering in Haiti. Crazy talk, sure, but I knew for certain that I wasn't going to land Mysty by sending her glypts from a thousand miles away. To bag a girl like that you have to make a serious move, and staying in the D.R. was for me a serious move indeed.

I think I might stick around, I announced when we were all driving back from what was left of Las Terrenas. No baffler on the burner and the heat was literally pulling our skin off.

Why would you do that? Mysty demanded. It's *awful* here.

It's not awful here, Alex corrected mildly. This is the most beautiful country in the world. But I don't think you'd last long. You're way gringo.

And you're what, Enriquillo?

I know *I'm* gringo, Alex said, but you're *way* gringo. You'd be running to the airport in a month.

Even my mother was against it. Actually sat up in her medicine tent. You're going to drop school—for what? Esa chica plastica? Don't be ridiculous, hijo. There's plenty of culo falso back home.

⊷⊶

THAT JULY A MAN NAMED Henri Casimir was brought in to a field clinic attached to Champ de Mars. A former manager in the utility company, now reduced to carting sewage for the camp administration. Brought in by his wife, Rosa, who was worried about his behavior. Last couple of months dude had been roaming about the camp at odd hours, repeating himself ad nauseam, never sleeping. The wife was convinced that her husband was not her husband.

In the hospital that day: one Noni DeGraff, a Haitian epidemiologist and one of the few researchers who had been working on the disease since its first appearance; brilliant and pretty much fearless, she was called the Jet Engine by her colleagues, because of her headstrong ferocity. Intrigued by Casimir's case, she sat in on the examination. Casimir, apart from a low body temperature, seemed healthy. Bloodwork clean. No sign of virals or of the dreaded infection. When questioned, the patient spoke excitedly about a san he was claiming the following week. Distressed, Rosa informed the doctors that said san he was going on about had disbanded two months earlier. He had put his fifty renminbi faithfully into the pot every month, but just before his turn came around they found out the whole thing was a setup. He never saw a penny, Rosa said.

When Dr. DeGraff asked the wife what she thought might be bothering her husband, Rosa said simply, Someone has witched him.

Something about the wife's upset and Casimir's demeanor got Dr. DeGraff's antennas twitching. She asked Rosa for permission to observe Casimir on one of his rambles. Wife Rosa agreed. As per her complaint, Casimir spent almost his entire day tramping about the camp with no apparent aim or destination. Twice Dr. DeGraff approached him, and twice Casimir talked about the heat and about the san he was soon to receive. He seemed distracted, disoriented, even, but not mad.

The next week, Dr. DeGraff tailed Casimir again. This time the good doctor discerned a pattern. No matter how many twists he took, invariably Casimir wound his way back to the vicinity of the quarantine zone at the very moment that the infected let out their infernal chorus. As the outburst rang out, Casimir paused and then, without any change in expression, ambled away.

DeGraff decided to perform an experiment. She placed Casimir in her car and drove him away from the quarantine zone. At first, Casimir appeared "normal," talking again about his san, wiping his glasses compulsively, etc. Then, at half a mile from the zone, he began to show increasing signs of distress, twitching and twisting in his seat. His language became garbled. At the mile mark Casimir exploded. Snapped the seat belt holding him in and in his scramble from the car struck DeGraff with unbelievable force, fracturing two ribs. Bounding out before the doctor could manage to bring the car under control, Casimir disappeared into the sprawl of Champ de Mars. The next day, when Dr. DeGraff asked the wife to bring Casimir in, he appeared to have no recollection of the incident. He was still talking about his san.

After she had her ribs taped up, DeGraff put out a message to all medical personnel in the Haitian mission, inquiring about patients expressing similar symptoms. She assumed she would receive four, five responses. She received *two hundred and fourteen*. She asked for workups. She got them. Sat down with her partner in crime, a Haitian-American physician by the name of Anton Léger, and started plowing through the material. Nearly all the sufferers had, like Casimir, shown signs of low body temperature. And so they performed temperature tests on Casimir. Sometimes he was normal. Sometimes he was below, but never for long. A technician on the staff, hearing about the case, suggested that they requisition a thermal imager sensitive enough to detect minute temperature fluctuations. An imager was secured and then turned on Casimir. Bingo. Casimir's body temperature was indeed fluctuating, little tiny blue spikes every couple of seconds. Normal folks like DeGraff and Léger—they tested themselves, naturally—scanned red, but patients with the Casimir complaint appeared onscreen a deep, flickering blue. On a lark, DeGraff and Léger aimed the scanner toward the street outside the clinic.

They almost shat themselves. Like for reals. Nearly one out of every eight pedestrians was flickering blue.

DeGraff remembers the cold dread that swept over her, remembers telling Léger, We need to go to the infected hospital. We need to go there now.

At the hospital, they trained their camera on the guarded entrance. Copies of those scans somehow made it to the Outside. Still chilling to watch. Every single person, doctor, assistant, aid worker, janitor who walked in and out of that hospital radiated blue.

⎯⎯◆⎯⎯

WE DID WHAT ALL KIDS with a lot of priv do in the D.R.: we kicked it. And since none of us had parents to hold us back we kicked it super hard. Smoked ganja by the heap and tore up the Zona Colonial and when we got bored we left the Dome for long looping drives from one end of the Island to the other. The countryside half-abandoned because of the Long Drought but still beautiful even in its decline.

Alex had all these projects. Fotos of all the prostitutes in the Feria. Fotos of every chimi truck in the Malecón. Fotos of the tributes on the Conde. He also got obsessed with photographing all the beaches of the D.R. before they disappeared. These beaches are what used to bring the world to us! he exclaimed. They were the one resource we had! I suspected it was just an excuse to put Mysty in a bathing suit and photograph her for three hours straight. Not that I was complaining. My role was to hand him cameras and afterward to write a caption for each of the selected shots he put on the Whorl.

And I did: just a little entry. The whole thing was called "Notes from the Last Shore." Nice, right? I came up with that. Anyway, Mysty spent the whole time on those shoots bitching: about her bathing suits, about the scorch, about the mosquitoes that the bafflers were letting in, and endlessly warning Alex not to focus on her pipa. She was convinced that she had a huge one, which neither Alex nor I ever saw but we didn't argue. I got you, chérie, was what he said. I got you.

After each setup I always told her: Tú eres guapísima. And she never said anything, just wrinkled her nose at me. Once, right before the Fall, I must have said it with enough conviction, because she looked me in the eyes for a long while. I still remember what *that* felt like.

⬥

NOW IT GETS SKETCHY AS hell. A lockdown was initiated and a team of W.H.O. docs attempted to enter the infected hospital in the quarantine zone. Nine went in but nobody came out. Minutes later, the infected let out one of their shrieks, but this one lasted twenty-eight minutes. And that more or less was when shit went Rwanda.

In the D.R. we heard about the riot. Saw horrific videos of people getting chased down and butchered. Two camera crews died, and that got Alex completely pumped up.

We have to go, he cried. I'm missing it!

You're not going anywhere, Mysty said.

But are you guys seeing this? Alex asked. Are you *seeing* this?

That shit was no riot. Even we could tell that. All the relocation camps near the quarantine zone were consumed in what can only be described as a straight massacre. An outbreak of homicidal violence, according to the initial reports. People who had never lifted a finger in anger their whole lives—children, viejos, aid workers, mothers of nine—grabbed knives, machetes, sticks, pots, pans, pipes, hammers and started attacking their neighbors, their friends, their pastors, their children, their husbands, their infirm relatives, complete strangers. Berserk murderous blood rage. No pleading with the killers or backing them down; they just kept coming and coming, even when you pointed a gauss gun at them, stopped only when they were killed.

⬥

LET ME TELL YOU: IN those days I really didn't know nothing. For real. I didn't know shit about women, that's for sure. Didn't know shit about the world—obviously. Certainly didn't know *jack* about the Island.

I actually thought me and Mysty could end up together. Nice, right? The truth is I had more of a chance of busting a golden egg out my ass than I did of bagging a girl like Mysty. She was from a familia de nombre, wasn't going to have anything to do with a nadie like me, un morenito from Villa Con whose mother had made it big selling hair-straightening products to the africanos. Wasn't going to happen. Not unless I turned myself white or got a major-league contract or hit the fucking lottery. Not unless I turned into an Alex.

And yet you know what? I still had hope. Had hope that despite the world I had a chance with Mysty. Ridiculous hope, sure, but what do you expect?

⎯⎯◦⎯⎯

NEARLY TWO HUNDRED THOUSAND HAITIANS fled the violence, leaving the Possessed, as they became known, fully in control of the twenty-two camps in the vicinity of the quarantine zone.

Misreading the situation, the head of the U.N. Peacekeeping Mission waited a full two days for tensions to "cool down" before attempting to reestablish control. Finally, two convoys entered the blood zone, got as far as Champ de Mars before they were set upon by wave after wave of the Possessed and torn to pieces.

⎯⎯◦⎯⎯

LET ME NOT FORGET THIS—this is the best part. Three days before it happened, my mother flew to New Hialeah with my aunt for a specialty treatment. Just for a few days, she explained. And the really best part? *I could have gone with her!* She invited me, said, Plenty of culo plastico in Florida. Can you imagine it? I could have ducked the entire fucking thing.

I could have been safe.

⎯⎯◦⎯⎯

NO ONE KNOWS HOW IT happened or who was responsible, but it took two weeks, two fucking weeks, for the enormity of the situation to dawn on the Great Powers. In the meantime, the infected, as refugees reported, sang on and on and on.

On the fifteenth day of the crisis, advanced elements of the U.S. Rapid Expeditionary Force landed at Port-au-Prince. Drone surveillance proved difficult, as some previously unrecorded form of interference was disrupting the airspace around the camps.

Nevertheless a battle force was ordered into the infected areas. This force, too, was set upon by the Possessed, and would surely have been destroyed to the man if helicopters hadn't been sent in. The Possessed were so relentless that they clung to the runners, actually had to be shot off. The only upside? The glypts the battle force beamed out *finally* got High Command to pull their head out of their ass. The entire country of Haiti was placed under quarantine. All flights in and out cancelled. The border with the D.R. sealed.

An emergency meeting of the Joint Chiefs of Staff was convened, the Commander-in-Chief pulled off his vacation. And within hours a bomber wing scrambled out of Southern Command in Puerto Rico.

Leaked documents show that the bombers were loaded with enough liquid asskick to keep all of Port-au-Prince burning red-hot for a week. The bombers were last spotted against the full moon as they crossed the northern coast of the D.R. Survivors fleeing the area heard their approach—and Dr. DeGraff, who had managed to survive the massacres and had joined the exodus moving east, chanced one final glance at her birth city just as the ordnance was sailing down.

Because she was a God-fearing woman and because she had no idea what kind of bomb they were dropping, Dr. DeGraff took the precaution of keeping one eye shut, just, you know, in case things got Sodom and Gomorrah. Which promptly they did. The Detonation Event—no one knows what else to call it—turned the entire world white. Three full seconds. Triggered a quake that was felt all across the Island and also burned out the optic nerve on Dr. DeGraff's right eye.

But not before she saw It.

Not before she saw Them.

EVEN THOUGH I KNEW I shouldn't, one night I went ahead anyway. We were out dancing in la Zona, and Alex disappeared after a pair of German chicks. A Nazi cada año no te hace daño, he said. We were all out of our minds and Mysty started dancing with me and you know how girls are when they can dance and they know it. She just put it on me and that was it. I started making out with her right there.

I have to tell you, at that moment I was so fucking happy, so incredibly happy, and then the world put its foot right in my ass. Mysty stopped suddenly, said, Do you know what? I don't think this is cool.

Are you serious?

Yeah, she said. We should stop. She stepped back from the longest darkest song ever and started looking around. Maybe we should get out of here. It's late.

I said, I guess I forgot to bring my lakhs with me.

I almost said, I forgot to bring your dad with me.

Hijo de la gran puta, Mysty said, shoving me.

And that was when the lights went out.

MONITORING STATIONS IN THE U.S. and Mexico detected a massive detonation in the Port-au-Prince area in the range of 8.3. Tremors were felt as far away as Havana, San Juan, and Key West.

The detonation produced a second, more extraordinary effect: an electromagnetic pulse that deaded all electronics within a six-hundred-square-mile radius.

Every circuit of every kind shot to shit. In military circles the pulse was called the Reaper. You cannot imagine the damage it caused. The bomber wing that had attacked the quarantine zone—dead, forced to ditch into the Caribbean Sea, no crew recovered. Thirty-two commercial flights packed to summer peak capacity plummeted straight out of the sky. Four crashed in urban areas. One pinwheeled into its receiving airport. Hundreds of privately owned seacraft lost. Servers down and power stations kaputted. Hospitals plunged into chaos. Even fatline communicators thought to be impervious to any kind of terrestrial disruption began fritzing. The three satellites parked in geosynch orbit over that stretch of the Caribbean went ass up, too. Tens of thousands died as a direct result of the power failure. Fires broke out. Seawalls began to fail. Domes started heating up.

But it wasn't just a simple, one-time pulse. Vehicles attempting to approach within six hundred miles of the detonation's epicenter failed. Communicators towed over the line could neither receive nor transmit. Batteries gave off nothing.

This is what *really* flipped every motherfucker in the know inside out and back again. The Reaper hadn't just swung and run; it had swung and *stayed*. A dead zone had opened over a six-hundred-mile chunk of the Caribbean.

Midnight.

No one knowing what the fuck was going on in the darkness. No one but us.

INITIALLY, NO ONE BELIEVED THE hysterical evacuees. Forty-foot-tall cannibal motherfuckers running loose on the Island? Negro, please.

Until a set of soon-to-be-iconic Polaroids made it out on one clipper showing what later came to be called a Class 2 in the process of putting a slender broken girl in its mouth.

Beneath the photo someone had scrawled: Numbers 11:18. *Who shall give us flesh to eat?*

WE CAME TOGETHER AT ALEX's apartment first thing. All of us wearing the same clothes from the night before. Watched the fires spreading across the sectors. Heard the craziness on the street. And with the bafflers down felt for the first time on that roof the incredible heat rolling in from the dying seas. Mysty pretending nothing had happened between us. Me pretending the same.

Your mom O.K.? I asked her and she shrugged. She's up in the Cibao visiting family.

The power's supposedly out there, too, Alex said. Mysty shivered and so did I.

Nothing was working except for old diesel burners and the archaic motos with no points or capacitors. People were trying out different explanations. An earthquake. A nuke. A Carrington event. The Coming of the Lord. Reports arriving over the failing fatlines claimed that Port-au-Prince had been destroyed, that Haiti had been destroyed, that thirteen million screaming Haitian refugees were threatening the borders, that Dominican military units had been authorized to meet the *invaders*—the term the gov was now using—with ultimate force.

And so of course what does Alex decide to do? Like an idiot he decides to commandeer one of his father's vintage burners and take a ride out to the border.

Just in case, you know, Alex said, packing up his Polaroid, something happens.

And what do we do, like even bigger idiots? Go with him.

Junot Díaz is the author of the bestselling novel *The Brief Wondrous Life of Oscar Wao* and the books *Drown* and *This is How You Lose Her*. His fiction has appeared in *The New Yorker* many times, and also in *Glimmer Train* and *African Voices*. He is the winner of the Pulitzer Prize, the National Books Critic Circle Award and most recently the MacArthur Fellowship. The fiction editor at *The Boston Review* and the co-founder of the Voices of Our Nation Workshop, Díaz teaches writing at MIT.

NONFICTION

EDITED BY

MAURICE
BROADDUS

INTERVIEW: VICTOR LAVALLE

MAURICE BROADDUS

Victor LaValle is the author of the short story collection *Slapboxing with Jesus*, three novels, *The Ecstatic*, *Big Machine*, and *The Devil in Silver*, and two novellas, *Lucretia and the Kroons* and *The Ballad of Black Tom*. He has been the recipient of numerous awards including a Whiting Writers' Award, a United States Artists Ford Fellowship, a Guggenheim Fellowship, a Shirley Jackson Award, an American Book Award, and the key to Southeast Queens. He was raised in Queens, New York. He now lives in Washington Heights with his wife and kids. He teaches at Columbia University.

———

How do you define horror and how much of the definition of horror do you think is rooted in a particular culture? That is, how well does what is horrific for one society—with their history, morality, culture—translate to another?

I'm pretty interested in this question. I grew up on horror; it's the reason I fell in love with reading, and yet there's such a wealth of cultural assumptions deeply embedded in the genre—at least the US, largely white version I grew up with—that I'm still regularly surprised by what's taken for granted as the positive, or the good, in a work of horror. Maybe this is just my way of saying that I often sympathized with the monsters a hell of a lot more than I did with the people I was meant to root for. This seems glib but I think there's a more serious idea hiding in there.

What makes a monster? Who has to be victimized for someone or something to be considered evil? I'd like to think there are some bedrock goals or beliefs that are universal, but even a cursory glance at world history—at the clash of various cultures—suggests otherwise. So maybe the only thing to rely on is a grounded perspective in either a narrator or a protagonist, one that communicates the values at play in a particular story. If those are clear then a reader might, I hope, follow any culture anywhere.

I'm particularly fascinated by how you come at genre as a person of color. Do you consider yourself a horror writer, a weird fiction writer, a literary writer, or do these labels not mean much when you sit down to write a story? What is it about Weird Fiction that keeps you coming back?

I consider myself a literary writer who's trying hard to become a horror writer. I fell in love with horror when I was young, and fell hard for literary fiction in my twenties. Now, I often feel like I'm trying to thread the needle between the two. I have noticed that my work never really begins as what I'd call "horror." By that, I mean that I spend time (sometimes too much damn time) creating a sense of normalcy, whatever that means for a story, before the horrific aspects start to accrue. I always want to understand who the people are, how they live, before I toss whole wheelbarrows worth of shit at them.

In the acknowledgments of *Big Machine*, you wrote, "Being a weird black kid can turn you a little crazy unless you have some role models." Who were your major influences, and how have they changed as you've grown as a writer?

When I wrote that line I was thinking, in particular, of the black eccentrics I'd come across in life, the ones who suggested that I was not some anomaly. Horror, as far as my reading went, was pretty much a wasteland for black writers. I'm talking the early eighties. There were heaps of white writers I loved, but the black folks were in short supply. And I wasn't a science fiction or fantasy kid, so I didn't come across Octavia Butler or Samuel Delaney, for instance, until I was in my twenties. So this meant I left literature behind in my quest to find a few guideposts.

A list of the weird black folks who meant the world to me when I was younger would include: Phil Lynott from Thin Lizzy, Fishbone (whole band), and Cochise from *The Warriors* (he was a gang leader and tough as hell, but if you remember his outfit alone, that made him qualify as someone I loved). Hell, I even loved Black Manta from the old *Super Friends* cartoon. As time passed, I figured out that I needed to find the weirdos who wrote books, too. I knew I wanted to be a writer, but still needed that kind of inspiration. This is how I came to discover writers like Gayl Jones and Ishmael Reed, Michelle Wallace and Ben Okri, and others musicians like Sun Ra and Nina Simone. They've meant the world to me.

I've read about how your Ugandan mother and grandmother were devout Episcopalians and how the legacy created by being raised Christian impacted the lens through which you see the supernatural and good/evil. How does faith intersect with horror in general, and for you and your work specifically?

If we're talking about one particular strain of horror, or literature, or culture— and that strain is Western culture—then it's pretty difficult to ignore/avoid the lasting effects of the Judeo-Christian faiths. One of the things I find most intriguing about Christianity in particular—one of the things I'm most grateful for—is just how flexible the faith turned out to be. I don't mean accommodating, certainly it's got as long a history as most other religions (or political systems) of ramrodding people into compliance. But I'm endlessly fascinated at how many other faiths or cultures find room to tuck snugly into Christianity, rather than simply being erased. I'm thinking of the obvious stuff like Christmas trees and Easter eggs, both well understood as remnants of earlier Pagan faiths, but also the ways that religions like Santeria and Candomblé and Voodoo (and many more) could hide in plain sight within the Christian faith. While of course there's a seemingly simple idea of good and evil within Christianity, I've been endlessly grateful to know, and believe, that the faith itself is actually much more complicated than pop culture depictions would ever allow. I think that's had a profound effect on my faith and my writing.

When you were growing up in Queens, you loved reading the horror stories of H.P. Lovecraft. When you were older, you recognized his level of racism. *The Ballad of Black Tom* seems like a conversation with Lovecraft by way of #blacklivesmatter. Its dedication reads, "For H.P. Lovecraft, with all my conflicted feelings." What drew you to Lovecraft in the first place? How did you reconcile with this "giant of the genre," despite his racism?

I grew up on Lovecraft, reading him long before I had any real critical faculties, and as a result I came to love him long before I understood what was repellent about him. In this way, he's a lot like a family member. I can't be the only person in the world who loves a family member but also understands that he or she believes in—and gives voice to—a hell of a lot of ugly personal and political opinions. And yet, you don't—or I don't—stop loving that person. How could I? He or she says terrible things about some group of people ("Left handed people can't be trusted!") and also helps me learn how to ride a bike. What do I do with such a person? It's going to be a complicated kind of love that results.

That's really what lay behind the writing of *The Ballad of Black Tom*. As an adult, I realize the point isn't to separate Lovecraft's writing from his prejudices, because his work is infused with, and informed by, those exact prejudices. In fact, his work wouldn't be as interesting if he wasn't such a profoundly prejudiced person. One of things he did incredibly well was to tap into a specific kind of fear—white, male, intellectual, upper class (if not wealthy any longer)—and turn that into a dreamy phantasmagoria that generations of readers and writers would eventually have to wander through. I like wrestling with that kind of thing rather than ignoring it.

Of course, I understand those people who never grew up reading Lovecraft and don't feel a particular need to start now. I'm not even sure Lovecraft digs his hooks into you as a reader if you come to him past a certain age. Most of the people I know who love him (even if they're critical of him) first encountered him at a younger age. Again, falling in love before the critical faculties have developed. For instance, I rarely find someone else's crotchety, prejudiced relative charming at all.

Do you feel a pressure or obligation, as a person of color, to your community when it comes to crafting stories? For example, a responsibility to represent well? Is this something you lean into or shy away from? In fact, should an artist have any social burden, when it comes to the work they produce?

This is a valuable question to argue about. Some readers have felt that my depiction of Tommy Tester in *The Ballad of Black Tom* ends up skewing too negative. By the end, Tommy has made some horrific choices and has, in many ways, become the monstrous black man the racist white characters assume him to be. So there's some question about whether or not I'm simply playing into those old stereotypes, or old narratives of black pathology. Just because I'm a black writer doesn't mean I'm absolved of the same failing.

But I'd argue that my job is simply to create characters whose choices are understandable. Not relatable. Not likable. And certainly not a credit to their race.

The danger in some of Lovecraft's stories (not to mention so many other writers in every genre) is that the non-white, or female, characters commit acts of horror and depravity for reasons that are impossible to understand. They act in ways that are truly evil and, thus, become inhuman. But you don't solve that problem by writing a bunch of damn saints. There are few things as dull as a "righteous" or "good" character. Sure, it may feel good to show the characters of color are purely good and on the side of justice (or something), but how is that any more honest than writing characters of color of who are comically evil? What I feel is missing most in depictions of any marginalized group is complexity. By the end of *The Ballad of Black Tom*, I knew things were going to go real bad for Tommy. I didn't see how they could go any other way. The point, instead, was to see if I could make a reader understand why a character like Tommy might lose his shit. If I could show him willingly choose destruction and death, but have readers come away feeling invested, feeling like they still understood him, then I would have pulled off one hell of a coup. It's easy to root for people who do good all the time. I've never met a person like that yet.

THE H WORD:
THE DARKEST, TRUEST MIRRORS

ALYSSA WONG

i.

I AM ELEVEN YEARS OLD when my mother asks me, *Why do you have to write such dark stories? Why can't you write something edifying?* At the time, I have no answer for her, and I mistake the tight line of her mouth for disapproval. I miss the concern in her eyes, the distress in the set of her shoulders.

I think about her question for many years. But at the time, I remember wondering, *What is edifying about stories that don't reflect the real world?*

ii.

I AM NINETEEN YEARS OLD when I am sexually assaulted.

We are standing outside of an apartment, and he is asking me to come in and enjoy the party. I tell him, *It's not my scene,* and *I'd rather go home,* and *I don't want drunk people groping me.* At that last one, he laughs and says, *Like this?* and then he crushes our bodies together, and his hands are all over me, and it is so awful that for a moment, I forget how to speak.

He has a history of violence. He has never physically hurt me before, but he has told me often how much he despises the Asian women who date white men, the Asian women who think they're too good to date him. He tells me that he refuses to acknowledge that I am hapa, because he does not want to acknowledge that I am mixed race.

You are a tiny lightning strike, he tells me once. *Small and fast and fierce. You could set the world on fire.* He is right—I am small, and I have a woman's body, and I wonder how much he thought he could get away with because of it.

He is right. I am fast, and small, and that is how I survive that night. But there are things—his attitude of entitlement toward my body, the racialization and sexualization of the violence he has inflicted on me, the fear and burning rage that bubble up in me later—that stay with me.

For a long time, I don't talk about it. But I think about them, and I write.

iii.

I AM IN CHICAGO, MANY years later, moderating a panel on the moral responsibility of the storyteller. One panelist brings up short stories by Angela Carter and Shirley Jackson. *These stories are so dark,* she says. She is right, and there is wonder and fear in her voice. *So bleak. To write something like that . . . it takes a certain rage.*

As I take notes on a piece of hotel stationary, I write down, in clean letters at the very bottom of the page, *a certain rage*. I underline that phrase several times. It touches something in me, resonates, deep and soft.

When the panel is over, I tuck the slip of paper into my journal for safekeeping. In the upcoming weeks, I take the paper out and reread it over and over again.

It takes a certain rage.

iv.

I AM JUST OUT OF college, and for the first time, someone tells me that what I am writing is a horror story. She says, *Have you read your own work? It's so full of violence and terrible people doing terrible things to each other. It's so scary.*

Another friend sits quietly at the lunch table. She doesn't say anything, but when I catch her eye, she nods. I realize, then, that instead of being put off by the ugly things I write about and looking at me with judgment and fear, she views them with the compassion and acknowledgment of someone who intimately understands. It is horror, yes, but it is a horror that we have both seen face to face.

That afternoon, I sit alone in my room to work on the workshop piece due that week. I have been trying to write a story about mermaids for about a year now, and as I go over my draft, I find the connection I've been missing.

I think about mermaids, and I think about bodies. I think about old stories about how sailors, horny and violent, mistook animals like manatees and dolphins for mermaids and imagined women's curves and pliant willingness where there were none. I think about the racist infantilization and fetishization of Asian women. I think about the epidemic of college sexual assault. I think about the stories that my friends have told me, quietly in the evenings, holding my arm so tightly for support that my hands go numb. I remember the feeling of him on my body, the feelings of betrayal and shock, the heat of him, the mixture of contempt and satisfied possessiveness on his face.

I write "The Fisher Queen."

I don't apologize for it.

v.

I AM TWENTY-FOUR YEARS OLD when a good friend of mine approaches me with a question similar to the one my mother asked me when I was eleven, all those years ago. But this time she says, *My mother is afraid because of the stories I write. She doesn't want me to have to go to a dark, sad place in order to write sad, dark stories. What do I tell her?*

Our mothers are always afraid. They want what is best for us, and they know the reality of how horrifying the world can really be. They don't want us to have to traverse imaginary horrors when the world is already full of real ones.

Tell her, I say, staring at the wall above my computer, *that the truth is, we don't have to go to sad, dark places to write our stories. We write our stories to cope with what we've already seen.*

We have always lived in this place, occupying our bodies and suffering the injustices and very real horrors that come with existing in hostile spaces. And so we write with eyes focused forward, because there is no way to not be who we are. Fiction gives us the tools with which to break our silence and name our demons so that other, unhaunted people can see them for what they are. To crystalize our monsters, and then to shatter them.

My stories are dark because I live in a dark place, and because to me, the most edifying stories are the ones that reflect, and then subvert, the given truths about the way the world deals with people like me.

Horror is only one storytelling mode of many. But it is my preferred mode of entertainment and exorcism, a space where fear can be manipulated and conquered, where terror and play, the real and the imaginary, can exist side by side. And when I write, I do so from a place I have always occupied, sitting quietly in peace with a certain rage.

————

Alyssa Wong studies fiction in Raleigh, NC, is a John W. Campbell Award finalist, and really, really likes crows. Her story, "Hungry Daughters of Starving Mothers," won the 2015 Nebula Award for Best Short Story, and her short fiction has been shortlisted for the Pushcart Prize, the Bram Stoker Award, the Locus Award, and the Shirley Jackson Award. Her work has been published in *The Magazine of Fantasy & Science Fiction, Strange Horizons, Nightmare Magazine, Black Static,* and *Tor.com,* among others. She can be found on Twitter as @crashwong.

TERROR, HOPE, FASCINATION, AND FEAR IN FILIPINO HORROR

ROCHITA LOENEN-RUIZ

A BOY RUNS THROUGH A forest. Focus on the boy and the fear on his face; focus on the amplified sound of his ragged breathing. Above him, the moon is full and bright. A shadow passes over the moon and a shriek sounds out as the camera pans back to focus on the boy running, pushing through thick foliage.

The above scene is from the episode entitled "Manananggal." It is one of three episodes in a horror movie anthology titled *Shake, Rattle and Roll*. The boy is Filipino actor Herbert Bautista, and in this scene he is being chased by a flying half-bodied woman who thrives by eating the internal organs of young boys. Herbert should not have been out in the forest. Indeed, it is way past his curfew.

The *Shake, Rattle and Roll* series, which first came out in 1984, is perhaps one of the most visible markers of how healthy the horror genre is in the Philippines. Since it first came out, this horror anthology has seen fifteen iterations and it continues to draw and to appeal to a broad public. There are other horror films that hit the box office and draw big crowds, but *Shake, Rattle and Roll* has become somehow symbolic for what it is that makes horror successful.

In the segment titled "Manananggal," we follow the main character as he moves through the terror of being hunted through the night. When morning breaks, the terror fades, as the monstrous being cannot continue its hunt in the day. It is during the day when the main character must work towards a solution, must hunt down the hunter, and must find a way to defeat the monster completely.

Papers have been written on the appeal of horror and on the role that horror stories play in Philippine society as well as in Philippine history. Writers, directors and academics have their own views as to why horror appeals so much to the masses.

In a country where more than a quarter of the population lives below the poverty line, where corruption and crime are rife, and where the masses have found themselves continually disappointed and disillusioned by politicians; in such a society where the poor are often left without recourse or without power, it is no wonder that horror as a genre thrives and lives well.

Horror, after all, is rooted in the desire to make things happen. As a genre, horror responds to the desire to make sense of what is inexplicable, and for many Filipinos, it is the way in which we come to terms with catastrophes and tragedies.

A good horror story allows the reader or the viewer to live vicariously and to experience the terror and the fear as well as the rush of adrenaline that comes from the strong will to survive. More than the love of being frightened or being scared out of our wits, is the drive to overcome and to continue on living.

It is perhaps, in some part, symbolic of the psychic trauma Filipinos have lived through and of the strength of the Filipino will. After all, we have lived through the very real terror of martial law and armed conflict. We know what it is like to feel impotent in the face of power. We know that the common man has little chance when going up against those who hold wealth and influence. We know this, and yet we continue to struggle and we continue to hope and even when we come face to face with certain death, we continue to fight to survive.

Hence we identify strongly with the young character in his or her struggle against the mythic hunter.

Film is not the only medium in which horror thrives. Literature and oral storytelling are time-honored traditions and many of the horror stories that we see today are rooted in these tales.

Local storytellers who mine local folklore and myth keep that self which is indigenous to the Filipino people alive. Local mythical monsters that come to us through the screen or through the page are made popular and find equal footing with monsters imported from Europe and America.

Where other genres can create a distance between reader and writer because of language, horror as a genre thrives because of the style in which it is told and because of the way in which the writers use language.

In an interview, Arnel Gabriel, publisher of the popular PSICOM True Philippine Ghost Stories series, says that the appeal of their series lies in the accessibility of language and style.

Most of these stories are told in the vernacular, they are often told in first person, and they are often classified as true-to-life.

But the horror tale is more than what is on paper. The horror tale grows and expands as it is passed on by word of mouth.

One of the most beautiful islands in the Philippines has a thriving and widespread reputation of witchcraft. Visitors are often warned not to spit anywhere, not to leave behind traces of their presence that witches can latch onto or they will be cursed. What form the curse takes is never explained except that it can be horrible.

To visit the island and to return from it without suffering any visible harm transforms the visit into something of a heroic adventure.

Tabloids often feature stories told by celebrities of their own ghostly or horrific encounters, and these stories lend veracity to first person accounts in pulp publications.

Many Filipino horror tales are rooted in animism and are also told with a social intent. Certain plants, trees, rocks or groves are inhabited by spirits, and we can gain their favor or be subject to their malice depending on our demeanor.

Ghosts can be benevolent or malicious. Houses can be occupied. Burial grounds are sacred, and restless spirits will not be quiet until justice has been done.

As a child, I remember my uncle telling us about ghosts who would haunt us if we didn't finish our food or of ghosts who would come out if we left too many crumbs on our plate or on the floor.

Naughty children would be taken away by the Tikbalang (a shape-shifting giant) and if we stayed out too late at night, the Aswang (a creature that separates at the waist and hunts by night) would come for us.

Pregnant women were warned against sleeping on their backs under a peaked roof because this made them vulnerable to the fetus-eating monster called the Tik-tik.

And then, there are women who stand out in a certain way. Being too different—perhaps too alluring or too intelligent or too knowing, could put a woman in danger of being called an Aswang.

There are also fascinating stories where men or women are courted and kidnapped by beautiful dwellers of the unseen world who are called Engkanto. Women who go into trances or who fall into seizures are said to be visited by Engkanto. Unexplained sudden death is sometimes said to be the result of such a kidnapping.

Whether such stories are horrific or romantic depends on how the story is told and who is telling it. And just like with any other tale, the horror story begs us to ask who the real monsters are and who the real heroes of the tale are.

The reasons behind horror's appeal to the masses are multiple and layered. At the heart of it, the love of horror can create a bond between lovers of the genre. We are in this together—it is a feeling that speaks to the communal nature of Filipino society.

Our intrinsic belief in the supernatural and the role of faith in daily life play into the popularity of the horror genre. And yet, despite the terror, the struggle and the fear, we continue to hold onto hope. Hope which looks towards the morning and the promise of redemption.

———

Filipino writer **Rochita Loenen-Ruiz** lives and writes in The Netherlands. She is a graduate of the Clarion West Writer's Workshop, which she attended as the Octavia Butler scholar. Her work has been published in a variety of online and print publications, and together with her sister, she put up the bookblog *Push*. She has written columns and essays including the Movements column, which was published on *Strange Horizons*.

HORROR, INSIDE OUT

JAYAPRAKASH SATYAMURTHY

SONG OF KALI BY DAN Simmons is a classic of modern horror. It regularly appears on lists of best horror novels, one of the few twentieth-century novels not by King, Straub or Jackson to do so. It is well written, well-researched and culminates in a jaw-droppingly apocalyptic vision of nightmarish evil casting a shadow over the world.

It's also deeply, unpleasantly racist.

I've encountered racism in horror stories before—I've read H.P. Lovecraft, and I've read *The Lair Of The White Worm* by Bram Stoker. I've been able to somewhat distance myself from it because of the remove of time between myself and the writers of these stories (although I don't believe "a man of his times" is a great defence. If anything, it includes a whole era in one's indictment). With the Simmons novel, it was hard to resort to this form of rationalisation. Simmons' *Kali* was launched into the world in 1985, the same year that my little sister was born. They have both been around for three decades now. One is an Indian woman; the other a massive misrepresentation of the nature of an Indian vision of feminine divinity.

Throughout the novel, Simmons refers to the "bitch goddess" Kali. Kali is linked to human sacrifice, to a vision of primitive, primal horror lurking among the teeming masses of an Indian city. As Simmons' protagonist works himself into an ecstasy of revulsion observing the abject poverty that is *absolutely* and *shamefully* a commonplace of Indian urban life, we can see how the scene is being set to expect the horrific, the brutal, and the downright evil in this setting.

Simmons and his protagonist extend their revulsion to the people of Calcutta. You'd think so much extant human suffering would promote some kind of compassion, some form of empathy. Instead, no Indian character here is allowed any sort of redeeming humanity except the woman who is married to the protagonist, and frequently expresses her contempt for India and her relief at leaving it behind (not unjustified statements, although those of us who remain behind are somehow able to live lives with some meaning and some fulfillment). The trope of the one "native" character who has any positive connotations being a woman who becomes the mate of a white man, and is thus saved from her lowly origins, is not uncommon in colonial tales of adventure. It's all over the Fu Manchu novels too, even if the love-object is sometimes further elevated by being a "Eurasian." It's sobering to find the stereotype alive and well in a novel published in 1985.

And yet, *Song Of Kali* is, so far as you don't focus on the real people and the real culture it obscures and devalues, an excellent, even superior novel. This has something to do with both the nature and origins of horror.

There are two main sources for the horrific in this genre: from inside and from outside. The horrors from inside could be from your past, from your loved ones, from inside your mind. They could be from outside—from outside your experience, your nation, your world, your cosmos. *Song Of Kali* is very much about horror from outside, even though the moment you stop and consider that India, even Calcutta (or Kolkata as we now call her), is not really outside, is somewhere on the same planet as Simmons and most of his readers (not an invalid point considering that Simmons also writes science fiction). I realise that we are all insular to an extent, that backwoods horror derives much of its power precisely from the fact that we know very little of the ways of those isolated denizens, and they know as little about ours. But backwoods horror that focuses on the ways in which people who live in small shacks in unpopulated, wild places is in its own way as dehumanising of real categories of people as is horror that draws on the unfamiliarity of foreigners and the writer's (and his chosen readers') misgivings or misconceptions about them.

I'd like to briefly mention Poppy Z. Brite's "Calcutta: Lord of Nerves" here. A far shorter story than Simmons', it shows us a part-Indian narrator, not quite a "Eurasian," but some kind of entry point for an American (and by extension, Western), audience into this far-off, to them, place. What we might describe broadly as a zombie apocalypse has taken over the world and our narrator finds himself back in Calcutta, where the horrors of poverty-stricken hordes and the horrors of zombie hordes slowly merge. There is a stark, striking vision here. And, after all the American and European suburban phantasmagorias of the zombie genre, there's no denying that there is something in the chaos, squalour and grime of our Indian cities that makes for a somehow appropriate place to play out such a catastrophe.

Brite's story again involves Kali; there is a remarkable journey into a Kali temple, into the veritable birth canal of the goddess and back out into the ravaged nightmare world.

You might get the sense that I like Brite's story more than Simmons'. You would be right. But aesthetics aside, Brite wins points by not demonising the people of Calcutta, not demonising my fellow Indians, your fellow humans. Because, while horror might come from within, when it is imposed upon you, upon your identity from outside, it becomes something more than a fictional hook for a horror story. It becomes a reminder of the prejudices and arrogant conclusions that allowed people who looked like Simmons to consider it their right, and even duty, to enslave people who looked like me, just a few centuries past. When I look at the corporate world today, I'm not sure that those attitudes have really gone away.

And that's when horror stops being from either within or without the tropes of a fictional genre. It even stops being something I can engage with fruitfully, as a fear or phobia that I might reasonably share with the writer or the writer's character. It becomes a re-enactment of the process by which colonialism (or its business-suited heir, globalism) becomes possible.

It is the point at which a work of literary horror becomes a horrible work of literature.

So far, I've told you about two American works of horror. I'd like to take a sideways step in the genre arena to something that is literary fiction in a magical realist vein that manages to work its way into a very similar space to the works of, say, Thomas Ligotti.

Naiyer Masud is a writer of Urdu short stories. He lives in the Indian city of Lucknow. Lucknow is a city in the north of India. It used to be a cultural hub, the seat of Nawabs—semi-autonomous Muslim princes ruling under the patronage of the Mughal emperors. Today, an aura of faded grandeur hangs around the old palaces and mansions of the city. Scions of aristocratic families often live in poverty, sometimes in the very homes of their wealthy forefathers, selling the furnishings and trappings of lost prestige piecemeal to get by. Masud sets stories in this city, in the decaying old homes and in the homes of the settled middle class; stories that juxtapose the uncanny and the everyday and blur the line between both. His stories could sit alongside those of Bruno Schulz and Thomas Ligotti with equal ease. Or perhaps, with equal unease. But you've probably not heard of him, even though his works have been translated into English. Well, no matter, he's not even that well known in India, despite English editions of his work from leading publishers.

Then there's Vilas Sarang. Described as a modernist, this Marathi writer gave his language its first substantial collection of truly weird fiction; a volume which appeared in English under the title *Fair Tree of the Void*. These stories mainly take place in the streets and crowded apartment buildings of Mumbai, although some unfold in a virtual realm like the scene of some of Kafka's tales or one of Borges' fantastic spaces. In one notable tale, the idols of the god Ganesha (the chubby, elephant-headed lord of beginnings) run away before the annual Ganesha procession can take place. People speculate that this means the god is displeased with them. There is a plague of rats, and it is speculated they are the mooshiks—the rat that is Ganesha's traditional vehicle, also liberated from duress as mere idols. A blind man keeps importuning the narrator, a photographer, for his passport photos. Criticised by staunchly social-realist critics for making a mockery of religion, this story deftly weaves together themes of urban crowding, spiritual unmooring, and a sprinkling of farcical humour. The ending, which I won't spoil because I want people to seek out Sarang's books and read them, is chilling.

Neither of these writers write conventional horror, or what would easily be slotted as weird fiction in the west. Horror and weird fiction, as it is understood in the western context, emerges from pulp fiction and the Gothic. The Gothic is itself a venerable tradition, which in turn has roots not just in previous forms but in in-depth psychology, as truly imaginative, symbolic fiction tends to. But the pulp roots have conferred a certain proud middle-browism (I am being generous) to swathes of practitioners and fans—this stuff is "just entertainment," and that is how we should judge it. Well, even so, it does not entertain me to have to read Orientalist claptrap anymore, or to read things that hinge on sexist, racist or homophobic stereotypes. I am interested in things that examine and do interesting things with those attitudes, just not in work that simply embodies prejudice as a primary worldview.

The world of weird fiction is vibrant today—I think there is a real renaissance taking place in the small presses. It's still a small world, and given the fact that so much of this genre is primarily an offshoot of American and English pulp fiction, it's a very Anglophone, very white world. What I hope for is that this small world can become a bigger one, that our inspiration, our exemplars, our practitioners, and our audience can become wider. That Masud, and Sarang, and so many more writers from Asia and Africa and Europe and South America can sit alongside the old Anglophone canon.

I wish this for all forms of art, of course. But I think it's very, very apropos when it comes to the literature of the dark, fantastic and horrific. Because when we're talking about horrors from within, and from without, we are ultimately talking about the stuff that moves and haunts all of us. Nothing is more universal than dread. (Maybe love; but there are lives that know dread but not love. I doubt the opposite has ever been true.) Maybe fear is healthy; what's unhealthy are fears that divide us amongst ourselves. Maybe as we learn to share our nightmares, in some way we can also learn to dream together.

In any case, the more the literature of unease becomes diverse and inclusive (mealy-mouthed words, but one shies away from the stridence of "the less white-dominated and west-centric"), the less chance there is that any given reader will simply have to read something that is horrific because of things the writer took for granted rather than because of the things the writer purposely put in there (or didn't; the unsaid is a prime vector of the horrific and the weird). And one day, the most horrific thing about books like *Song of Kali* will simply be that we had to settle for them at all.

———

Jayaprakash Satyamurthy is a writer, musician and animal welfare worker. He lives in Bangalore, India, with his wife, several dogs and a horde of cats. He writes weird fiction, a little poetry and a lot of Facebook status updates. He has one chapbook of short stories and poetry, *Weird Tales Of A Bangalorean*, available from Dunhams Manor Press.

THE THING WE HAVE TO FEAR

CHINELO ONWUALU

"Fear is the most powerful emotion in the human race and fear
of the unknown is probably the most ancient. You're dealing
with stuff that everybody has felt; from being little babies we're
frightened of the dark, we're frightened of the unknown."
—John Carpenter

I'M GOING TO ADMIT, WHEN it comes to horror, I'm a bit of a baby. When I was younger, I would cower behind the couch whenever a horror movie came on, ready to duck if it got too gory or scary. As an adult, I am the person who won't watch a horror movie by myself—and I only read scary stories in the light of day. I am more of an outside observer of the genre than a dedicated fan. However, as the aesthetics of the horror genre have begun to move into the mainstream of Western entertainment, American pop culture has gotten darker. For instance, the immensely popular cable series *Game of Thrones* is known for its scenes of rape, mutilation and murder, while superheroes like Superman, once known for his unambiguous goodness, kill their enemies on screen. Horror is now universal, and this has made me wonder about its fundamental appeal. I have to ask: What is it about being frightened that is so alluring to Western audiences?

The idea of horror is not new. As the website filmiq.com notes[1]: "Monsters, murderers, demons and beasts have been around since antiquity, ghost stories told 'round camp fires since we learned how to talk." However, the roots of the genre we recognize today can be traced to the Gothic Horror literature of the late 1700s coming out of Europe and the United States. These were works designed to create moods and atmospheres which would unsettle and disturb the reader. Feelings of disgust, distress and fear are universal, but what people associate with these emotions—particularly the images that will elicit these emotions—differ across time and place. Every culture has its own understanding of what is disgusting and who to be afraid of, and these anxieties are reflected in the scary stories they tell. To write this essay, I conducted a cursory examination into the roots of the genre, and I was discomfited by what I found. Beyond the psychology of why the West loves to be frightened, it was much more disquieting to find out exactly what the West was frightened of. Because it seemed, for all intents and purposes, that the West was scared of me. More precisely, the West is scared of people like me: Africans and people of African descent.

This fear of blackness is evident in nearly every interaction the West has had with Africa: From slavery to colonialism, to historically racist immigration policies[2] which used a variety of strategies to keep black people out of First World nations (except when they were needed as temporary labor), and the hysterical reactions to the Ebola crisis in West Africa a few years ago[3]. It is most glaring in the West's interactions with the black communities within its countries, in the disproportionate violence meted out on black bodies[4]—from lynchings[5] to police shootings[6]—to the systematic erasure of black families[7]. That the West has chosen Africa and its people as the repository of its fear is telling. Nigerian author Chinua Achebe explains it best when he said there is a "desire—one might indeed say the need—in Western psychology to set Africa up as a foil to Europe, as a place of negations at once remote and vaguely familiar, in comparison with which Europe's own state of spiritual grace will be manifest."

Achebe made this assertion as part of a critique of Joseph Conrad's *Heart of Darkness*[8], a book some consider to be one of the canons of Western horror. In the book, Africa is portrayed as the antithesis of civilization, "a place where man's vaunted intelligence and refinement are finally mocked by triumphant bestiality." The horror writer who best embodied the Western fear of the African other was H.P. Lovecraft. Considered to be one of the fathers of modern horror, his work has influenced writers such as Mike Mignola[9], Alan Moore and Jorge Luis Borges, as well as film directors like Guillermo del Toro and Joss Whedon[10]. However, Lovecraft was virulently racist. In his writings he depicted Africans and those of African descent as barely human, incapable of rational thought, and inherently disposed to evil. His racist dread and fear of the non-white other fueled his depictions of cosmic horror.

Yet neither Lovecraft nor Conrad's racism have dimmed the veneration of their work in the canon of Western literature. This Achebe attributes to the fact that: "white racism against Africa is such a normal way of thinking that its manifestations go completely unremarked."

Today, when Africans and people of African descent (in fact, most non-white people) are shown in horror, their suffering is rarely considered as important as that of whites. In his review of the horror film *The Shallows*[11], writer Nico Lang calls out a sub-genre of horror which he calls "white survival porn." These are works in which white travelers to foreign countries find themselves in peril—either by the foreign other or by hostile natural forces. In these stories, though, "the trials of [the] Caucasian tourists are treated as more important than the suffering of the people of color around them" and "acts of selfless generosity [offered by the locals] are treated like services to which wealthy Western travelers are entitled." In horror, the fear of blackness is transmuted into the dehumanization of black bodies with blacks being literally turned into monsters. For instance, both the creatures in *Alien* and *Predator* are played by people of African descent. Alternatively, their presence is tokenized and they are put into the narrative only to be the first to die[12]. Or they are simply not featured at all. As scholar Tiffany Bryant points out in her essay "Horrifying Whiteness,"[13]: ". . . the invisibility of non-white bodies inadvertently reinforces the importance of the visibility of whiteness as the norm—not showing other demographic representations of the American society denies the existence of racial and ethnic difference."

This refusal to depict Africans—to pretend that they and their pain do not exist—is an important part of the fear of blackness. By devaluing Black lives to the point of disappearance, the West can continue to think of itself as fundamentally good and benign. Erasure is a way for Western society to distance itself from its subjugation, exploitation and genocide of Africa and its peoples. As long as the bodies ravaged by slavery, colonialism and racism don't show up, the West can continue to indulge in the fantasy that *it* is the innocent under threat from the evil other[14].

And this fantasy of a besieged West is becoming increasingly prevalent and, I believe, one of the reasons why horror is becoming more popular. Psychologist Dr. Glenn D. Walters identifies three primary factors in the allure of horror[15]: tension, relevance and unrealism. Tension can be created through craft, writing words or creating a visual atmosphere. Relevance means the fears depicted have to matter to the audience viewing it, while unrealism means that, on some level, the audience must know that what they are watching is not real. According to Walters then, the West tells these stories of horrific blackness in order to feel safe from them. As filmiq.com puts it:

"Horror movies require us to face the unknown—to understand it and make it less scary. They allow us to see our fears and put them into context, to play 'what if,' and in doing so, they shape our belief systems, how we see each other and ourselves. They are a safe place to explore, and for some, just a good bit of fun."

If horror is indeed a way for frightened populaces to help make sense of a scary world, then the West needs to evaluate *what* exactly it is scared of. The "other" is not the darkness at the heart of Africa or its peoples; the true monster is the assumption of superiority that underpins Western understandings of the world. In the West, a palpable real rage has been growing among populations who are afraid that they are no longer at the top of the heap. It is this anger that fueled the United Kingdom's recent referendum to leave the European Union and the nomination of the nakedly racist Donald Trump as a US presidential candidate this week. This anger has been co-opted by what British feminist writer Laurie Penny calls "manic trolls and smug neo-fascists."[16].

These are agents provocateur who are using the fear and disenfranchisement of ignorant populations for their own advancement. As Penny notes:

"They are pure antagonists unencumbered by any conviction apart from their personal entitlement to raw power and stacks of cash . . . They ventriloquise the fear of millions into a scream of fire in the crowded theatre of modernity where all the doors are locked, and then they watch the stampede, and they smile for the cameras." By depicting us as the boogeyman, the West is kept from dealing with the true horrors that are devouring their societies. But for those of us who see ourselves distorted in its nightmares, we know that the Western world is not a safe place. Already the rise of far right political parties and ideologues that spew hateful rhetoric with impunity has led to the deaths of hundreds of people of color across Europe and in the United States. Many in these societies have identified the monster—and they are coming for me. And that, more than any slasher, ghost or alien, is what keeps me up at night.

———

1. *Filmiq.com:* "A Brief History of Horror": bit.ly/1DIijAE

2. "Globalized anti-blackness: Transnationalizing Western immigration law, policy, and practice" by Vilna Bashi: bit.ly/2bAmPrG (PDF download)

3. *The Guardian:* "The problem with the west's Ebola response is still fear of a black patient": bit.ly/2bQCWiE

4. *Gradient Lair:* "Epistemic Violence, Erasure and The Value Of Black Life": bit.ly/1pWT9nJ

5. *Kalamu.com:* "Truly by Persons Unknown: Racial Erasure": bit.ly/2bjgo8P

6. *Propublica.org:* "Deadly Force, in Black and White": bit.ly/1eDu1AE

7. *Aljazeera America:* "The legal erasure of black families": bit.ly/1LZRuea

8. *Massachusetts Review:* "An Image of Africa: Racism in Conrad's 'Heart of Darkness'": bit.ly/1veUE2N

9. *CBR.com:* "H.P. Lovecraft and the Horror of Comics": bit.ly/2bZsPez

10. *Wikipedia:* "Old Ones (*Buffy the Vampire Slayer*)": bit.ly/2blC7S1

11. *Salon:* "Yet another white lady in jeopardy: "The Shallows" and Hollywood's empathy gap": bit.ly/296TkNi

12. *TV Tropes:* "Black Dude Dies First": bit.ly/1jdUSkN

13. *Off Screen:* "Horrifying Whiteness: Slasher Conduct, Masculinity, and the Cultural Politics of Halloween": bit.ly/2bSvK6L

14. *The Atlantic:* "Why Sci-Fi Keeps Imagining the Subjugation of White People": theatln.tc/1imATlr

15. *Filmmaker IQ:* "The Psychology of Scary Movies": bit.ly/107xujX

16. *Medium:* "I'm with the Banned": bit.ly/2cbF0Gt

Chinelo Onwualu is an editorial consultant living in Abuja, Nigeria. She is a graduate of the 2014 Clarion West Writers Workshop, which she attended as the recipient of the Octavia E. Butler Scholarship. She is editor and co-founder of *Omenana*, a magazine of African speculative fiction. Her writing has appeared in several places, including *Strange Horizons, The Kalahari Review, Saraba, Brittle Paper, Jungle Jim, Ideomancer,* and the anthologies *AfroSF: African Science Fiction by African Writers, Mothership: Tales of Afrofuturism and Beyond, Terra Incognita: New Short Speculative Stories from Africa,* and *Imagine Africa 500*. She has been longlisted for the British Science Fiction Awards and the Short Story Day Africa Award. Follow her on Twitter @chineloonwualu.

HORROR IS...NOT WHAT YOU THINK OR PROBABLY WISH IT IS

CHESYA BURKE

ALL RIGHT, BOYS AND GIRLS, *we're going to have an adult conversation. This isn't Racism 101. If you don't "see race" or don't know why the very idea is offensive, this essay isn't for you. If you know racism exists, but don't understand it's not about individuals calling other individuals "colored" or other offensive words, and don't understand how it's about the anti-black system in place to oppress blacks and other minorities, then this essay is going to be above your head. Save us both the headache and the angry email that you will be prone to write me because your bigotry is showing. I publicly post all racist commentary. Enter and engage at your own risk.*

"Horror is not a genre, like the mystery or science fiction or the western. It is not a kind of fiction, meant to be confined to the ghetto of a special shelf in libraries or bookstores. Horror is an emotion."

—*Douglas E. Winter*

ANYONE FAMILIAR WITH THE HORROR genre is familiar with this quote. In fact, the Horror Writer's Association (HWA), a professional writing organization within the field, donned this quote on t-shirts for many years, and still, as of this writing, holds this quote up as the proud "rallying cry for the modern horror writer." In other words, this quote is seen as the "true" and pure definition for any work seeking to call itself horror.

Except when we're dealing with minority writers. Too often, when it comes to Black and minority writers, this definition of horror is often twisted and contorted until it is no longer acceptable. Or more bluntly, Black and other minority writers are not allowed to simply create a "horrific emotion" within their (white horror) readers and be welcomed into the fold, instead there are always more and higher hoops that these writers must jump through (hoops dictated and controlled by the mainly white male readers and writers) seemingly with the sole purpose of excluding them.

For the sake of argument, however, we will not rely on one quote to define horror. Although this has been enough for white writers to find inclusion in the genre in the past, it seems this quote by Winter is not enough for many white readers and writers to accept one of the most notable works of fiction by a black writer. Dario Argento, the Italian film director, is famously quoted as saying, "Horror by definition is the emotion of pure revulsion. Terror of the same standard, is that of fearful anticipation." For Argento, too, horror is grounded in emotion, as well as revulsion and the anticipation of fear.

With these quotes from people who famously deal in horror for a living, I think we can understand horror to fundamentally be an emotion, the anticipation of fear that it creates within the participant. Horror, of course, is and can be many more things than this, but this is its definition at the fundamental level that even white men have willingly accepted. So, while you, as an individual reader or writer, can add many differing definitions to what you believe horror should be, you cannot take away these basic, essential principles that have long been established as horror, simply to exclude certain writings or writers.

So what, then, of the magnum opus of books? The Pulitzer Prize-winning novel of horrific revulsion, *Beloved*?

Now mind you, Toni Morrison is not waiting in the sorrow, dark corners of her tiny bedroom in her little shotgun house, for horror to welcome and accept her. I think her Pulitzer is more than enough to get her through the dark, lonely nights. But, that is irrelevant. The point is that if this mammoth work can regularly and systematically be overlooked for not being horror-enough for white readers, what does this say about horror and who is included? What does it say to upcoming writers of color who don't write about the middle class white family fighting against malevolent forces? What of the black writer that writes of welcoming those forces into their lives, as it is less horrific than living under white oppression? What of the minority writers that pen tales of torture and horror at the hands of white abusers simply because of their race, nationality or religion? Because horror seems to have built an entire sub-genre around women being tortured simply because they are women. And what of the tales of horrific murder, bondage, and racism in the vein of *Texas Chainsaw Massacre, Saw* or *Hostel?*

These are important questions, because in February 2016 Tor.com published an article titled, "*Beloved*: The Best Horror Novel the Horror Genre Has Never Claimed" (bit.ly/2aT0MP3). In the article, Grady Hendrix, the author, compares *Beloved* to *The Handmaid's Tale*, which unlike *Beloved* and the horror genre, is openly welcomed as a work of science fiction. Hendrix goes on to say that while Atwood's novel is often listed on the best of science fiction lists, *Beloved* is "rarely if ever seen on lists of 'Best Books in Horror.'" The author goes on to discuss why horror has not accepted *Beloved*, concluding:

> Horror has walked away from the literary. It has embraced horror movies, and its own pulpy twentieth century roots, while denying its nineteenth century roots in women's fiction, and pretending its mid-century writers like Shirley Jackson, Ray Bradbury, or even William Golding don't exist. Horror seems to have decided that it is such a reviled genre that it wants no more place in the mainstream. *Beloved* could not be a better standard-bearer for horror, but it seems that horror is no longer interested in what it represents.

True to its title, the comment section (Tor readers, and thus genre readers) went about jumping right back through those hoops to exclude *Beloved* from being horror. Readers tended to agree that the novel is horrific, however, they cite "author intent" (in other words, it wasn't Morrison's intent to write horror, so the novel is in fact not horror), that the novel is not "fun" and many compare *Beloved* to Lovecraft and Stephen King to prove that it is not worthy to be considered horror.

And yet, in neither of the definitions cited earlier is it stated that the author must have intent, make it "fun" for the reader, nor be H.P. Lovecraft or Stephen King to be considered horror. Including these things, I'm not even sure Lovecraft or King are writing horror.

But Hendrix has overlooked one very important fact. Race. Toni Morrison is black, has only black characters and *Beloved* is about the black experience.

Think about it. The idea that white male writers must be used to define horror, and then juxtaposed to those who are not white male writers to define what is included in horror, but more importantly excluded from horror, is absurd and honestly, quite racist. Not only that, but one of the writers, H. P. Lovecraft, was a known racist and xenophobe. This seems to suggest that for some horror readers, racist writing can in fact be horror, but anti-racist writing, which *Beloved* is, cannot be included in the definition of acceptable horror.

So now we must truly ask ourselves why, when we have defined horror in a very specific way for so long, are we now changing the perimeters to exclude this, and no doubt, other works of fiction by and about black peoples?

In other words, what does it mean to define horror by the writings of white men? What does it mean for the cannon of horror to almost exclusively be white? Is this intentional or not?

Well, to the observant reader, defining horror by the writings of white men means one clear thing: exclusion. It means that horror writing has in the past (and willfully into the present, if you listen to some readers) been defined by Western ideas. It is too often in the genre that horror is seen as an invasion of some outside force that must be exorcised in order to restore balance. When you see this, and only this as horror, you leave out those whose worlds are already defined by outside forces (e.g. the white gaze), and often use an invasion of another force as a welcomed reprieve from systemic oppression. When you have historically seen the black, the dark, the other as scary, you create an entire genre around fearing them and their cultures. Does Voodoo, loas or perhaps entire countries (Haiti) and continents (Africa) come to mind? When you define horror by white men, you not only exclude others, but you vilify them. You see, in the end, horror still must be "scary," and who and what, you should ask, are more scary to white men than black and brown people?

When you define horror by the writings of white men, the white men become heroes and everyone else is a villain.

It is no surprise then, when you, white men and women, say that horror must be "fun," you are saying that you do not want to be confronted with stories that make you uncomfortable. The stories that may force you to confront your history and your continued participation in the subjugation of others. It is so perfect a ploy to silence certain voices. In no other way that I have ever seen would horror fans claim they want to be coddled, to be entertained in a fun, pleasurable way when engaging with horror fiction. Except when blacks are involved. Because when blacks are addressing whites, they too often must "change their tone" to be considered acceptable. Blacks often are forced to entertain whites (as if a minstrel in a show), to make the racism they experience palatable for whites to digest. Claiming that blacks must write fun things for whites to read is basically telling them to don blackface and give you a great, entertaining, funny story that will not offend, confront or make you uncomfortable.

Now, quick! Name for me one of your favorite horror novels or stories that doesn't offend, confront or make you uncomfortable.

Furthermore, I tell you that intention is irrelevant. Not the intention of the author, because Hendrix already addressed this point in his essay, but the intention of the horror genre itself. It does not, in fact, matter if those trying to exclude *Beloved* from the ranks of horror are in fact racist and mean to do so or not. The outcome it still the same. Blacks and other minority writers are still excluded, their types of writings are still not accepted as horror, and they are still villainized. And you, white people, are still your own heroes.

So, make no mistake, I do not accept your idea that works of horror should be compared to those of white men (and, in the case of Lovecraft, an outright racist, at that) or must be fun to be justified, and I will not allow you to define an entire genre through your simple-minded views.

You may remain forever stubborn, bullheaded and racist. And you may get old and scream about the new kids fucking up your garden of good lightly digestible horror fiction, and you may die. But horror will move on without you—you can be part of the progression or stay your ass right in the 1980s where you belong.

———

Chesya Burke has written and published nearly a hundred fiction pieces and articles within the genres of science fiction, fantasy, noir and horror. Her story collection, *Let's Play White*, is being taught in universities around the country. In addition, Burke wrote several articles for the *African American National Biography* in 2008, and Burke's novel, *The Strange Crimes of Little Africa*, debuted in December 2015. Poet Nikki Giovanni compared her writing to that of Octavia Butler and Toni Morrison, and Samuel Delany called her "a formidable new master of the macabre." Burke's thesis was on the comic book character Storm from the X-Men, and her comic, *Shiv*, is scheduled to debut in 2017. Burke is currently pursuing her PhD in English at University of Florida. She's Co-Chair of the Board of Directors of Charis Books and More, one of the oldest feminist book stores in the country.

ARTISTS GALLERY

DANSE, REIKO MURAKAMI

MARCH, REIKO MURAKAMI

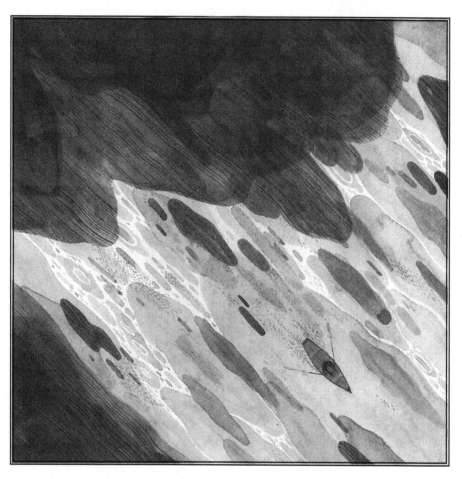

GOING HOME, MAGGIE CHIANG

HEAD IN THE CLOUDS, KIMBERLY WENGERD

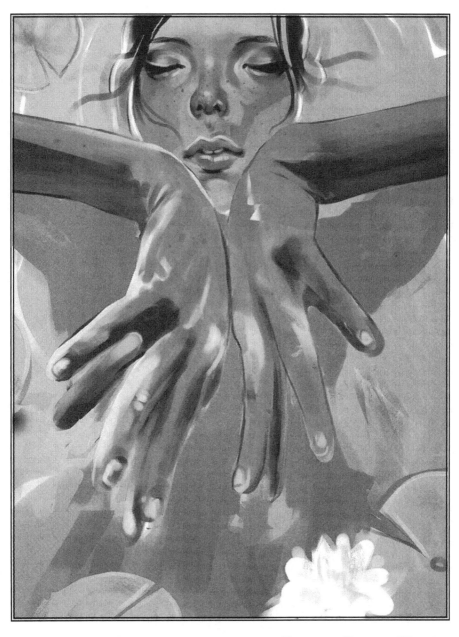

Drowned, Kimberly Wengerd

R.I., SainaSix

Sakura, SainaSix

AUTHOR SPOTLIGHTS

EDITED BY

ARLEY
SORG

AUTHOR SPOTLIGHT: NADIA BULKIN

CHRISTIAN A. COLEMAN

While Dimas undergoes a tour guide's ultimate nightmare of losing his tourist group, he tells a series of ghost stories nestled in the frame of a larger ghost story. Tell us about how you came up with this idea and Dimas's character.

I should start off by saying that I wrote "Wish You Were Here" as a response to "Safe Haven," the short movie set in Indonesia that was part of the *V/H/S 2* anthology. I include it in a long, sad history of horror movies that thoroughly other-ify a real place, much like the *Hostel* series and *Turistas*—stories about innocent tourists ruthlessly attacked by a savage and borderline inhuman local culture. Not only are the real power dynamics of the tourism industry fairly savage, but I've always found the most effectively terrifying travelogues to be ones where geographic dislocation only unpacks some darkness hidden inside the traveler, like *The Sheltering Sky* or *A Passage to India*.

So I focused on a non-local tour guide, besieged by personal demons, who discovers that his tour group has brought along their own demons. Of course, the tour group believes that they're the ones getting the crash course in exotic mysticism; hence their repeated insistence that their guide essentially exoticize himself and "tell [us] a ghost story."

Some of the stories Dimas tells are actually terrifying because they reference violent historical events. How challenging was it to balance the horrors of the past with the supernatural menace in this story?

I'm all about the interplay between the "natural" horror of current events and the "supernatural" horror of ghosts and demons. I think the combination makes for a richer, truer story. I also think that, frankly, it's important to remember that large swaths of the human population have been subjected to real horrors—genocide, ecological disaster, systemic discrimination—and their horror stories are going to look a little bit different from, you know, *Poltergeist*. Dimas's ghost stories are reflective of the sorts of stories that I was told as a kid in Indonesia, many of which were imbued with the kind of tint, or taint, that comes from a long history of political violence, from colonialism to authoritarianism and beyond. This is all part of how I approach horror, but political science is also my day job. I think everything's political. I think being apolitical is political.

The narrative is as much about storytelling as it is about the scars of history, grief, and ghosts. There's the meta-referential nod halfway through about the denouements expected of ghost stories. Is this meta-reference also a means of commenting on the legacies of colonialism?

I hadn't intended it that way, but I think it absolutely applies to the legacy of colonialism. In my view, a huge part of the postcolonial experience is the need to create a triumphant, simple Hero's Journey about your nation's past. It's usually a quixotic project, to be sure. But as I wrote it, I was thinking about the hopeless quest for neat endings and predictable arcs and explanations in our ghost stories, which is so ripe for disorientation and confusion and discomfort.

I had conflicted feelings about Rose. I sympathized with her grief, but couldn't help seeing how selfish she was for taking advantage of Dimas's hospitality and his culture to overcome her loss. Like the other tourists, she didn't truly engage his country or its history. What does she mean to you in terms of the West and its relations with Southeast Asia?

All of the tourists represent different slices of the way the West has interacted with Southeast Asia—from Melissa's desire for entertainment and amusement to Josh's desire to prove his intellectual superiority, from Ben's clueless bumbling to Rose's cold, calculated pragmatism. For sure, Rose has no interest in engaging with the local culture. Of all the tourists, she's probably the least interested in engaging, because she's on a singular mission to heal her own inner wound. Her approach is utilitarian, extractive, and exploitative—absolutely! But you know, at least Rose has no pretense. She's the only one who calls the tour what it really is: a chance for the tourists to demand anything from their host country.

On your website, you wrote that your work could be summed up in these three songs: Sisters of Mercy's "Lucretia My Reflection"; Fever Ray's "If I Had a Heart"; and Massive Attack's "Voodoo in My Blood." Were there any specific songs that inspired this story or powered you through writing it?

Glad you asked. There certainly were. Mainly, it was "Manifest Destiny" by Zola Jesus for the combination of both a lamentation and a militant drumbeat (the anthem of postcolonial nationalism, if there ever was one), and for the desperate demand that anchors the song for everything, essentially, to be all right again. For me, this story is all about that plea. Like a lot of my stories, it's about grief and trauma, and the way it makes you rethink what you thought was possible—it's impossible I can be expected to go on this way—and—it's impossible that this is the way the world looks now. And yet here you are: living in the impossible. Making bargains you never thought you'd make.

AUTHOR SPOTLIGHT: GABRIELA SANTIAGO

JEREMY SIM

First of all, congratulations, Gabriela, on creating this wonderfully haunting and riveting story. Could you tell us a little about how the story came to be?

Thank you! I really did find a rock with the word "EAT" scratched into it in jagged letters in the dumpster behind my apartment.

Also, just before that, I had read the brilliant *Life is Not a Shoujo Manga* by my friend and fellow Clarionite / Tiny Bonesaw Isabel Yap. I fell absolutely in love with the way that story uses fandom and tropes simultaneously as a smokescreen and as a lens, the way truths are revealed by talking around them and explaining the way things are not, narration via negation. (As of this writing, *Life is Not a Shoujo Manga* is still available to read for free online at *Interfictions*; go check it out!) So I immediately knew that I wanted to try something similar; I just needed something solid like a voice or a plot or a character to hang the technique on. And then I found the rock with the word EAT scratched into it in jagged letters along with a heart and some patches of finely crosshatched lines. And a stuffed baby alligator. And a satchel with sixteen perfectly good drill bits. And three mutilated pianos. And more compasses, binoculars, and X-Acto knives than one person should ever really need. I took some of these things into my apartment and started to write.

One of the things that struck me most about the story was the way the narrative starts out clear and logical, then descends into stark madness. However, the element of logic is still present throughout—it feels like the narrator is actively struggling to explain away a horror that ends up unexplainable. What were some of the challenges in pulling off this style?

I had a lot of fun exploring this style; I'm glad you think I pulled it off! The unreliable narrators that I like best are those who are actively struggling to tell the truth; a really big influence on the way I wrote myself in this story was Justine Larbalestier's *Liar*, which is still my favorite of her books for the way it constantly upset my expectations while never making me lose sympathy for the protagonist. However, a narrator who wants to tell the truth but is terrified of the consequences ends up going on a lot of tangents, so there was the challenge of going through and cutting the 1,200 words of tangents that didn't either a) fall into the main themes as I identified them: consumption, writing/storytelling, truths and lies, surveillance, racism, representation in media, or b) get referred back to later, e.g. the alternate universe in which my mother became a geologist. Shout-out to another talented

Clarion friend, Marie Vibbert (the same Marie I mention in the story), who helped me cut another hundred words after that!

Another challenge was maintaining a balance between the evidence I presented for different interpretations of what is going on, trying not to tip my hand as to whether I was writing with an ultimately supernatural or mundane explanation in mind, and at the same time trying to write with enough sincerity that the reader hopefully doesn't feel like I'm just jerking them around and hurl my story across the room in annoyance; trying to be mysterious enough that the story didn't feel too pat, but revealing enough that the reader didn't feel cheated.

Probably the biggest challenge was not explaining too much. It's something I'm still working on after years of being told, by beta readers who didn't typically read speculative fiction, that I wasn't explaining enough.

I found the constant blurring of reality and fantasy in this story really interesting. Were there any aspects of the story, or perhaps some of the narrator's thoughts on being a writer, that draw on your own experiences in real life?

That would be telling!

But I will say that the narrator is literally me.

And "Far Beyond the Stars" is the best episode of television ever created.

Also, my big sister really did qualify for a mission to Mars.

My favorite line in the story is when the narrator compares the act of writing to "an anguished scream of realization that magic is not real." How much do you feel this way about writing and speculative fiction in general?

That was how I felt in high school and college. Nowadays, my writing tends to be more about either "the little places where possibilities live"—celebrating all the small and secret hidden in-between things that aren't magic, but are close enough that they might as well be—or about "you have to write Uhura over and over again, because she was here and she was real and you're here and you're real, you're real, you're real!"—trying to fight against the way marginalized groups get erased from the mainstream cultural narrative. This story in particular was very much about the anxiety of not seeing yourself reflected in fiction, and the way it can feel like you're physically being erased, subsumed, or consumed.

So I guess it is still sometimes a way of shouting out my pain into the universe— just not generally about the existence of magic anymore.

What's next for Gabriela Santiago? What are you working on now?

I have a short story coming out in *States of Terror, Volume 3*; it's partly about what it means to love children who are not your own, and partly about a giant snake-fish. I'm currently working on several other short stories in sort of a Lazy Susan rotation where I write about a thousand words on each of them at a time. In addition to my short fiction, I'm editing the billionth draft of a novel about an art-school dropout who becomes the reluctant sidekick to a Manic Pixie Dream Guy who accidentally fractured his self and scattered the pieces all over the greater Chicago area.

I also love performing my work, so you can find me around the Twin Cities at The Calof Series with Patrick's Cabaret, the OUTspoken! queer open mic, and The Not-So-Silent Planet speculative fiction open mic.

AUTHOR SPOTLIGHT: VALERIE VALDES

CHRISTIAN A. COLEMAN

You begin your story similarly to Jay McInerney's *Bright Lights, Big City*. Second person is often a highly contended narrative mode, dismissed as gimmicky. You use it to great effect here, allowing the reader to inhabit the dead-end reality of the "you" character. Why did you decide to use it to tell this story?

It felt right to tell a story about a service-industry worker in the second person because such people are frequently ignored or dehumanized in their daily lives. When I worked in a movie theater, customers would walk up to the concession stand and start barking orders at me like I was a kiosk instead of a human being. So I wanted the reader to, as you say, inhabit the character more fully than first or third person would allow. There's an immediacy and intensity that comes from second person when it's done well, if you can clear the hurdle of the reader rejecting the POV like a bad organ transplant.

I found your story more saddening than frightening because the terror is rooted in existential dread rather than the supernatural, gore, or violence. The "you" character is doomed to work this Sisyphean movie theater job until death. Tell us where this idea came from.

This began as a story for an anthology where the only mandate was to write horror that included a particular element; the rest was up to me. I didn't feel like writing something gory or violent at the time, so those ideas went into the notebook for later. When I'm brainstorming, I like to dredge my own life for anything that can be useful and, like I said, I worked in a movie theater for years. I have a lot of fond memories, but it was hard work for long hours and little pay, and the odds of advancement were minimal.

There's this perception that minimum wage jobs are temporary, that they're for young people in college who are going to earn their degrees and get "real" jobs and move up in the world, allowing the next teenager in line to take their slot. That's garbage. Life is Sisyphean. Most of us are pushing a rock up a hill; the only differences are the size of the rock, the slope of the hill, and the view from the top before the damn thing rolls back down. Thinking about that certainly horrifies the crap out of me.

What on earth was going on in theater 12? The ambient sucking and breathing noises, the constant close-up shots of the girl drinking wine or soda in the

movie, the lack of AC—I don't think I'd last more than five minutes in there.

Theater 12 is the embodiment of the soul-sucking nature of the job. It always felt like on the day when I was least equipped to deal with things going wrong, I'd be stuck working until oh-dark-thirty, the ice machine would break, we'd run out of popcorn oil, some film would get stuck and have to be cut apart and taped back together while a bunch of customers screamed at the projection booth, and the AC would be out as the icing on the crap cupcake. Cleaning a hot theater in the summer in Miami sweats the life out of you.

I'm happy to let readers interpret the situation how they like—I've probably said too much already—but I'll add that the inspiration came from the Arctic Monkeys song "Arabella." There's this great moment at the end: "Wraps her lips 'round the Mexican coke / Makes you wish that you were the bottle / Takes a sip of your soul and it sounds like . . ." And then these wailing guitars come in, and I get chills every time. I won't say the song correlates strongly to my story otherwise, but I wanted to recreate those chills.

You bookend the story with the image of the shark-teeth smile, suggesting that the "you" character and floor manager Yamilet are part of an ongoing cycle of Sartrean hell. Was there any way they could escape, or was there something bigger and insidious keeping them trapped forever?

I'd like to think there's a shot at escaping, but again, life is Sisyphean. It takes an enormous effort and not a little bit of luck to break this kind of cycle on an individual basis. That's the world we live in. Until we acknowledge collectively that the labor system is flawed and work to improve it for everyone, it'll be rocks and hills all the way down. People like the protagonist will be stuck in the same job, or make lateral moves for microscopic benefits, in order to maintain the scraps of security such positions offer them. People like the manager will cling to limited authority because it's the closest they'll ever come to having any real power over their own lives or others. At the same time, reality isn't so simple and people aren't so easily reducible—this is horror, after all, not a documentary. Someone can work retail or wait tables until they die and still be happy and fulfilled, because they enjoy their work or they have other things outside work that bring them pleasure. But lack of choice and opportunity can lead to the kind of stagnation I'm exploring, and I do think that's a problem society isn't adequately addressing.

Do you have other forthcoming works we can look forward to?

Plenty of works in varying stages of completion, but none have found a home yet. Still pushing my own boulder and hoping for a nice view at the summit before I have to chase it back down and start over again.

AUTHOR SPOTLIGHT:
RUSSELL NICHOLS

ISABEL YAP

"The Taming of the Tongue" is a story that explores multiple themes, including hope, betrayal, losing one's voice, and yearning for true freedom. I noticed you selected a very specific place and time for this story. What first led you to exploring this idea?

Four years ago, I was living in India with my wife, riding camels across a desert in Rajasthan. This got me thinking about different modes of travel. And I asked myself: What if I had to ride in the mouth of an animal to get somewhere? Weird. Not enough to jump-start the story, though. I came up with the theme of voicelessness (a recurring theme for me as a writer of color). The question evolved: What if a voiceless person had to ride in the mouth of a monster to escape . . . something? Still not enough. Later on, I was doing research for another project, reading the Harriet Jacobs memoir, *Incidents in the Life of a Slave Girl*, and I read, "Dr. Flint swore he would kill me, if I was not as silent as the grave." I knew then that this was the right place and time for the concept and theme.

One of the primary sensory details running through this piece is tension. In every moment, I worried about Cat's safety, and who she could trust. Did you know Cat's ending before you wrote it?

Most definitely. I'm the type of writer that needs to know the ending. It might change over time, but I want an idea of where I'm going. Problem is, my endings usually don't work for readers. I've gotten hundreds of magazine rejections, mostly form letters. But if an editor does give me feedback, 99% of the time they will say, "the ending is too abrupt." Seriously, that should be the name of my future collection. But these are the types of endings I like. This one took me a few drafts and good feedback to get just right. Truth is, Cat told me how and when she wanted her journey to end. I'm just the journalist.

I tried to do research on whether a zwelgen was an existing mythological creature or folktale, and I couldn't find anything besides the Dutch word meaning to guzzle/gulp down/revel in. How did you come up with this monster?

Here's the thing: I don't write much horror, and I've never written historical fiction. I knew if I was going to challenge myself with genre and period (and second-person POV), I had to go all the way. So I set out to create an original monster, with its own mythology, real enough to make readers wonder if this thing truly existed in folklore. That was the mission. All I knew about the zwelgen starting out was the travel-by-mouth bit. Everything else evolved as I was writing.

You left the US in 2011 to travel from country to country. How have your travels changed the way you approach writing or generating ideas for fiction?

Basically, my wife and I live out of our backpacks. We plan ahead where we can, but mostly we just go where the wind blows. Right now, we're housesitting in Puerto Rico. Six months from now, maybe we'll return to Mexico. Or go back to Southeast Asia. Who knows? When it comes to writing, I take the opposite approach. Not that I've got binders full of character bios, but like I said, I need to know the ending before I start writing. So for me, this freestyle lifestyle reminds me to be more open with where my ideas want to go and let my characters be my guide instead of doing my usual control freak thing.

In addition to fiction, you write in various forms, including screenplays, graphic novels, and nonfiction. How do you decide which form a certain idea should take? Are there any upcoming projects you're particularly excited about?

Ideas like to play games. They'll come to me, talking all sexy like, "Take me, I'm yours." That's it. No hello. No specifics. And I'm blindfolded, mind you. So I might think the idea wants to be a short story, come to find out it really wants to be a travel essay or a play. For example, I wrote a short film script about married fugitives in the Louisiana bayous, which grew into a TV pilot, then I realized it would be a better graphic novel. That's life. And even though it feels like a waste of time, I'll admit the process always helps me refine the piece. As far as upcoming projects, I'm working on a screenplay about a society where sleeping is illegal, but that might end up being a one-act play. Or a piece of flash fiction. Or maybe nothing but a tease.

Do you have any advice for writers of color, especially those who would like to try writing horror?

Disclaimer: My wife's the scream queen; I usually write science fiction, so I'm just visiting here. But I will say, real life is scary. Police killing black men and black women, natural disasters, mosquito-borne viruses, terrorism, etc. Reality strikes without warning. The horror comes from the unpredictability factor, i.e. fear of the unknown. In fiction, people of color have too often been cast as that unknown. But our unknowns feel different. Our demons look different. Collectively and individually. In "The Taming of the Tongue," for example, Cat's story is definitely her own, but I related because that psychological trauma is personal to me—the monster as a metaphor for my own fear of not being heard. So don't stop writing. Keep telling your stories because one of the scariest things is the blank page.

AUTHOR SPOTLIGHT: NISI SHAWL

CHRISTIAN A. COLEMAN

In this story, stagnant water seems to be a harbinger of death and self-destruction. Is it a metaphor or commentary on the favoritism and implicit colorism in Dory's family that drives Calliope to murder and suicide?

As an author, I'm not all that qualified to tell readers what is or isn't a metaphor. I can tell you that the experience of writing about stagnant water in "Cruel Sistah" drew largely on my fascination with secrets and the forbidden. Also, astrologically, I'm triply connected with the stagnant water archetype. And water is seen as a medium between the spiritual and material realms in countless traditions around the world. That's all I can tell you; the rest is left as an exercise, I guess.

You compress three distinct points of view—Calliope, Dory's spirit, Byron—while zooming out from Dory's murder through each POV shift. How did you decide on this structure?

For me, this compression of viewpoints maps onto the de-coalescing of boundaries that I imagine must be part of what you feel after death. Your body is gone, which is how you keep track of yourself as separate. I wanted to share that same elision of perspective through the story's structure. It was a very conscious attempt on my part, and I'm glad you picked up on it.

I love the scene where Byron's handcrafted gimbri gives voice to Dory's spirit so she can divulge her demise through song. Tell us where this idea came from.

Actually, the singing instrument is the core of the ballad I lifted this plot from, "Cruel Sister." In the sixteenth-century version, it's a harp, and the musician and lover are different characters. But yes, totally not an original idea.

What about the ballad drew your attention?

The entire story, not just the song, is inspired by "Cruel Sister." There are many, many songs on the same theme, by many different titles. What attracted me was the plain, unalloyed, chilling hatefulness of the crime and the equally chilling retribution—though I carried that part a bit further in my story. The song "Cruel Sister" ends with the ghostly accusation, as does most of its ilk, but I wanted to show the aftereffects of the murderer's horrific action. The song in "Cruel Sistah," by the way, is loosely based on W.C. Handy's "St. Louis Blues."

Asimov's **originally published "Cruel Sistah" in 2005. What meaning does it have for you now in 2016? Has it changed over the years, especially with regard to the results in** *Fireside Fiction's* **#BlackSpecFic report on anti-black racism in SFF publishing?**

As you age, objective time slows. To me, the original publication of "Cruel Sistah" seems not that long ago. I can remember when waiting a week for my first ballet lesson seemed intolerable. Now, no—my take on a story I published eleven years ago hasn't undergone much of a transformation. I *have* noticed a difference in the reception black authors receive in the field within the span of my professional career. A positive one. But the arc of this change, it is long, and the progress way slower than it needs to be. May I live to see the rate of positive change in the field pick up a bit more velocity.

AUTHOR SPOTLIGHT: PRIYA SHARMA

CORAL MOORE

There's a bending of time at work in "The Show" as we see glimpses of Martha's past interwoven with what's happening in the present of the story. What were the reasons you chose those moments from her past to highlight?

The past haunts Martha. It's shaped who she is, and everything has led her to filming in that cellar and all that follows. For both myself and the readers, I needed those moments of sibling envy and rivalry, desperation, and grief for us to understand the woman Martha has become, and the importance of what's happening to her now. Take those elements out, and the whole thing falls flat.

The aspects of gore in "The Show" are restrained rather than garish, though the content lends itself easily to going either way. Was that a conscious choice you made when writing this story?

I wanted there to be a detached, voyeuristic feeling to the violence. It suited the strangeness of Martha seeing past events, as well as the theme of this being a TV show. I felt what I'd written was explicit enough to let the readers fill in any gaps. Much of what I write falls into the horror category, but I'm not a big fan of huge amounts of gore. I like my horror to be much quieter, but hopefully no less brutal.

Martha is an interesting character, the charlatan who becomes the genuine article. Is that a type of character you've used before, or was there a particular inspiration for her in this story?

There are a lot of shows about filming in allegedly haunted sites. My influence was the UK show *Most Haunted*, where buildings were visited by the regular presenter, a historian, a parapsychologist, and a medium. I always found watching the mediums especially interesting. The controversies around the show are well-documented, and Martha grew from those. I liked the idea that she'd suppressed a lot of herself to survive, and I wanted to write about that.

What are you working on now, that we can look forward to reading from you in the future?

I've just had a story out in *Black Static* issue 53 (ttapress.com/blackstatic) called "Inheritance" (my own take on Gothic themes) and a story reprinted on *Mithila Review* (mithilareview.com) called "Egg" (a fairy tale). The latter is part of the *Mithila Review's* Asian SF special, and the whole issue is free to read online, including a roundtable discussion.

Next year, I've a story called "The Crow Palace" in Ellen Datlow's "Black Feathers" anthology (original avian horror). There's some other stuff I can't talk about, and other than that, I'm working on pieces for my own anthology. Many thanks for including "The Show" and for interviewing me here.

AUTHOR SPOTLIGHT: TERENCE TAYLOR

JEREMY SIM

Terence, I found this story chilling on so many levels. It was so good. Could you tell us a little about how the story came to be?
Well, thank you! I was very happy with it when it was done and am glad to see it get a new readership. It started with a similar relationship with a friend's husband, with frequent long phone calls between states. There was a dark period in our lives when we were both dealing with work issues, or more accurately, lack of work, and on occasion I would feel him sliding into a darker place. After getting off the phone one particularly bad day, I wondered what would happen if he ever just went off the deep end, and what could I do at a distance to help? That was the seed that initially started me working on the story.

One of the story's strongest aspects, I think, is the characters: Dean and Lynn and the protagonist Greg just feel so real that it makes the narrative that much more frightening and immediate. Is there a story behind the development of these characters?
They started with the friend who had inspired the story, as described, for Dean, and then I added other aspects until he was no longer an Irish-American Californian with anger issues, but a southern guy from New Orleans with rage issues. My father also had a hair-trigger temper, which I inherited, and it has always been an aspect of his and my character that I wanted to explore in my writing.

I had visited New Orleans for the first time on New Year's 2005, and it seemed a great setting for a "racist ghost" story, and I had a friend from Louisiana who could fact-check me. Then I made Dean's wife a black woman, for reasons I needed in the story, her character based on a good female friend and fellow writer, and Greg was based on myself at the time. I had never actually worked in production with my buddy, but Dean's job was based on his, and Greg's was made into one that fit into that. So I took reality and reshaped it to fit what I needed for the story.

I started it long enough ago that I really have to think to remember some of the progression, but I know it was essentially to be about these three characters and one's decline, but then as I was working on it, Hurricane Katrina happened. I was stunned as I watched the TV coverage and the escalation of damage and death, then the horror stories of what was going on in the stadium where survivors were being warehoused, the politics of the levees . . . I started to think I should change the setting of the story out of respect, but then realized as events unfolded that it actually strengthened the story and its themes, put them against a large-scale disaster that reflected the smaller personal themes of the narrative. I had something to say about it, and the event became an integral part of my palette for the story. My idea of "racist ghosts" raised from his past by Dean's digging through his family home actually seemed to be rising in New Orleans that month, and the growing crisis started folding itself into the story and made it much stronger than I originally expected.

One of the things that also inspired the story was the KKK photo in Washington, D.C. that Dean sends to Greg. The photo is real—seen at a shop called Arcana in the East Village on a visit with an artist friend who bought things there for conceptual installations—and I was so freaked out by it that I talked the owner into letting me bring in a scanner to scan it in sections to restore, with the promise that I would give him a copy on disk and in print. It has been an occasional hobby and new cloning brushes in Photoshop are helping me make better progress, so he should get it soon, years late. But I scanned it at a high enough DPI that I could see the expressions on their faces, including the women and children. The ordinariness of the event, the casual display of the American flag at the base of the Washington Monument, Klan costumes, and picnic-like atmosphere of the revelers scared me more than anything else; that it was just a simple social event for them, despite the organization's history.

It was kept in the store because the owner's wife told him when he found it and brought it home that it was it or her in the house—one had to go. Greg's reactions to it and its growing significance as he feels they are watching him while the storm builds was part of the texture of the story that made it work for me. I occasionally wondered if I really wanted it hanging over my head as I work, but those who do not remember the past are doomed to repeat it, so I will be taking it to a framer to experience Greg's encounter soon.

I really connected with the way the "horror" elements in this story knit closely with real-life horrors that we see around us every day: racism, homophobia, natural disasters, abuse, and so on. What were some of the challenges in writing a story encompassing so many painful topics?

The first, of course, is creating a plausible base reality to set it in. I like my stories taking place in as real a world as possible, regardless of how alien they may be, filled with prosaic details that are familiar enough to let the reader sink into it. A few years ago, I re-read a novel of my mother's I'd read as a kid, *The Master and Margarita*, by Mikhail Bulgakov. It was a stunningly sharp satire on Soviet life, with strong supernatural elements folded into a starkly real representation of their urban life. My first novels were in the same mold, set in the late '80s and then a millennial New York, infused with supernatural elements that were oddly plausible in context. It wasn't until I re-read the Bulgakov that I realized where I got that sensibility.

Once my stage is set, the unnatural horror is interwoven with real-world horrors to make the fantasy elements more real, more dangerous, as the impact is then felt in our world, not that of imagination. Klansmen and ghosts are scary on their own; dead Klansmen whose ghosts influence the living and turn friends into foes are scarier. Whenever I can blend elements to ramp up that impact, all the better. The challenge is in using them well in ways that focus and amplify what you want to say. It is a delicate balance between making sense and going for sensation. Any uncomfortable feelings evoked as I write only help—the more uncomfortable the subject, the more discomfort it raises in me, the more I know readers will react.

My first published story, "Plaything", was about a lawyer assigned to defend two men having sex with a robot that looked like an eight-year-old girl. Exploring the moral question of whether it was a sex toy or pedophilia creeped me out every time I worked on it, and that was how I knew it would be effective. If you want to discomfort others, your own comfort can't be of concern. The story has to make you feel what you want readers to feel.

As a writer of color yourself, I imagine your experiences, thoughts and emotions on some of these topics are so much vaster and more complex than can be contained in a single short story. Do you ever find it difficult distilling that down, so to speak, for the purposes of a story?

We are all kaleidoscopes of experience and reaction, and it is from that that I draw the stories and themes in my work. Whether about people of color or not, I am a gay writer of color, and all my perceptions and sensibilities are filtered through that reality along with an ability to see outside myself. Being both black and gay, I've often been outside of either culture because of my inclusion in the other, and that has made me an outsider who sees the world at a slight distance that often gives me more objectivity and insight.

I enjoy writing stories about characters as far from me as possible, knowing I can offer a view of them that writers more like them might not see or be as honest about. The amount of me that goes into any one story is as much as is needed to tell that particular story. The tale tells me what and how much to use, and distillation is less of a problem than might be expected, for that reason.

As part of this special People of Colo(u)r Destroy Horror! issue, do you have any advice for developing writers of color who may have just read your story and aspire to write a story like this one day?

Keep writing. Never give up. Never surrender. I wrote for decades before I took it seriously enough to achieve the published work I have accomplished in the last ten years. There was a lot of waste, but it had to be written to get here. There are always bad stories that have to come out before you get to the good stuff, and it is a pain, but never a waste, and even failures can be recovered later when you have the skills to fix them. Be fully aware of the world, step outside of yourself to see it as others see it so you can write from that point of view as well as your own, and never feel limited by who or what you are, to only write from there. Be free to be anyone in your work you need to be to tell the stories you need to tell. You will always be you—who you write is individual to you and your insights and just needs to consider all possibilities in the world.

What's next for Terence Taylor? What are you working on now?

I've been lucky to have three stories in print this year, the last, "The Catch", coming out this fall in John Joseph Adams' and Douglas Cohen's *What the #@&% Is That?* anthology, and an essay on Samuel R. Delany's *Dhalgren* in the People of

Colo(u)r Destroy Science Fiction! issue. This has put me back on the path to finishing my *Vampire Testaments* trilogy, as I work on *Past Life*, which leaps another twenty years into the future and brings Zora Neale Hurston to Hollywood for a reunion with her vampire ex-lover, Turner Creed, and picks up our world in "present day" 2027, after two decades of Tom O'Bedlam's attempt to break down society, as our heroes, human and otherwise, deal with a host of issues I am currently evolving.

The hardest thing for me is that I have terribly high expectations for the third movement of my literary symphony, and that I am leaping into the void to try things I haven't dared. To cut loose from all you know to fly into the unknown is both terrifying and ultimately gratifying, if you can let yourself trust your muse enough to try. I often remind myself that after a leap of faith, falling and flying feel the same, so I must give myself the benefit of the doubt as I wait to rise.

After that, I have a Terry Pratchett-ian science fiction/fantasy series set in Park Slope that I want to try, so the journey continues. I also have a regular review column in *Fantastic Stories of the Imagination*, called *Read Me!*, where I'm clearing my shelf of that pile of genre novels we all have that I have been promising myself to read. My creative life is full for the moment.

AUTHOR SPOTLIGHT: JUNOT DÍAZ

ARLEY SORG

There's a lot here about class, race, and culture, especially the sense of being wedged between identities, and of existing on the fringes in a place of clashing identities and mutable definitions. There's also this POV character who is kind of self-absorbed, and who, while suffering under his placement in the social structure in some ways, reflected for example in his sense of Mysty being out of his league because he's neither white enough nor wealthy enough, and who is more than conscious of these structures, is also content enough to play his part within them and perpetuate them, rather than subvert them or challenge them. Why does the central character play along, rather than rail against, these social systems? And how do these elements represent your experiences growing up (or even today)?

Why does anyone abet systems that oppress? Why do so many of us have solidarity with elite structures that don't give two shits about us? As any sixth grader will tell you, in contexts of extreme conformity "going along" with shit is often so naturalized the idea of resisting is not even on the table. This is a character, though, who is a lot more complex than that (one hopes). He is critical about the deeply unjust world he inhabits but that in itself is not enough to sever his longing to join the ranks of this world's "winners." Here we see Berlant's concept of "Cruel Optimism" at work. How in the middle of an environmental and social collapse people can still be invested in "compromised conditions of possibility" or "clusters of promises."

Now me, I grew up in a far different context than the narrator; I had very different kinds of mentoring which gave me opportunities for different kinds of ways of thinking and feeling. Which is not to say that I didn't pass through my period of self-loathing, of identifying and longing for wealth and whiteness and their many privileges. I most certainly did, me and almost every single person of color I know. As Fanon understood, internalized racism is the darkness that all us people of color have to face and vanquish if we are ever going to lead healthy lives. Our narrator in "Monstro" is on the road to that self-liberation but he ain't quite there yet.

One of the things I admire about this piece is the conversational style of narrative, but more specifically, the use of a culturally mashed-up language: easy-going strings of phrases punctuated with cuss words and seasoned with Spanish, then the tossed-in GRE words, and finally, enhanced by the speculative near-future terms. The language of the piece well-represents the conflicting cultures of the POV character. How has language been important to you in terms of identity and connecting with people or places?

Conflicting culture or simply hybridic creolized culture? This is after all the Caribbean, where hybridity has been a central paradigm for centuries. Never underestimate the Caribbean's cannibalistic power (per Joaquim Pedro de Andrade): in the Caribbean we could reconcile the Black Tongue of Mordor and Quenya in two generations flat. One of the particular joys of SF and fantasy books for me has always been when writers layer in invented or archaic language into English to create a heteroglossic density. When I was reading as a kid—70s and 80s—the world I lived in was heteroglossic but the only places I found that reality reflected was in certain SF and fantasy books. *Dune* and *The Lord of the Rings* and *The Book of the New Sun* and *Watership Down* made sense to me and despite their fantastic strategies (and perhaps unwittingly) were truer to the worlds I was living in than any other kind of fiction I was encountering. These books required you to be actively present in the language, not only to be reading but to be *translating*. Even if you weren't an immigrant, when you live in a multicultural space, surrounded by multiple languages, multiple traditions, multiple idioms, multiple registers, language was not a matter of passive absorption like watching TV—language required an active relationship, like dance. Required participation. And I guess I wanted to evoke that reality in the work, however glancingly, to reach across to all those books that guided me.

For me, I have this sense of the setting being the most important place in the world, at least, within the context of the story, if that makes sense. Sort of, the way that most stories in the US have this inherent kind of US-centric feeling, as if all events revolve around US importance; in this piece, despite the occasional comment about how people were more interested in what was happening in other places, it still reads as D.R.-centric, and D.R. becomes this extremely relevant place in the moment. I spoke with another author recently who, when translating their book to English, changed the setting for their US version to a US city. In the conversation around diversity, do you think diversity of "place"/ setting is just as important as diverse representation among characters?

Diversity of place is of course essential. Anything to decenter the Eurocentric North as the default center of the universe is always welcome. But not all representations of "diverse" places are equally swell. Eurocentrism comes in many forms, after all. When it comes to the speculative genres (and not just them) white writers have been textually adventuring in "exotic places" (read: full of people of color and other subalterns) for as long as adventure has been a genre. That's a familiar style of colonization. It's not just blackface, yellowface, and brownface that victimize—it's also the politics of hegemonic folks appropriating our topos in their texts—what we might call blackplace, yellowplace, and brownplace. Me, what I would like to see more of is stories set outside of dominant geographies written by people of color. That would be awesome, a welcome change and would not only decenter the White West and raise important questions about appropriation, it would counter some of the weird bullshit that arises when outsiders write "the foreign." Everyone can write anything they want—but there are political consequences to every choice we make in our narratives and in unequal worlds such as ours some folks are allowed to visit places and leave easily because of their privileges and some of us cannot. Bottom line is our textual maps are not as diverse as they should be and are often drawn by the same white folks—what we need, most definitely, are other types of maps. What we need are new maps. Imagine what discoveries might we make, what horizons might open if the mapmakers were actually the people who for centuries were the ones always being mapped?

Going back to the notion of our kind-of self-absorbed POV character: One of the things that fascinates me here (but also rings true) is the way that, while these terrible things are happening, the characters engage with them on the level of them almost being a novelty; or, perhaps, as moments to exploit. Early on, in the narrator's reflecting, this is explained as being related to his age. At the same time, these characters have been victims of different sorts of abuse. Do you feel like individuals within our cultures are, generally speaking, shifting towards a more self-absorbed, self-interested way of interacting with the world and events? Or have we always been this way, and we are just more brazen about it? Or, perhaps, is the narrator right—this is just a mark of youth, and in maturation, we tend to grow more compassionate?

The cruel irony is that these Dominican characters are talking about Haiti, which is only a short drive from where they live! But in their conceptual universe Haiti might as well be another planet, another galaxy. This inability to grasp the situation, the suffering, of poorer darker people, this aphasia of sympathy, is common to our global order; how we see in this day and age is actively not to see what's really going on. A lot of this has to do with the outcome of neoliberal socializations and spatial practices, with how deeply networked we've become (in a Delany turn of the phrase) and how as a consequence we've lost much of our contact spaces. We could always say a generation has become more selfish, more solipsistic, but there's a lot of social work that goes into making that happen. The question always is: in a society that prizes only inhuman values, how do we learn sympathy and compassion? Sometimes we need to be humiliated by our philosophical shortcomings before any learning can take place, and the plan was for this character to face such a reckoning.

Even though this is written as part of a longer project, I actually really love the way it ends, because it points beautifully to the nature of the characters, in their reckless pursuit of excitement and fame, and their exploitative interest in the pain of others: "Just in case, you know, Alex said, packing up his Polaroid, something happens." What are some of the projects you're working on now that we can look forward to?

God, I ain't working on nada. I'm a bum.

Thanks so much for the story. I personally think the writing is amazing. Thanks, also, for your time!

Thank you for the opportunity.

IN THE NEXT ISSUE OF
NIGHTMARE

We have original fiction from Tananarive Due ("Migration") and Sandra McDonald ("When You Work for the Old Ones"), along with reprints by Michael Shea ("The Horror on the 33") and Tim Pratt ("Fool's Fire").

We also have the latest installment of our column on horror, "The H Word," plus author spotlights with our authors, a showcase on our cover artist, and a feature interview with author Jack Ketchum.

It's another great issue, so be sure to check it out. And while you're at it, tell a friend about *Nightmare*. Thanks for reading!

SUBSCRIPTIONS & EBOOKS

If you enjoy reading *Nightmare*, please consider subscribing. It's a great way to support the magazine, and you'll get your issues in the convenient ebook format of your choice. You can subscribe directly from our website, via Weightless Books, or via Amazon.com. For more information, visit nightmare-magazine.com/subscribe.

We also have individual ebook issues available at a variety of ebook vendors, and we now have Ebook Bundles available in the *Nightmare* ebookstore, where you can buy in bulk and save! Buying a Bundle gets you a copy of every issue published during the named period. Buying either of the half-year Bundles saves you $3 (so you're basically getting one issue for free), or if you spring for the Year One Bundle, you'll save $11 off the cover price. So if you need to catch up on *Nightmare*, that's a great way to do so. Visit nightmare-magazine.com/store for more information.

STAY CONNECTED

Here are a few URLs you might want to check out or keep handy if you'd like to stay apprised of everything new and notable happening with *Lightspeed*:

Magazine Website
www.nightmare-magazine.com

Destroy Projects Website
www.destroysf.com

Newsletter
www.nightmare-magazine.com/newsletter

RSS Feed
www.nightmare-magazine.com/rss-2

Podcast Feed
www.nightmare-magazine.com/itunes-rss

Twitter
www.twitter.com/nightmaremag

Facebook
www.facebook.com/NightmareMagazine

Subscribe
www.nightmare-magazine.com/subscribe

ABOUT THE SPECIAL ISSUE STAFF

Silvia Moreno-Garcia, Guest Editor-in-Chief & Original Fiction Editor
Silvia Moreno-Garcia is the author of *Signal to Noise*, a tale of music, magic, and Mexico City which *The Guardian* has called "a magical first novel." Her debut collection, *This Strange Way of Dying*, was a finalist for The Sunburst Award for Excellence in Canadian Literature of the Fantastic. Her stories have also been collected in *Love & Other Poisons*. She has edited several anthologies, including *Dead North* and *Fractured: Tales of the Canadian Post-Apocalypse*. Her latest book, a Mexican vampire novel called *Certain Dark Things*, goes on sale October 25, 2016. She blogs at silviamoreno-garcia.com and tweets @silviamg.

Tananarive Due, Reprint Fiction Editor
Tananarive Due is the recipient of The American Book Award and the NAACP Image Award and has authored and/or co-authored twelve novels and a civil rights memoir. In 2013, she received a Lifetime Achievement Award in the Fine Arts from the Congressional Black Caucus Foundation. In 2010, she was inducted into the Medill School of Journalism's Hall of Achievement at Northwestern University. She has also taught at the Geneva Writers Conference, the Clarion Science Fiction & Fantasy Writers' Workshop, and Voices of Our Nations Art Foundation (VONA). Due's supernatural thriller *The Living Blood* won a 2002 American Book Award. Her novella "Ghost Summer," published in the 2008 anthology *The Ancestors*, received the 2008 Kindred Award from the Carl Brandon Society, and her short fiction has appeared in best-of-the-year anthologies of science fiction and fantasy.

Maurice Broaddus, Nonfiction Editor
Maurice Broaddus is the author of the *Knights of Breton Court* urban fantasy trilogy: *King Maker*, *King's Justice*, and *King's War* (Angry Robot Books). His fiction has been published in numerous magazines and anthologies, including *Asimov's Science Fiction*, *Lightspeed Magazine*, *Cemetery Dance*, *Apex Magazine*, and *Weird Tales Magazine*. Some of his stories are being collected in the upcoming *Voices of the Martyrs* (Rosarium Publishing). He co-edited *Streets of Shadows* (Alliteration Ink) and the *Dark Faith* anthology series (Apex Books). You can keep up with him at his website, MauriceBroaddus.com.

Terence Taylor, Podcast Host

Terence Taylor (terencetaylor.com) is an award-winning children's television writer whose work has appeared on PBS, Nickelodeon, and Disney, among many others. After years of comforting tiny tots with TV, he turned to scaring their parents. In addition to horror and science fiction short stories, Terence is author of the first two books of his *Vampire Testaments* trilogy, *Bite Marks* and *Blood Pressure*, and has returned to work on the conclusion of his trilogy, *Past Life*. He has recently appeared in *Fantastic Stories of the Imagination*, *Lightspeed's* People of Colo(u)r Destroy Science Fiction! and the *What the #@&% Is That?* anthology. Find Terence on Twitter @vamptestaments or walking his neighbor's black Labrador mix along the banks of the Gowanus Canal and surrounding environs.

Arley Sorg, Spotlights Editor and Special Issue Coordinator

Arley Sorg grew up in England, Hawaii and Colorado. He went to Pitzer College and studied Asian Religions. He lives in Oakland, and most often writes in local coffee shops. A 2014 Odyssey Writing Workshop graduate, he works at *Locus Magazine*. He's soldering together a novel, has thrown a few short stories into orbit, and hopes to launch more.

Christian A. Coleman, Author Spotlight Interviewer

Christian A. Coleman is a 2013 graduate of the Clarion Science Fiction & Fantasy Writers' Workshop. He lives and writes in the Boston area. He tweets at @coleman_II.

Coral Moore, Author Spotlight Interviewer

Coral Moore has always been the kind of girl who makes up stories. Fortunately, she never grew out of that. She writes character-driven fiction, and enjoys conversations about genetics and microbiology as much as those about vampires and werewolves. She has an MFA in Writing from Albertus Magnus College and is an alum of Viable Paradise XVII. She has been published by *Vitality Magazine*, *Diabolical Plots*, and *Zombies Need Brains*. She loves aquariums, rides a motorcycle, and thinks there is little better than a good cup of coffee.

Isabel Yap, Author Spotlight Interviewer

Isabel Yap writes fiction and poetry, works in the tech industry, and drinks tea. Born and raised in Manila, she has also lived in California, Tokyo (for ninety-six days!), and London. In 2013, she attended the Clarion Writers' Workshop. Her fiction has been published by Book Smugglers Publishing, *Uncanny Magazine*, *Tor.com*, *Shimmer*, *Interfictions Online*, and *Nightmare*. You can find her on her website (isalikeswords.wordpress.com) or on Twitter at @visyap.

Jeremy Sim, Author Spotlight Interviewer

Jeremy Sim is a Singaporean-American writer and author of more than a dozen short stories, most notably in *Beneath Ceaseless Skies*, *Cicada*, and *Crossed Genres*. He is a graduate of Odyssey and Clarion West writing workshops, where he was awarded the Octavia E. Butler Memorial Scholarship in 2011. He currently lives in Berlin, Germany, where he moonlights as a freelance video game writer and editor. On a normal day, he can be found making spreadsheets, overanalyzing things, or trying strange new ice cream flavors—sometimes all at the same time. Find him online at jeremysim.com, or on Twitter at @jeremy_sim.

Pablo Defendini, Art Director

Pablo Defendini is a designer for hire. He mostly works on user experience, product design, and strategy for websites and mobile apps, with a little book design and art direction on the side. Occasionally he'll do some illustration and some printmaking for his own amusement. You can see his latest work at defendini.com. He also gets really nerdy and technical exploring new forms for building digital comics out of HTML and CSS at digitalcomics.co. He helped launch tor.com and ran it for its first few years, before moving on to work for companies that sit in the overlap between publishing and technology, like Open Road Media and O'Reilly. Pablo was born and raised in San Juan, Puerto Rico, lives in New York City, and works with clients all over the world.

Maggie Chiang, Illustrator

Maggie Chiang is a Taiwanese American full time artist and part time dreamer. Inspired by both places real and fictitious Maggie's illustrations evoke a longing for adventure and the pursuit of the unknown, exploring impossible landscapes and places unseen. A central theme of her art is the relationship between humanity and nature, oftentimes the underlying thread that ties together her work and establishes her individual artistic voice.

Reiko Murakami, Illustrator

Reiko Murakami is a U.S. based fantasy illustrator and concept artist who works in digital painting. She was born in Japan and grew up in Virginia after her family moved to the U.S. when she was 15. While studying at Rhode Island School of Design, she started to work in the video game industry. After graduation she spent a few years working as a full time concept artist, then in 2012 she decided to move to Tokyo, where her family is originally based, to expand her experience in the digital art and illustration industry. After spending a few years as a freelance fantasy illustrator working with various clients from both countries, she decided to move back to the U.S. and now she has settled down in Boston. She is currently working as a full time video game artist at a local video game company while spending some time for personal art projects and freelance illustration jobs.

SainaSix, Illustrator

SainaSix (sainasix.com) has been drawing since the age of five. Born in Paris, she initially wanted to become a fashion designer but her love of mangas led to her interest in visual narration and character design. After graduating from art school in Paris, she left for Tokyo where she began a career in animation. Her work is informed by her African heritage and Asian influences. SainaSix loves to play with lines and shapes. They are her inspiration to build the world of her dreams. SainaSix currently lives in Tokyo where she is an art contributor for fashion magazines and also showcases her work at private art exhibits.

Kimberly Wengerd, Illustrator

Kimberly Wengerd is an illustrator and designer, and is studying graphic design at the University of Akron. She was born in Canton, Ohio in 1994, and works predominantly with digital painting and leans toward creating surreal portraits full of vivid colors. Typically her works are a mixture of horror and fantasy, and she enjoys combining both of these elements into something otherworldly and sometimes even humorous. When she's not drawing, she enjoys taking long walks in nature and catching up on new TV shows and video games. She posts paintings and sketches on her site: facebook.com/kimberlywengerdart.

Additional Special Issue Staff

We made every effort to involve POC production staff whenever possible, but, as with the Women and Queers Destroy projects, we involved some allies on the production side of things. (Note: Copy Editing, though it has "Editing" right in the name, is actually a production job. Similarly, Audio Editing is a production task as well.) So the following folks worked on this special issue, but are not necessarily people of color.

Publisher
John Joseph Adams

Associate Publisher
Christie Yant

Managing Editor
Wendy N. Wagner

Podcast Producer
Stefan Rudnicki

Audio Editors
Jim Freund
Jack Kincaid

Copy Editor
Melissa Hofelich

Proofreaders
Devin Marcus
Coral Moore
Liz Colter
Mike Glyde
Julie Steinbacher
Carson Beker
Esther Patterson

Book Production & Layout
Matthew Bright
of Inkspiral Design

Crowdfunding Logo Design
Julia Sevin

WHAT THE #@&% IS THAT?
edited by John Joseph Adams & Douglas Cohen

Fear of the unknown—it is the essence of the best horror stories, the need to know what monstrous vision you're beholding and the underlying terror that you just might find out. Now, twenty authors have gathered to ask—and maybe answer—a question worthy of almost any horror tale: "What the #@&% is that?" Join these masters of suspense as they take you to where the shadows grow long, and that which lurks at the corner of your vision is all too real. Includes stories by Laird Barron, Scott Sigler, Seanan McGuire, Jonathan Maberry, Alan Dean Foster, and many others.

Saga Press
Horror / Nov. 1, 2016 / 368 pages
trade paperback / 978-1481434935 / $16.99
ebook / 978-1481435000 / $7.99
www.johnjosephadams.com/wtf

COSMIC POWERS
edited by John Joseph Adams

A collection of original, epic science fiction stories by some of today's best writers—for fans who want a little less science and a lot more action—and edited by two-time Hugo Award winner John Joseph Adams. Inspired by movies like *Guardians of the Galaxy* and *Star Wars*, this anthology features brand-new stories from some of science fiction's best authors including Dan Abnett, Jack Campbell, Linda Nagata, Seanan McGuire, Alan Dean Foster, Charlie Jane Anders, Kameron Hurley, and many others.

Saga Press
Science Fiction / Apr. 18, 2017 / 400 pages
trade paperback / 978-1481435017 / $16.99
ebook / 978-1481435031 / $7.99
www.johnjosephadams.com/cosmic